My Angel the Devil

Dan Agbeje

For Lucia, My Angel, Never the Devil

Book I: Preconception

1.

"Allah-Hu-Akbar!"

A chill ran down Fatima's back. The eerie, haunting but beautiful voice of the *Muadhin* cut through the afternoon rush. The *Adhan* always had that effect on her. She looked around and noticed it seemed to have the same effect on many. People who only a few seconds ago were calling out wares in high-pitched voices fell quiet, their visages unconsciously taking the form of self-effacement.

She knelt on a plastic woven mat with a broom placed in front of her knees. Her mother stood in front of her, tipping a basket of maize kernels. The warm afternoon breeze blew lighter unwanted particles away and allowed the heavier kernels to drop onto a clean cloth on the mat.

"Allah-Hu-Akbar!"

Fatima could hear sounds from her household that would only mean preparations for the short walk to the mosque. Her mother did not join them for although she was one of three wives to a Muslim man, she was allowed to keep her Christian faith. Fatima herself did not rise and her mother raised an eyebrow at her. The kernels seemed to have stopped mid-air.

"I'm going to the market later."

Fatima was not yet married so was not imposed a faith by a husband and her father did not see the need to insist on his daughter's religious preference. As a child, she had followed siblings and mothers to the mosques or churches never favouring one or the other. Recently, her mother had noticed an increasing preference towards the local church.

"I see." Her mother smiled with a slight gleam in her eye. "Take Hassan and Musa with you, and don't be late to return." As Fatima made to rise, the eyebrow went up again. "I thought you said 'later?'"

"I need to prepare," Fatima replied sheepishly, kneeling back down.

"I am sure he can wait. Finish here first." The gleam turned into a smile. "Don't worry, he seems a patient boy."

"I do not know who you speak off," Fatimah replied.

"Really?" her mum asked, pouring more kernels and not waiting for an answer. "I was fifteen once you know?"

2.

Madagali was situated in a valley that at mid-Harmattan season, held in its soil some of the limited rainfall that had fallen in the wet season. There was a sense of green when one looked towards the east at the Cameroonian border just twenty kilometres away. Ram and goats took advantage of the greenery and grazed the savannah-like fields. Sparrows danced happily in the air swooping into rooftops. To the south, the rocky and almost treeless Mandara Mountains rose like guardians looking over the town.

Madagali was not a large town by area but like most Nigerian towns, had a high population density. Almost twenty thousand people called it home with the Marghi and Fulani the most predominant. A major highway that linked the South and Eastern states of Nigeria to the North passed through the centre. The junction of roads was where the central market stood, receiving, unloading, packing and loading goods 24 hours' a day.

With the afternoon prayers almost halfway through, you would expect the mostly Muslim town to be devoid of human activity. This was not the case, for as Fatima and her brothers walked towards the market another side to the town beckoned. It started as a niggling din of human activity, promising to drag them into the bowels of organised chaos.

***

Fatima's mother, Rekia was Kanuri from Daura, a distinct ethnic group of northern Nigeria. When one looked at Fatima, she was instantly identifiable, for she had the perfectly shaped oval face of the Kanuri, noticeably softer facial features and much fuller lips than the locals. On each cheek, just above her prominent dimples, she also had two

3

pairs of traditional line tattoos identifying her heritage. A gold ring hung from her left nostril and her lips were painted silver with black linings. Non-Kanuri features were her lighter complexion and the pointier nose she inherited from her father.

She wore the traditional *Hijab*, exposing only her face. Her slender frame was covered in traditional attire with spiral pink, red and orange patterns, the cuffs exposed delicate painted *Lalle* fingers. On her feet, also painted in *Lalle*, she wore cured cowhide sandals with a cleanness that defied the dusty walking track.

For a girl approaching her sixteenth birthday, Fatima was often called *Amariya*, new wife. She never disputed this, as it was a sign of respect. It was better to make the mistake of calling a woman a young wife than calling a young wife an unmarried woman. People often had to atone for such mistakes.

Fatima's half-brothers stood on each side; Hassan, the eldest walking proud for he was popular here, and Musa, the youngest, clutching Fatima's handbag.

Although they used the rear entrance to the market, it was still packed with people. Sellers and buyers could be heard screaming and yelling, calling out prices, refusing and then accepting; sometimes not. It appeared chaotic but a closer look revealed a refined art of negotiation as well as a game of persuasion. Fatima stopped to watch a mobile phone seller haggle with a customer.

"*The price too small. I no buy am like that,*" the seller said.

"*Na wetin I get be that. Take am or leave am,*" replied the potential buyer.

"*Haba! Mana? Add 2,000 I beg?*"

Fatima smiled to herself, the price was now 500 less than the previous offer.

"*Ah!*" Potential Buyer responded, "*You no want make I eat or feed my children?*"

Fatima noted the buyer did not look like he had any children. In fact, he seemed her age; most boys married at nineteen.

"*Look...,*" the seller said, taking a more serious tone. "*Add 1,800. Open market for me*".

"*Okay. See, last na 1,000 I fit add. Last!*" Potential Buyer responded, emphasising 'Last' for good measure.

"*Chei!*" yelled the seller. "*Too small, Yankuri, too small!*"

"*Haba! Why you dey shout?*" Potential Buyer responded. "*Okay, one-five?*"

"*Me? I no gree,*" seller says, shaking his head. "Too small."

"*Na wetin I get be that,*" buyer says. Walking away.

Fatima knows the deal is already sealed.

After a few steps the seller calls out, "*Okay, look as per na you. No problem. Bring your money...*"

Fatima was not sure her time was worth the savings of the buyer, but this was the way of haggling. N*o pain in trying. Right?* It was fun to watch while she took time to calm her ragging nerves. She and her entourage walked on.

The phone vendors gave way to cowhide and trinket sellers and she took a deep breath. She loved the smell of leather and it was strong here. Rows of sandals, slippers and leather shoes were strewn all over the pathway. Although she would have loved to have seen the new styles on offer, she ignored the calls from sellers and continued on.

She walked through the body of people, exposing a skill of walking in the crowd whilst having a buffer of personal space. She noticed her brothers had stopped and were caught up in a somewhat one-sided heated conversation.

She paused at a jewellery stall to admire some earrings, trying not to stand close enough as to seem to be eavesdropping. Besides, she could guess what Musa was worried about.

Dambé was a traditional Hausa martial art with a vague history she could never confirm. Some said fourteenth century, others claimed earlier. Similar to kickboxing, fighters took a cat-like stance and circled each other looking for openings to cause damage. One hand was raised in front as a shield and grapple, while the other, the sword arm, was pulled back to be used to punch or jab. Historical recollections had fighters' arms and shins wrapped in a resin and glass shards dipped cloth.

Public exhibitions had more relaxed rules, but it was still a dangerous sport. Hassan was one of the best within his age group, something their father frowned at, although Fatima suspected was proud of.

"Father will ask after you and I refuse to tell him where you are!" Musa said. Unlike his brother, he abhorred violence.

"You don't need to tell him anything. Say you left me with friends at the market." Hassan replied calmly.

"What about food..."

"Don't worry, have mine." Hassan interrupted. "I will just watch. I have no fight today."

"But…"

"Musa," Fatima called. "Your brother will only watch," she turned to look at Hassan. "Don't worry he won't fight, and if he does, you should worry for his opponent." It was more a warning than a compliment and Fatima hopped her best maternal look added measure.

Hassan nodded, took a side exit and was soon lost in a mass of bodies.

***

Fatima and Musa walked past vegetable sellers, lines of fish and poultry, dashed quickly through meat sellers - which both always found uncomfortable - and finally to a restaurant in the central motor park.

Just as the main market was the heart of the Madagali, The Motor Park, situated in its middle was the market's heart. Trucks drove in from across Nigeria to unload goods which found their way into local stores and the hands of consumers. Vegetables and fruits came in from Jos, while cattle were loaded in trucks bound for Lagos.

Madagali Market Motor Park was shaped like a large 'U' with two gates at each end. One for entry and the other exit. The inner part of the curve was the main activity hub and was packed with people yelling destinations, trucks being offloaded and street hawkers advertising their wares.

Shop fronts lined the outer 'U' and consisted of branch offices of transport firms, a fairly big convenience store and smaller shops. In the middle of it all was a restaurant, their destination.

As Fatima saw the sign 'Ngozi's Kitchen' she felt her racing heart's increased pace.

Ngozi's Kitchen was a large establishment that catered for hundreds of people. The restaurant had two sitting areas. One was a front section where a customer could sit under a patio with a clear view into the loading and unloading bays. This was a favourite spot for drivers and travellers who preferred to keep an eye on things. The sitting arrangement consisted of low benches and tables customers shared by sitting in line.

Further inside, the restaurant catered for a different clientele. Customers here preferred a more relaxed environment, especially after a hard day's work or a very long trip. The tables sat two or four people and several flat screen televisions which hung from the walls were always tuned to football and *Nollywood* channels. A few ceiling fans and air conditioner units added to the activity hum as they struggled to provide cooler ventilation.

Musa took the lead and rather than head for the entrance, walked to the side of the building seeking access to the rear. Fatima followed, anticipation building in every step she took.

"How do I look?" she asked Musa's retreating back.

"You look very beautiful!" Musa said without turning around.

"You didn't even look!" she cried, catching up with him and playfully punching him on the back.

"You have asked me several times," he smiled. "And like I said, you look great! *WALAHI!*"

They both laughed and continued walking.

The rear of the restaurant was functional, a few drums and several water tanks marked the washing spot. Next to that was a dry storage area for stacks of firewood, coal and wooden crates. Across from this was a pit toilet. Fatima knew customers had access to more modern facilities inside and this was only for staff.

They approached a cooking hut that stood in the centre of the yard where a lady stood over one of several steaming pots. She stirred the contents with a ladle, tasted the brew and tilted her head as if consulting an oracle. Seemingly satisfied, she smacked her lips, covered the cooking pot and moved to the next.

Her name was Ngozi and this was her kingdom. An Igbo woman from eastern Nigeria, she was much heavier set than the women of the north. She was also of a much lighter complexion and possessed much rounder features. The way she wore her traditional attire was different from the locals.

While Fatima would wear hers as a gown, sometimes covering up with a chest high wrap, Ngozi wore three pieces of the same design. One wrap was tied across her waist, another over it across her hips and a blouse made of the same material as the wrapper. Covering her hair, using the same material was a *hair-tie* tied in knots that resembled flower petals.

A stern look crept into her face as she tasted another pot's contents. She and the oracle seemed to have agreed the taste did not meet standards, she turned around and in Igbo berated someone who was still inside the cooking hut.

"*As-salamu 'alaykunna,*" Musa interrupted.

"*Wa'alaykumu salaam...*" Ngozi responded automatically, turning to see who dared disturb her flow of insults. Her face instantly brightened as she saw Fatima and Musa.

"Ah! My daughter come through!" Gone was the stern expression and a motherly one softened her face. "And I see you have brought my little husband!"

You could tell Musa was so shy, he willed the ground to swallow him. For some reason though, Fatima knew her brother was quite fond of Ngozi. *Or was it her cooking?*

"Good afternoon, Ma," he responded. "Your food smells nice as always".

Mmm definitely the food, Fatima thought.

"And you look well, as always."

Ah, good comeback little brother.

"Good afternoon, mother," Fatima said, curtsying with her knees as a sign of respect. "You look busy; can I assist?"

"Don't be ridiculous!" Ngozi responded. "Go sit under the shade there and I will send some food to you."

"Oh! We are fine Ma, no need to feed us," Fatima replied, Musa seemed ready to disagree.

"And let my little husband starve to death?" Ngozi said in mock display, she must have noticed his distraught look. "God no! Go sit. Where is Hassan?"

"He is watching…"

Ngozi interrupted. "Don't tell me he has gone to participate in that horrid game!" She shook her head. "They should start calling him Hassan Chan." Another head shake. "Go sit…"

The stern look was back and Ngozi turned to a young girl who had just walked out of the cooking hut. "What? You will just stand there and look pretty? Where is the *maggi...*?"

Fatima moved on, Ngozi was back in her element and they were already forgotten. They walked to a bench and table that was placed across a side wall under some shades. This was where workers shared their meals. Fatima took a seat facing the action while Musa sat across from her.

After a little more good-natured berating, Ngozi walked into the restaurant. The young girl, her victim, called out to them, smiled and waved at Musa. He bowed his head and waved back.

"*I don't want no shy boy,*" Fatima sang to Musa, mimicking a popular western song. He tried to kick her under the table but his legs were too short and they both laughed.

***

Fatima always felt as if, for a moment her heart had stopped, and breathing was an effort.

Ike's presence seemed to obscure everything else, for a million things went through her mind. His eyes seemed to glitter when he saw her, his body language spoke of wanting to pick her up and elope.

Most of all, when he was around, she felt as if everything was okay. The smile that lit his face was always genuine, he was always truly happy to see her. Ike walked up behind Musa and playfully jabbed him in the ribs.

"Hey, it's my little father!" Ike said. Despite having lived in northern Nigeria all his life, he still retained a strong Igbo accent. He turned to Fatima, "and the most beautiful girl in the world."

"Ah, already the sweet Igbo tongue has started." Fatima replied, smiling.

"Please, don't shoot the messenger, oh!" he sat next to Musa. "What do you think Musa, am I right?"

Musa palmed his face. "Not again!" he replied. "Yes, she is."

"You don't look bad yourself," Fatima said to Ike. "And I see your university wife is feeding you well".

"University wife *ke*?" Ike responded. "No, this is me making sure I look good for you and my mother, otherwise you guys will complain I'm too skinny."

Ike took Fatima's left hand in his. A taboo for an unmarried Hausa woman, although as Musa noted this *particular* woman didn't seem to care.

"As I have always told you Fatima, run, hide, you will always be *Nkem*."

Fatima smiled. *My Own.* Musa conveniently found something interesting in his own fingers.

"Musa, how are you doing?" Ike asked. "Am I going to be yelled at because of yesterday?"

The previous day Musa had come to inform of today's visit but had been accosted by seniors from his school. When Ike had intervened, Musa was on the floor been kicked by the group of boys. One boy stood apart holding on to a bleeding nose and Ike had instantly become involved.

"If I wasn't so happy to see you after four months, I would be a lot angrier with you. You are not a bushman to just join a fight?" Fatima said.

"I didn't think it was a fair fight," Ike said, downcast. Why did she make him feel like his mother was telling him off? "One against three?"

"And he called me *Yan Daudu*," Musa said, almost in a whisper.

Yan Daudu was a Hausa term used to describe a man who had a flawed masculinity. Due to the perception of masculinity in the Hausa culture and indeed most of Nigeria, the term was mostly used in derogatory forms and Ike understood why Musa reacted with a punch to the nose. Musa's softness and mannerism were likely to be the bane of many fights to come. Ike felt sympathy for that.

Although Musa was Fatima's half-brother, he was more similar to her than Hassan his blood brother. A softness Ike prayed came from their father as he intended to ask for Fatima's hand and hoped to survive the ordeal.

His mother used that particular moment to interrupt with food. She dropped a plate of *Akpu* and *Afang* soup in front of him and he released Fatima's hands and sniffed the food.

"Mmm... Mother I missed your food," Ike said.

"Well I better take advantage of being able to cook for you before my daughter takes over. I have tasted her food and I have no chance," Ngozi winked at Fatima.

"*Nne*! You are too kind," Fatima responded. "Let me help you get the rest." She stood up.

"No, sit down. You have not seen my son in a while. Enjoy the moment." She turned to Musa. "Little husband, you come and help."

Ike washed his hands in a bowl that sat on the middle of the table. *Akpu* was a popular starch dish made from cassava flour. The dish was usually accompanied by a soup and in this instance, Ngozi had chosen a leafy vegetable soup of the Efik tribe of Eastern Nigeria. Ngozi had cooked it with stock fish, goat meat and some traditional spices to give it a distinct Igbo taste.

Fatima knew this was one of Ike's favourite dishes. She sat back and watched him mould a small ball of *Akpu* in his hand and expertly add pieces of vegetables, goat and fish to the mould. He leaned forward, she opened her mouth and he dropped it in, he licked his fingers and went on to preparing a much larger one for himself.

And just like that the two love birds were like couples that had spent decades together. Fatima folded her legs into the bench, she dropped her hijab to her shoulders, leaned forward and washed her hands. Ike paused, like a dog, he sniffed the air.

"Mmm… I missed your scent," he said, stuffing more food in his mouth.

"You smell like food," she responded. They both laughed and continued eating.

Musa walked out of the restaurant followed by Ngozi's minion. She walked past him with a plate of food and he leaned forward and stopped her.

"Let's sit inside for a minute," he said to her.

Ngozi followed behind with some drinks. "Yes, those two are already husband and wife. We just haven't been told yet," she gestured with her head. "Come eat your food inside.

3.

Across the fence of her house, Rekia was absently watching two he-goats butt heads, when a boy came storming past and stopped at the end of the street. She did not like him. His name was Alihu, a very unhappy eighteen-year old boy, oppressed by his elder brother's shadow.

The boy was raving, obviously upset about something and another boy with a bandaged nose was trying to catch up with him.

Rekia recalled hearing from her sister-wives that Alihu's father was a rather stern man who employed the use of a horsewhip for discipline, applying it to his children and workers alike without regard. She totally disagreed with this and her husband always said,

"When you treat a horse badly, it will always behave badly, for it is all it knows." He often added after a pause, "Although it is hard for some to know what bad is."

The poor child with the bruised nose was probably someone to whom Alihu's father had just taught a *no-doubt good old-fashioned* lesson.

Ignoring the fracas, she looked at her watch. Her daughter and sons would be home soon and she needed to get ready for dinner.

It was her turn tonight to prepare the evening meal but after cleaning grain all day, she did not feel like cooking for a household of fifteen people. So, she had taken on the opportunity to give Fatima's visit to the market a reason. Although, she did not think her daughter *actually* needed one.

She had given her some money for dinner for the whole family. An expensive treat from Ngozi's kitchen but hopefully enough to soften what she knew was coming from her daughter and Ike's expectations.

***

Halfway through the meal, Fatima had her fill and sat back to watch Ike devour the rest. He ate quietly with the occasional smacking of lips while she filled him in on missed local gossip. When he finished eating, he washed his hands, dried them and took her hands in his.

"Fatima, I don't know how to say this so I will just go ahead and say what I feel," He paused.

This was serious, Fatima thought to herself, Ike lose his tongue?

"Ever since I met you, you are constantly on my mind. I want to see you all day and even when I do get the chance to do so, I realise that the way you make me feel even though it is scary, is intoxicating in a good way." He squeezed her hands gently.

Another pause? This was definitely a first for Ike. Then it hit her, he was about to ask for her hand.

"Even in uni I thought about you. All I wanted, was to hear you laugh and watch you talk."

This was ridiculous, yet another pause? "Yes," she said, interrupting him. "Yes, I accept. I will be your wife."

"Ah!" he laughed. "Did I look that much in trouble?"

"I could not bear to see the sweet-tongued Ike lost for words. And you were taking too long. Besides, when we do get married you can tell me everything. Again and again and again, every day for the rest of our lives!"

A Few minutes later, Fatima collected her family's dinner and in good faith argued with Ngozi on taking payment. Eventually, Ngozi accepted half of the payment.

As she left, Ngozi whispered to her, "You have my blessing; you make him so happy."

***

On the walk back, Fatima thought about Ngozi's comment to her. Ike must have told his family what he was going to do. She thought of their parting.

I hope to see you in church on Sunday. He had said to her.

Fatima smiled, her mind twirling with thoughts of a wedding. Musa's presence was foggy next to her. The rest of the world was - very much non-existent.

A wise man once said to Fatima. *Nothing good, lasts forever.* She could not remember who, but she was sure he was wise because what he had said made perfect sense, a sense not realised until you were in the thick of it.

Fatima was yanked out of her wedding daydream by a boy slamming into Musa and grabbing Musa by the neck. Without thinking, she lashed out.

"*Walahi*! It is little Alihu coming to make his miserable life everybody's problem!"

Alihu was still holding a struggling Musa by the neck but the yelling had stopped and only silence greeted her outburst.

Even the boy who stood behind Alihu with a bandage across his nose held his peace. Shock apparent on his and everyone's face.

"*La-ila- ila-la-hu*," Alihu replied, "You infidel, you think I am not a man? You think I am that dog eater?" he pushed Musa aside and stepped towards her.

"Alihu!" a voice called out.

They all turned to see a tall, slender man walking towards them. It was Alhaji Sani, Alihu's uncle.

Sani had watched and heard the drama unfolding. The boys' rage, valid in his opinion was just what he needed. "Come, take me to your father," he said to Alihu.

Alihu dropped his hand to his sides and bowed to Sani. He straightened and leaned towards Fatima and whispered.

"The day I make you my wife, is the day that I will fuck you like the dog he eats."

Fatima bit back a retort. Alihu was dangerous and the look in his eyes was a look of a devil. Musa had recovered and sensing a truce he relaxed. He and Fatima greeted Sani.

"For such a fine package, young lady, you need to learn some manners," Sani said walking past them.

Fatima watched the three retreating backs. She refused to be unhappy, especially today and after Sani and Alihu had gone far enough to her liking, she said to Musa.

"Come, let us go and enjoy your wife's food."

***

Alihu paced back and forth mumbling to himself in his bedroom where his uncle had told him to await summons. He glanced at his watch. Whatever they were talking about was not as important as what he had on his mind.

Fatima's father was friends with his father, well more like acquaintances but *surely any father would want to marry into his family?* Everyone knew his family was rich. Their home was the biggest on the street. A one-hectare compound that housed multiple dwellings including the main house with ten rooms and three guest-meeting rooms. All of his father's wives had their own houses for their young and female children while his father and brothers stayed in the main house.

Alihu had told his uncle his intention and his uncle agreed to help. He would make Fatima his wife. *Ko da Karifi ko the yaji.*

The door to his room opened and a male helper stood waiting to be addressed.

"Is my father ready for me?"

"Your father wishes to see you."

Alihu brushed past and shoved the boy aside.

***

Alihu was just shy of six-foot-tall, broad shoulders and instead of muscles like his elder brother, was fat filled. He was a notorious bully. Where his brother, Hamza, was witty, Alihu was aggressive. He never referred to himself as a bad person, he saw only jealousy when others saw disgust.

High school for him was the local government secondary school. He excelled more from his teacher's fear of failing his father than smarts. His brother on the other hand was in second year at the University of Maiduguri. Rather than join him there, Alihu was refusing further education.

He walked into a private lounge room with drapes so thick they kept the sunlight out. Covering the walls were paintings of various landscapes, local to the north. The main painting to the left was of a group of Fulani herders across a river landscape. His father and Sani stood looking at the painting.

"Alihu," his father said. It was not a question, simply an acknowledgment of his presence. "I hear you fight for a girl?"

Sani made to respond but Alihu's father raised his hand for silence.

"A man does not fight for women." He turned and stared down at his son. "Women, fight for him."

"That! Dog-eater gives her the right to…" he did not see the slap. It came out of nowhere. A backhand slap that sent him staggering backwards.

His father's hand was back at his side. "Excuses as always," he said and turned his back. To Sani, he asked. "Alhaji, so this is the boy you wish to make a man?"

"He is a man," Sani said. "He just needs to realize that. Give me six months with him and I assure you, he will not disappoint."

Alihu's father looked at the painting again. "Our family has come a long way," he said to himself. He turned and faced Alihu. "You have always failed me. Always." He let that sink in. "Your uncle believes there is hope for you. But I doubt it."

"Father, let me honour you. Let me prove that I am twice a man!" Alihu yelled. The pain of the slap already forgotten.

"Be twice the man you are now, and you will have honoured your family," his father walked next to him and placed his hands on Alihu's left shoulder. "This is your last chance. If you fail, do not return even your dead body."

4.

Ike walked into the church in his Sunday best and paused at the entrance. The church could hold two hundred people or so and it was almost to capacity. Three rows of pews facing the altar lined the main sitting area. On the far left you had the row reserved for men, on the far right there was another row for women and in the middle, a mixed sitting for male, female, young and old. Finally, benches with a capacity of fifty people were set up just beyond the entrance. This was reserved for late-comers.

The interior walls of the church were painted white with images of Jesus, Mary and baby Jesus hanging next to wooden miniature crucifixes. At the front of the church, on the right of the altar sat the pastor, his wife and helpers. To their left the choir and band stood, already singing songs of praises to welcome worshipers.

Ike spotted Musa seated at the edge of a middle row pew. Fatima sat to the left of him with a free space reserved between them.

He made his way to them, greeting family friends and acquaintances along the way. He came to the edge of the pew and Musa rose to let him through. This was the first time he would sit with Fatima. Usually they sat close but in different pews or across from each other, both on pew edges.

The feelings every time he saw her flooded back and today was especially nerve racking as she managed to look beautiful, modest and sexy all at once. She wore a tight-fitting gown made of colourful traditional cloth, her hair was wrapped in a *head-tie* and a small piece of cloth was draped over her head and shoulders. The gown had a V-neck that was not scandalous enough to kick her out of church but revealing enough to show some cleavage.

Ike noticed all this in the seconds it took him to take his seat and he sat down quickly hoping his body had not already betrayed him. Her perfume wafted into his nostrils and he realised the battle with his body was one he would not win today.

"You look beautiful," he whispered to her.

"You always say that," she replied a smile on her lips. Her *Lalle* was gone but she had painted around her eyes and her lips were covered with a light brown lip-gloss. "And you smell like food," she added.

He laughed. "Well, you also look…" He lowered his voice more. "Very… very sexy."

She giggled. "Idiot, you are in a church."

"And God agrees." He turned to Musa. "*How far? Any more troubles?*"

Musa thought about the incident on the way home from the restaurant but he and Fatima had agreed not to tell Ike. He had not known the boy he punched in the nose was Alihu's cousin and considering Alihu and Ike were just waiting for a moment to fight each other he let it go.

"No, no more troubles. How is your mother?"

"She is fine. She should be here already." Ike spotted her sitting with a group of women. He noticed Fatima's mum was among them and prayed it was a good sign.

The pastor called for opening prayers and his congregation settled. The choir ended their praises and the church service began.

***

Fatima had come with an extra cloth of her gown's design that she used to cover her chest when she came to church. She placed this over her thighs and put her fingers underneath. Ike noticed this and slid his left hand under. They clasped hands, faces straight and looking at the altar. He traced his fingers over hers, his mind already far away. Thoughts of the church, although still in his subconscious were as distant as water to a fish in its habitat.

He turned to look at her and realised he should not have done that.

She was staring ahead. He looked downwards to her neck and instantly wanted to bury his face there; taking in her scent and lightly brushing her neck with his lips, one reason because he loved the feel of her skin and another just to hear her moan.

Her gown had slipped and he could just see the curve of one of her breasts. He imagined slowly dragging his kisses further down her chest. Kissing, until he reached under the breast he just saw and matching his tongue to the curve under

19

it. Licking, kissing all the way round and slowly continuing on to her other breast. Taking this one from the top, tracing his tongue around it then delicately around her areola, kissing, licking and finally taking her nipple in his mouth. He could just hear her moan, her back arched towards him, fingers buried in his head and him feeling the nipple harden in his mouth.

He did not intend to stop there, he had to taste her other nipple and this time as he sucked it lightly, his fingers would be playing with the other. As her breath became quicker, he would continue downwards with his tongue. His fingers now replacing his tongue on her nipple. Taking in the scent of her flat stomach and the taste of her on his tongue. He felt that by the time he got between her legs, her hips would already be grinding up to him. He would kiss her there, multiple small kisses to tease, moving his hands to spread her legs and then taste her, slowly dragging his tongue upwards and then down. Looking up at her, the view of her head thrown backwards between her perfectly shaped breasts, he would slip his tongue inside her…

"...Let us pray."

The cut of the pastor's voice brought him back and as everyone in the church closed their eyes, she turned to him with a look that seemed to know his thoughts. She moved the cloth on her legs to cover his groin and squeezed him as her fingers brushed over his hardness. Good thing it was brief; Ike knew if she continued he would have spilled his seed.

∗∗∗

Olu was a well-known teacher at Gwoza Government Girls College, an all-girls secondary school Fatima and most girls in the community attended. The school was located fifty-kilometres north of Madagali, at the outskirts of a small town called Gwoza, and was a popular choice for parents with the mind and resources to educate their children.

Olu liked to catch up with parents of his students, giving them personal feedback and getting a little information on their living environments. His peers often commented

that he went overboard but Olu had a passion for teaching.
He was from Western Nigeria, a long way from home and
only saw his aging parents twice a year. A painful sacrifice for
contributing to an increase in the education levels of northern
Nigerian girls.

The church service had just ended and Olu stood
under a tree talking to Rekia and her friend, he could not
remember her name but recalled she owned a fledging
restaurant in the town's motor park. Usually his conversations
were about school or his students, not this time. He was
trying to determine if Rekia had any information on the
disturbing news of young boys taken to bush camps for some
form of training. He was not sure why but the rumours did
not sound good.

"So you have not heard anything. Maybe your
husband has mentioned something?" he asked Rekia.

"Not really," Rekia responded.

She seemed distracted but Olu pressed on. "A boys
bush camp maybe?"

Rekia, thought for a few seconds. "Now that you
mentioned it, I do recall my husband telling his sons not to
pay any heed to an Islam training should they be approached.
He did not elaborate though," she said.

"Islam training… I see." Before Olu could respond, a
boy interrupted them.

"Good afternoon, Ma," Ike said to Rekia. He turned
to Olu. "Good afternoon, Sir."

"Ah, Mr. Olu," the woman with Rekia addressed him.
"My name is Ngozi and this is my son, Ikechukwu. He is
currently in his final year of university."

"Pleased to meet you my son." Olu shook hands with
the Ike. "Well, ladies. I must leave you now. Please extend my
regards to your husbands."

Olu waited for their respective responses and walked
off seeking more information on his worries.

"Mother…"

"Ah, Ike," Rekia interrupted. "Your mother said you wish to come to my house to see us. Is something wrong?"

Ike could not tell if Fatima's mother was joking. He could have sworn his mother promised to soften the fall before he spoke to Rekia.

"Mother." *Was he supposed to call her that yet?* He continued, back straight. "I would like to ask you for a very special gift." The gleam in Rekia's eyes told him what he needed to know. *So this was where Fatima's cheekiness came from.*

"A gift, eh?" Rekia asked, her eyebrows raised. "Please tell me what this gift is?"

"You have a very beautiful daughter." *Was his voice getting hoarse?* "In fact, she just may be the most beautiful girl in the world and I will very much like to spend the rest of my life with her." He was quite proud of the rehearsed short proposal.

"Really? As what?" Rekia asked, again with a straight face.

"Mother!" Fatima cried out from behind him. *How long had she been there?* Ike thought. "You know what he means!" She came and stood next to him. Not touching but close.

"Err… No." Her mother said. Ngozi could barely hold a straight face but remained silent.

"I would like to ask for your daughter's hand in marriage," Ike blurted out.

"Oh, I see," Rekia replied as if a great revelation had been made known to her. "Well, what does this young woman say?" she turned to Fatima.

"Depends on how good a husband he promises to be," she replied smiling at Ike.

The women could not hold it anymore and all broke out laughing. Rekia touched his shoulders. "Yes, my son. Come to the house on Wednesday evening next week and I will let my husband know to expect you and your parents." She tapped his nose. "You can breathe now."

Ngozi hugged Fatima and they said their goodbyes. Fatima turned to Ike, said her goodbyes and walked off with Rekia. Ngozi held her son's hand and led him to the car.

"She will make a strong wife."

***

Hassan circled his prey like a cat. The circle of people around them who watched in silence were forgotten. He glanced at his opponent's feet, judging the skill. Some said you could tell how skilled a Dambé fighter was by looking at their stance. To others like Hassan, it was one way to fool an opponent.

Hassan lashed out with his sword arm. The crowd broke its silence. His opponent stepped back, dodging the blow then responded with a kick. If Hassan had not been probing and skilled enough to expect the counter, the kick would have caught him in the temple. He ducked and continued circling.

The crowd settled back into silence. Some had expected the blow to connect, others, including Hassan's trainer knew Hassan only meant to probe.

The fighters continued to circle, their feet moving like a shuffle, legs wide, sword arm back and shield arm forward. This was Hassan's third fight for the day and his opponent's first, the boy would have bribed for the slot.

Hassan was tired and knew he had to end this quickly but he wanted to keep his undefeated record so he remained cautious.

He shuffled forward, his opponent shuffled backwards. He circled, he quickly shuffled forward again, lifted his knee in a kick but thought better of it and dropped his feet bending his ankle as if he had miss-stepped.

His opponent saw this and jumped forward with a sword arm punch. Hassan stepped to the side, used his shield arm to catch the sword arm, tugging forward and downwards, he unbalanced his opponent who turned trying to get back his stance. Hassan's kick was already well on its way and it connected to his opponent's temple. The boy crumbled to the floor.

23

The Old Man walked with Hassan. Although he was a popular sight at Dambé fights, nobody seemed to know much about him. He was Kanuri for sure, as was clear in his features. He had the build of a fighter and the scars on his knuckles further proved that, although pointing to a much darker version of the sport. He had thinning grey hair, deep-set eyes that seemed to see all and a gait of one who had a bad leg.

Three years previously, before Hassan had become a skilled fighter, the Old Man had approached Hassan saying he could train him for a fee. After their conversation, Hassan had asked around about the Old Man, but no one knew much.

For as long as the ring in the market existed, the Old Man was always there. Hassan would not be surprised if the Old Man spent his last day watching a fight.

Despite the limp, Hassan noted the Old Man looked fit enough to take on boys his age. There was still a lot of life in the Old Man, Hassan thought to himself.

"…That was a risky move," the Old Man said. "What if his punch was also a probe?"

"I took the risk as I was already exhausted, Old Man," Hassan replied. "And hey, I learnt from the best, remember."

"No, I simply guide. A Dambé fighter is born with his sword arm first," The Old Man replied. He changed the subject. "Have you thought about what I said?"

Hassan sighed. "I keep telling you those you speak of do not exist!"

He loved the Old Man, but this subject, which had become more frequent in the past few months, always annoyed him. At first, he had taken it seriously but after not getting any more information from others he had taken it as the Old Man's fabrication.

"Young Man!" The Old Man held him back. Hassan noted the strong grip; he would not be able to break the hold no matter how hard he tried. "I do not ask you if you believe they exist! I simply ask if you will fight!"

He met the Old Man's piercing eyes. "Warriors, you say. Mercy, they will not have. Poised like demons to take our land, ready to behead our fathers, rape our mothers and marry our sisters?" Hassan's eyes were venomous but his voice remained calm. "You ask if I will fight." He shook his arm from the grip and luckily the Old Man let go. "I will destroy them. Let them come."

He turned and walked off. "See you on Wednesday," he said without looking back.

The Old Man watched him leave. A rare smile came to his face. "I hope you are enough. At least to hold them back," he said to no one in particular.

He turned around and headed in the opposite direction.

5.

Rekia woke up before the cock sang its first morning call and by the time the *Muadhin* called for the morning prayers, she already had chicken killed, prepared and simmering in a clay pot. The main course would be the traditional Hausa peanut soup served with *Tuwo Shinkafa*.

She sighed, Wednesday had come quicker than she had hoped for. Fatima was also up, tasked with ensuring the family compound was clean and presentable enough to receive guests.

Typical of many northern Nigerian homes, her home was designed in a way that meant visitors came through the main gate to an open compound with resting areas. Two massive *Dongonyaro* trees stood in the centre with mats placed in their shades. Members of the household either used the shade to rest from afternoon chores or to receive visiting guests. Facing this was a veranda with chairs and a table, a favourite spot for her husband when he returned from farming duties. Currently he was at the rear, supervising the killing of a cow to be used for *Suya* and *pepper soup*.

Past the balcony was a fairly large room popularly called a *sitting-room*. Here more official or prominent guests were catered for. It was furnished with middle-eastern furniture and rugs that reflected the Arabic influence on northern Nigeria. On the walls mixed with family portraits were wood carvings of masquerade masks and animals. This was the room where Ike's family would be received.

Past this and also part of the same structure, was Rekia's husband's private rooms. It contained two sleeping areas, a bathroom with its own toilet, an ablution room, a private sitting room and a study.

This part of the house opened to the rear compound with three independent properties for wives, children and some of their close relatives. At the centre was a kitchen and food storage.

Situated just before the surrounding fence were pens for chickens, sheep, turkey and more storage. For rear access, a pedestrian gate was used and it had a sign that read *'Ba Shiga'*, No Entry. It was used for family only, and the sign was a clear indication that women beyond its point were not appropriately dressed to be seen by non-family members.

Rekia was happy with how well her husband had taken the news. She had been providing some subtle hints for the past few months, so he expected the visit. She knew him well and although it did not openly show, he was pleased with the match. He even provided an insight into the history of Ike's father's transport business and profitability of Ngozi's restaurant ventures.

Rekia's Sister-wives were in full festive mood. They had all woken early to help with the preparations with everyone seemingly knowing where help was needed and when. Their children had been cleaned and dressed in traditional Hausa clothes. The girls wore a long flowing caftan with colourful embroideries around the collars and cuffs and the early afternoon sun reflected their bright faces and gold-plated earrings. The boys wore a similar long flowing caftan with no embroidery and the only jewellery to be seen on them were gold plated cufflinks.

Musa approached Rekia, a big smile on his face. He seemed to be the happiest person in the house and Rekia could understand why.

Fatima was his immediate elder sister and although from a different mother, Fatima had taken care of him as a baby. Always there to help his mother with him and their bond grew as strong as siblings born of the same parents. Sometimes Rekia felt the bond seemed even stronger.

"Are you the one marrying today?" Rekia addressed him. "Look how well you are dressed!"

Round bright face still holding the smile, he made a spin and stretched his hands. "Do I?"

Rekia folded her hands and nodded, a smile on her face.

"It is a beautiful day to look good. Besides, I don't want Ike to think he is the only good-looking boy in da house!"

This was another thing that surprised her. Musa had taken a shine to Ike, accepting him as easily as a brother. Usually he protected Fatima like a pup protecting its sick mother.

"Are you sure it is not for the young girl that works with Ngozi?" She laughed at his reaction.

"Ah… Well that too," he replied, face to the ground. "But I don't see her as Ike sees Fatima."

"Oh! Please do tell, how does this rascal see my daughter?" Sensing the trap, Musa laughed and ran off.

***

Fatima had never been this nervous in her life. Even when she and Ike first kissed she could swear what she felt now was much worse. Things seemed to be turning out as bad as the first kiss too. Awkward with the kiss but *chaotic* with today's arrangements.

Worse, she just did not seem to be getting the message across to the woman styling her hair. She wanted

27

much thinner braids, but the woman was giving her medium sized ones.

She sighed, two hours to go for the hair, it was almost done and all that was left after that was a bath.

Hours later, hair done and body scrubbed, she stood in front of the full-length mirror in her mother's room. She dipped her fingers into a perfumed oil jar and applied the oil to her body, slowly massaging it into her skin. When she got to her stomach, she turned to her sides and pushed her stomach out. She imagined it full with Ike's child and smiled to herself.

A sound of broken glass brought her back and she yelled out in Hausa, asking what happened. Hearing an unlucky pair of buttocks being smacked and one of her mothers berating someone, she knew it was already taken care off.

Her caftan, although similarly styled to everyone else's, was of a much finer silk and dyed in multiple flowing colours. This identified the silk as one that came from the famous Kano dyers. The main body of the caftan was a dark, almost pink purple that flowed downwards to her knees and merged with black. The flow was not a straight colour change but a chaotic mixture, resembling a splash of colours. The neck of the caftan, its cuffs and the hem were designed with silver and gold coloured threads. The embroidery was an elaborate design of sun and hibiscus flowers.

She put on a pair of leather sandals her mother had given her. A gift from when her mother had also been introduced, one Fatima would now keep until her daughter's time. She picked up her earrings.

"Look at my beautiful daughter."

Fatima turned to face her father, Usman Turaki, standing at the door. She gestured in greeting, bowing her knees, but he waved her on. He stepped up to her and held her by the shoulders, a look of pride in his eyes. He took one earring from her and helped her put it on. "Are you sure this is the boy you want to marry?"

"Yes, Papa. He is a loving and caring man. Very strong and he will give you stronger grandchildren."

Her father laughed.

"I am very sure," she added.

"Well, I'm glad. He seems nice enough," Her father paused as if he wanted to say more, instead he collected the other earring from her fingers and helped her with it. He turned her to the mirror and stood behind her. "Better hurry up then as they are already here."

She yelped and grabbed her necklace, *where had the time gone!* Her father stepped out of the room. She knew why he seemed sad, he was about to lose a daughter.

She finished her preparations and a few minutes later when her mother came for her, she was ready to be introduced.

Although Fatima had been running, when she got to the sitting-room entrance she stopped, caught her breath and walked in slowly. This was just an introduction, so she did not need a veil to cover her face. She stepped into the room and found herself directly facing Ike and his family.

Everyone in the room stood and she had to stop herself from bolting back into the corridor. She had not thought about the number of people in attendance and as they stood regarding her, it dawned on her that not only was most of her household here, so also was the household of her future husband.

Ike's family wore the traditional attires of their Igbo origin. Ike's Father, Chibuike Amadi stood in front of his wife and Ike. He wore a black velvet shirt with gold patterns that Fatima could not place. They seemed like a combination of a Lion's head, a family crest and a drinking calabash. The length of the shirt sleeves ended just beyond his elbows, neither a short sleeve nor a long sleeve. On his wrists, he wore ceremonial beads that identified him as one with a chieftaincy title and several gold rings occupied most of his fingers. He smiled at Fatima and took off his woollen traditional cap.

"Ah I see!" His voice was deep and with a more prominent accent than Ike. "My son has chosen the jewel in your house!" Fatima squatted in front of him in greeting, he placed his right hand on her head and blessed her. "My wife told me you are beautiful, but now I fear there may not be anything we can offer my friend here to part with such a beautiful gift!" Fatima stood up, smiling brightly at his compliment and Chibuike stood aside for his wife to step forward.

Ngozi was dressed to occasion in what seemed to be a very expensive white lace blouse with flower patterns. Her hair was covered in a gold *Ichafu* head-tie, styled like a round flair at the back that must have been difficult to get into any vehicle. The *Ichafu* almost covered her ears, showing the gold and diamond earrings that hung from them. Around her neck, she wore a gold and diamond crucifix in addition to much bigger red beads than those found on her husband's wrists. For her wrapper, she had chosen to wear a blood red material and, on her feet, some low-heeled gold leather sandals.

"My daughter." She hugged Fatima and blow-kissed her cheeks. "You look very lovely today." She stepped aside and Fatima was facing her future husband.

Ike was bare-chested with a set of red beads around his neck, wrists and ankles. A red strip of cloth that seemed to be made of a chiffon like material was wrapped around his waist completing his simple attire. Fatima wondered if there were shorts underneath the wrap and had to hold herself back from taking a peek.

He seemed to recover from the sight of her, flexed his chest and bowed deeply.

"*Nkem*, you are the most beautiful girl in the world," he said.

Fatima's father laughed. "So this must just be window dressing if she is already yours!" He waved to interrupt Ike's apology. "Don't worry, I am sure it will be so. Please, all of you, sit."

As everyone settled into their seats, Usman Turaki stood and a hush filled the room. Fatima smiled inwardly, her father always had a commanding presence. He looked around the gathered faces not frowning but not smiling either, it gave the meeting a serious air and silence eventually prevailed.

"We are gathered here, today," Usman began, "to receive the family of my very good friend Chief Chibuike Amadi." Ike's father raised his right hand and nodded at the gathered faces. "Is there anyone here who does not believe the Amadis' should be welcomed?" the faces remained silent. "Chief Amadi, the floor is yours."

Chibuike stood up and a young man stepped forward holding a calabash decorated with rope-like patterns in red and yellow and polished with a light brown sheen. In the calabash, placed on top of banana leaves, were three kola nuts. He cleared his throat and began.

"First I would like to thank you, Alhaji Usman Turaki, for receiving us to your beautiful palace." Chibuike collected the calabash from his assistant. "As it is our custom, we bring *Oji* to share with your family and both our ancestors." He stepped forward with the calabash. "Please pick one." Usman glanced into the bowl and selected a nut at random. Chibuike received it from him and handed the calabash to his assistant. He placed the selected nut in his left palm and using his right thumb broke the nut. It separated into three pieces. He showed it first to Usman then at the gathered faces.

The women raised their voices in exclamation making hollering sounds with their tongues and fingers over their mouths. The kola nut breaking into three pieces was a good omen. One piece for the gods, and two pieces for the parties hoping for an agreement.

Chibuike waited before he continued. "Alhaji, my family and I have come here for two reasons. First to thank you for your ongoing friendship to our family. We all know how hard it is now for families across different ends of the country to still have the bonds that we have. For this we thank you."

Usman nodded in response.

"Secondly, my son, Ikechukwu Amadi rushed to his mother some years back and said to her that he has seen a beautiful fruit at the top of the tallest tree in town." He paused for dramatic effect. "She came to me and told me this and I asked, 'Please tell me my lovely wife, where is this tree?' When she responded, I said to her that boy is an idiot." He smiled and the room laughed with him. "Not only did he choose the tallest tree! He selected one guarded like the fortress of Queen Amina!"

This time Usman joined in the laughter. "We cannot choose our children's paths. We can only guide," Usman responded. "Please, go on."

"Ikechuckwu come forward!" Chibuike said turning to address Ike. As Ike stepped next to him, he continued. "As you can see, even though they do not have to live as we men used to in our days he is not a bad specimen." He placed his hand on Ike's shoulders and gestured him forward. "He is strong, works hard and is in his final year at the university."

"I greet you, my son," Usman said.

"So, my friend, I and my son stand before you to request for the hand of your most prized fruit, Fatima Turaki."

The women raised their voices again, one of them would soon be *Amariya,* a joyful thing.

Ike stepped forward and knelt at Usman's feet. "Father, I promise to cherish and take care of your daughter with all my strength and for the rest of my life."

Usman waited for silence and beckoned Ike to stand. "Well met, my son, but as you are aware" he turned to Rekia. "Fatima is not only my daughter. Please meet my third wife Rekia Turaki."

On cue, Rekia walked forward and stood next to her sitting husband. "We greet your family and well-wishers of Chief and Mrs. Amadi. Welcome to our humble abode." Chibuike and his entourage replied to her greeting.

"I have known Ngozi Amadi for as long as I have been brought from my house in Borno to marry my loving husband. I consider her as my sister and I was pleased when she told me that her son wishes to marry my only daughter." Some of the women in both sides of the table had already started tearing up. Rekia continued. "I present to you the fruit Chief Amadi mentioned and the love of my life, Fatima Turaki."

Once again, the women made the hollering sound, only stopping when Fatima made it to her mother's side. She greeted the assembled guests starting with Ike's parents, thanking them for coming and wishing them God's blessings.

As she finished, her father cleared his throat and asked her, "Fatima, this boy who seems brave enough to stand before me asks for your hand. Do you wish to marry him?" Once again, a hush fell across the room.

"I do, Papa," Fatima replied.

"Then it is settled, I give my blessings," Usman raised his hand to interrupt shouts of jubilations that had already started. "But before I allow both our families to discuss the bride price, dates and all those things you women love to talk about when you smell a wedding…" Laughter. "I ask you all, please eat, drink and enjoy, for today is a day of joy and the first day of the rest of the lives of our children."

Rekia sighed with relief, the first part of the introduction ceremony was finished, already someone was beating a drum and she scanned the crowd identifying the culprit to be Musa, she smiled.

Servants walked into the room with plastic plates, cutlery and cups. The men and her husband were to be served in his private sitting room, Ngozi, her female relatives and Rekia's sister-wives would be served in this room. The remaining attendees and children were to be served at the front of the compound where chairs, tables, food and drinks were already waiting. At that moment, she knew the negotiations would go well. Good deals always came from full stomachs.

***

Ike stood facing Fatima, around them people moved about and went on with the celebrations but they stood staring at each other. He, with the half smile Fatima was always fond off, and her with smiling eyes he always missed.

"Want to go for a walk?" he asked her.

"That would be nice," she responded.

He turned and led the way towards the front of the house. The children and other guests were already eating, chatting and celebrating outside. As Fatima came out behind Ike, some of the girls among the guest greeted her presence with the hollering sound the women made earlier. Fatima smiled at them and after a moment they returned to whatever they were doing, the *Amariya* to be, briefly forgotten.

They walked towards the least lit Dongonyaro tree. The mats had been removed from under the trees for use in the sitting room. Fatima leaned on the tree trunk facing the gate, she knew it was situated in a way no one from the house could see her and Ike took the initiative and came to her.

He hugged her and it instantly felt right, a place he always wanted to be and what he wanted for the rest of his life. He could not help it so he kissed her briefly. It was one of those kisses that left the recipient to accept or deny. Fatima accepted it. She took him in. Accepting him like a lost love. Then he stared into her eyes, kissed her forehead.

"I love you more than anything in the world," he said.

"Really?" she asked.

"Really," he responded and made to kiss her again.

"More than anything?" she stopped the kiss with palms to his chest.

"Yes," Ike looked into her eyes. "Nothing matters. I will always love you."

Without knowledge of what would be, they became lost in each other's embrace.

The kiss was better than their first, better than all they had previously shared. It was a feeling Fatima did not want to

34

end. After what seemed like hours, although in the real world
was barely minutes, she withdrew.

"I love you too Ike," she said to his questing eyes. "I
will always be yours."

They kissed again and would have continued if not
for interruptions. Musa had walked to the tree. He cleared his
throat to gain their attention.

"The deliberations have finished," he said with blank
face disregarding what he saw.

Fatima turned to Ike and said. "I have something for
you," she moved her hand to her brassiere. The boys looked
away. "A show of undying love."

Ike looked at what she offered and loved it. It was a
silver eternity pendant, styled in the universal pattern of eight,
each side had a black string attached to the ends. He extended
his arm and she knotted the gift around his wrist.

"Eternity," he said looking at the pendant when she
had finished. "I have something for you as well." He
removed a chain from his side. "Don't worry. I am wearing
shorts; it is not where you think it is from."

The chain was also silver with a small pendant
attached to both sides of the chain. Unlike hers, the pendant
was a word, *Otu*. "It is what we are. One," he tied the chain
around her left ankle. "Don't worry, the chain is almost
unbreakable."

When Ike had stood up, Musa said, "You guys are
needed." They walked with him towards the main house,
"Hassan arrived just after you left. He insisted on a reduced
bride price."

***

The sitting room was packed. Fatima walked to her father's
side and Ike to his. The room was tense, as the visitors did
not know of the bride price deliberations.

Usman stood up, adjusted his caftan and spoke in a
clear voice. "My friend, like all Igbos, has negotiated a hard
bargain. I know how much my daughter helps her mother
and tried to make sure that her parting will not impact my

35

wife's life too much." He smiled at Rekia, a rare public display. "But we are happy with what has been offered." He gestured at Rekia.

Rekia stood up, trying not to show any emotion. She moved to Fatima, held her shoulders then hugged her. "This is the only daughter I have," She began, with tears in her eyes.

Fatima could not help herself and began to cry.

"Like an eagle, I must let my brood spread its wings"

The women gathered also began to cry, tears streaming from their eyes.

"Ikechuckwu Amadi, we accept your request to marry our daughter."

6.

Alhaji Sani leaned back into the very comfortable arm chair. He took his eyes off his host's lips and admired the chair, moving his buttocks in it and massaging the arm rest. He glanced up at his host and nodded in response to whatever the man was saying.

They were in the presidential suite in Hilton Abuja, a large three-bedroom penthouse with unattractive views of the city below. The suite was the best the Hilton had to offer and a glance around proved why. The floors were covered with a lush Persian carpet, the furniture was Victorian splashed with gold and the walls had paintings that looked very expensive.

His host was from Saudi Arabia, a prince whom Sani judged was probably too far from a throne's inheritance to ever get the chance of sitting on it. Yet, he was still important and Sani sat in the comfortable chair listening to the man's dribble.

Garuba and he did not care why the Saudi family invested in their venture. Oil profits or political gain, it did not matter. Sani was willing to listen to the prince for as long as the man wanted.

"So now that we are agreed that no links should lead to my family, I am willing to start the payments."

The prince was an overweight man in his mid-forties and seemed to have trouble breathing. Sani wondered if it was due to the oversized stomach that screamed for freedom from the white caftan or a lack of lung capacity. *Probably both, or worse* he thought. He waited for the man to catch his breath.

"Thank you, your eminence. We are in your debt."

"Do not be silly, this is simply a business deal and we ALWAYS deliver." A pause to catch his breath. "We are more worried about your capacity to meet your end of the bargain," the prince added.

Sani noted the intensity in the man's pig-like eyes. This was one never to cross. "We have already begun to do so," he replied. "As I have shown you, we are well prepared. In a few months' time you will see the strength of our resolve."

The prince nodded. He snapped his fingers and a man in a black suit standing behind him walked into one of the bedrooms. After a few seconds the man walked out with a briefcase and left it at the feet of his prince. Sani noticed the butt of the gun that briefly showed under the bodyguard's jacket.

"Expecting trouble?" Sani asked.

The prince glanced up at him then at his bodyguard. "One should always expect trouble; we are in Nigeria after all."

It was said so matter-of-factly that Sani simply nodded.

The prince opened the briefcase and flipped it around to show its contents. Sani nodded and smiled. The prince shut the briefcase and handed it over to his bodyguard who took it and placed it next to Sani's feet.

"Next time we meet, your eminence, you will realise how capable we are." Sani picked the briefcase up and stood. "Also, you will be happy with our gifts," he looked around the suite. "The Hilton is great but not discrete enough, we will host you and you will be amazed at what we offer for your pleasure," Sani winked. "Nigeria after all is young and sweet."

***

Sani whistled a tune in the elevator. He was glad the meeting was over, the prince was important, dangerous even, *But by Allah he talked too much.* The elevator pinged and Sani stepped into the foyer.

The penthouse suite had a private elevator with security scanners. Sani took the exit, ignoring the smiles of the security staff. His men were waiting for him and stood up from chairs as he walked to them. He handed one of them the briefcase and walked towards the hotel exit.

A black Toyota Land cruiser with tinted windows was already waiting, engine running and a door opened for him. Sani stepped in, and the car sped away, tyres squealing.

Book II: Hearts of Hate & Greed

39

1.

He ran.

It was a run of desperation, one born of fear mixed with a potent dose of self-preservation. The branches that stung his face and body were ignored. His bleeding bare feet were not even considered. His chest begged for respite, but his adrenal glands were already in overdrive.

He continued to run.

In desperation, he chanced a quick glance across his back. He heard his pursuers as they crashed through the Sambisa forest after him.

They were close.

Every act sanctioned by Allah is of compassion, the Imam had said.

Even if it is with pain... death? he had asked.

Yes, for with pain we are cleansed. In this life or the next.

He remembered thinking on that before asking, *so how do you know an act of compassion by man is an act sanctioned by Allah?*

His imam had looked uncomfortable, then replied, *compassion is in us all and you will know what is right.*

What he had seen, what he was told to do and, in some cases, what he had done was not right. In his heart he knew this. So, he ran.

The arm came from nowhere. The force of it slamming into his chest. The velocity of his run lifted him upwards and then backwards. He crashed into the forest floor like a sack of grain.

"You disappoint me." He knew the voice; it was the father of all devils. The rest of his pursuers caught up with them, some of them panting almost as hard as him. He made to stand but the shock of the fall reminded his body of all he ignored.

The owner of the voice knelt next to him. "Never fear, for even in death you shall do the will of Allah."

A sharp object with serrated edges was placed on his neck and as his head was being sawed off, the last thing he

40

recalled were dark eyes. Humanity, if ever existed, had faded from the eyes of his killer a long time ago.

***

Olu had left the school in Gwoza as early as he could. The first bus was to leave at dawn and he was the first on it. He had spent the previous week thinking on what he would say and who he should say it to. Eventually he decided he would see the police superintendent in Madagali. The man although not from his own home town, was still Yoruba. The high-ranking police officer would surely allay the fears of a kinsman.

The pothole riddled road was so bad passengers held their tongues for fear of biting them off. The stressed-out Toyota HiAce engine and the local radio station blaring through busted speakers, made up the journey's soundtrack. After a brief stop for brunch at a rail crossing packed with street hawkers, the journey continued.

Olu was dropped off at the town's motor park. It was a bit of a walk to the police station, but he did not mind. The walk would allow him to mull over what he had to say.

***

The Madagali district police station was situated at the base of a hill that some will notice, strategically divided the town's elite from the rest of the community. On one side, towards the hill and indeed covering the whole hill was the government reserved area. It was here the town's exclusives such as Alhaji Usman Turaki and his family lived. On the other side, leading downwards, was a road leading to Madagali's town centre.

The police station was surrounded by a waist high block fence with a main gate that had a separate vehicle and pedestrian access. The vehicle access was barred with a steel pole attached to a concrete block on one end to act as the weight for a fulcrum.

He headed for the pedestrian access guarded by a fierce looking officer. He greeted the officer and told him he was here to see their boss. The officer no doubt thinking it

41

had something to do with school business, waved Olu
through.

Inside the station grounds, staff motorcycles and cars
were parked to one side and a gravel driveway led to the main
station building.

As he got closer, Olu could already hear the shouts of
accusations and pleas of those who had come for one case or
the other. It was almost mid-day and already the station's
waiting room was crowded. Some waited to be seen, others
were in conversations with officers and a few were at the
counter. Olu spotted an entry to the offices next to the
counter and walked to it, standing next to the door as if he
was expected.

One of the officers finished with her clients and
walked towards the back office entry. She saw Olu waiting
and greeted him. When he told her who he had come to see,
like her colleague, she pointed Olu to the right office without
asking if he was expected. He thanked her and walked to a
door at the end of the corridor, knocked, waited for
acknowledgment and stepped in.

The police superintendent, Mr. Folami, was free. He
was at his desk eating lunch and watching a football game on
a TV hanging from one of the walls. Olu noticed the office
was cool, this room was probably the only office with an air-
conditioner.

The police chief seeing Olu stood up and extended
his hand.

"*Bawoni Oremi!*" Folami greeted in Yoruba taking Olu's
Hand in his. "*Ope ti mo ti rie!*"

"I am fine, sir," Olu responded in Yoruba. "Yes, it has
been a long time, you are a busy man and so I have not
disturbed you."

"Come on now, we always have time for our brothers
and sisters. Last I remember, my wife was trying to marry you
off to her cousin." Both men laughed, remembering the
incident.

After a few more pleasantries, Folami asked him to sit. "So how can I help you?"

Olu sighed. His host sensing an important conversation took a more serious demeanour.

"For months now," Olu began. "I have been hearing some rumours..."

"Ah, you should know me, Olu. Rumours are not my thing." Folami interrupted.

"That I know, *Oga*. You and I are both educated men..." *You, secondary school, I post graduate.* "But like every rumour that you hear more than twice, we both know there may be an element of truth. So I looked into it further."

"What was this rumour?" Folami asked.

"Well, there have been reports of young men taken into camps in the Sambisa forest for some form of Islamic training. They range from boys as young as eleven to men as old as thirty. From what I can determine, it seems to be for radicalisation."

"I have heard this before. Only last week I sent a car to check it out. The officers that returned did not seem to see anything out of place. From what I was told it is like a boys' scout training."

"That is what I thought." Olu leaned back in his chair. "But during my investigations, I met a few people. Some had not heard anything, others had, but warned their sons not to get involved."

"Wise parents," Folami interrupted and got back to his lunch.

Olu continued. "I eventually met someone who convinced her grandson to join. She is an old woman who lost her daughter to malaria a few years back. She has been taking care of the children ever since, earning a living selling yams."

"Why did she encourage the boy?" Folami asked through a mouth full of food.

"She was convinced that her grandson would learn the ways of virtue, the training was free and at his spare time while he worked, he would be paid." Olu paused. "It was a gift from God and she gladly accepted. The boy is eleven, the eldest and she needed the support."

"Well, we can't really do anything if she approved." Folami said, gesturing with open hands.

"I know that." Olu smiled despite the conversation. "Last week, she came to me in tears. Her grandson had not come to visit for almost two months. The money he usually sent had stopped coming and when she tried to contact the training school, she was given the run around. She said she felt something was wrong and kept on asking the recruit officers who regularly came to town. She said she would not rest until she knew where her grandson was."

"Interesting," Folami said. "Please continue, there is obviously more."

"She left me, still in tears vowing to go to the camp and demand access to him. I pleaded with her not to and said I would come and see you first."

"Very wise," Folami said but Olu raised his hands in the air.

"She didn't listen. Yesterday I went to tell her I was coming here and her relative who lives with them said she left the day I spoke with her. She has been gone a week."

There was silence in the room for a few minutes before Folami came to a decision.

"Okay, what I would like to do is send some officers to the camp, a few more than two this time. I will say we are looking for missing persons."

"*Oga*, thank you so much!" Olu was satisfied with the response.

"There have been some fights with herdsmen and some farmers so we have to look into that first. But I assure you this is next on the list. Maybe next week?"

Olu agreed, saying how this was more than he expected and thanked Folami again. "It is okay my brother; it is what we are here for. Please give me your number and I will keep you posted."

Olu left the station with a much lighter heart, he would be able to make the return trip in good time and he had the police on his side. The day seemed brighter.

***

Idris Ahmed always referred to himself as a tactician. If any asked what made him so sure, his quick response was his chess proficiency.

Chess was not a popular game in his community so Idris spent his spare time teaching peers his own version of the game. The meaninglessness of winning over novices did not register on his ego channel so the list of the defeated continued to rise.

He was always quick to say; *Chess was a tactician game, I am the best player around and so am the best tactician, period.*

Idris did have his moments; after all chess did require some forward thinking and considerations. Such moments made some believe his claims and he soon found himself promoted to his level of incompetence.

Just thirty-two years old, he was the leader of fifty combatant men; well more like ten as the remaining forty were boys under fifteen. Still, he often found the time to lecture them on tactics, the importance of planning and how great he intended to make them.

Unfortunately, his prestige was not widely accepted and not all within the group trusted in his abilities. No matter, he was willing to make the effort to win their hearts.

The man seated in front of him, dressed in civilian clothes, was a private in the Nigerian Army. The soldier was refilling his cup from a three-litre keg that sat on the floor next to his chair. It contained palm wine, a juice tapped from the neck of palm trees and allowed to ferment throughout the day. The longer it was kept; the sweet drink became a more potent alcoholic drink.

Idris tried not to show his disgust and kept an accommodating expression. Alcohol was against his doctrine and on a normal day he would have the man flogged for his evil indulgence, but he needed the officer. It was all part of

45

his grand scheme. He waited for the man to once again empty his cup.

The officer belched loudly, refilled his cup and smiled at Idris, showing snuff-stained teeth. "I think fifty thousand Naira is not bad. Especially for what you want to do." Another swig from the cup.

Idris was surprised the man was still standing. In fact, the man was not even slurring his words yet. He sourced the palm wine from a good seller asking for a mid-morning brew, still sweet but with enough punch.

"How is the palm wine?" he asked, ignoring the man's comments.

"The best I have had in years!" Another belch. "Thank you!"

They were in a hut in one of the hamlets between the Sambisa forest and Chibok. Three months ago, Idris and his men had quietly liberated the hamlet from its ways of sin and made it their first outpost. Apart from a change towards a stricter modified way of Islam, all seemed normal.

He had had the soldier followed to ensure he was alone and even had him searched before their meeting.

"Fifty thousand seems like a lot," Idris said, finally addressing the man's comment.

"Not for what you want," the soldier replied. "It guarantees what you want and it makes sure that I can start afresh somewhere far, far away."

"Join us and I will make you spend the rest of your days in abundance," Idris said, leaning forward in his wicker chair.

"And miss the joys of…" the soldier lifted the palm wine filled cup. "And the warmth of *Ashawos?*"

"You do not need the elixir of sin or the warmth of prostitutes. You will have many wives and enjoy a good healthy life under Allah."

"Thank you for your offer but I humbly decline. If you want my help it is fifty thousand." The soldier drank from his cup, eyes meeting Idris's.

Idris waited for the man to refill his cup once again. It seemed the soldier had all the intention of finishing the keg of wine. "Okay, I will give you half now, and half when this is over."

"No, no." Vigorous head shake. "By the time it is over, I assure you I will be long gone. I want it all now."

Ah, so the Nigerian Army did not always recruit idiots? "Okay." Idris said and pulled out two bundles of money from his caftan.

If the man was wise, he would have accepted the compassion of Allah and joined their cause. Now, he did not intend to allow the man to live long enough to spend his spoils. Once the man was no longer useful, he would personally behead him.

"Spend it wisely and I expect you to do what I intend you to."

"I will." The money disappeared into layers of clothing. "Now if you don't mind, I will finish this beautiful drink and head back to the barracks."

"It is your body," was all Idris said and walked out of the hut.

2.

The Sambisa forest is one of those natural beauties that seems to have no right to be where it is. This is more obvious if you approach it from the south. You would have driven through a receding tropical landscape as you got further north. Big trees disappeared giving way to smaller trees, which in turn became shrubs and soon the major flora became more *elephant* grass than anything else. Stumbling on a forest, although not like the lush green of the south, was like driving into a different world altogether. The Sambisa stood like a portal, one of the last few oases before the Sahara.

The portion of adjoining land not cleared for farming was lined with big native trees, four-foot grasses and broad-leaf ferns. Despite the human encroachment, the forest was always teeming with wildlife and hunters often returned with antelope, monkeys and other *bush-meats*. There was even the occasional hunting of hyenas-or worse that had caused turmoil in surrounding hamlets, attacking livestock and children.

It was a jungle and if it looked game, regardless of species, it usually ended up being so. Knowing this, the locals created well marked paths that snaked through the forest for their uses. These paths usually lead to popular hunting grounds and water sources.

Locals also knew not to wander too deep into the forest. "If there are no paths, you are on your own."

***

Well past the locally known area of the forest and about fifty kilometres towards the Cameroonian border was where Idris Ahmed and his gang called home. Access to it was not public knowledge, in fact, most locals were unaware of their presence.

This allowed the community to thrive; carving out sections of the forest to build communal areas, mud residences, two mosques and even a garage to store and repair cars.

It was not simply a case of clearing a large space and building on it. The structures were distributed; a visitor could easily spend days in a mud hut not knowing there was another just four meters away.

Sentries always patrolled the camp's perimeter in silence. The order was to only attack if there was a threat, otherwise they came back with a report. The daily perimeter patrol was also a productive way to prepare recruits for a life in the forest, dropping them into the alien world of Mother Nature's sounds in her purest form. For the newly arrived, it was also the beginning of a month-long initiation process.

On his first night, a recruit was led to the camp's main communal area. He was then blindfolded and taken to an uninhabited pre-selected part of the forest and instructed to only remove the blindfold when he felt alone.

Eventually, fearing the unseen or fear of not knowing one's attacker, the recruit-to-be worked up the nerve and removed the blindfold. Next to him, lying on the mossy forest floor would be a jug of fresh water and a machete. If he returned to camp, he became the newest member of the gang.

The lost ones, on the other hand were never even searched for as the Sambisa usually claimed them in one way or the other.

The successful recruit would then spend four weeks patrolling the forest, at which point, due to the adaptive evolutionary nature of humans, he would become more at home in the forest.

***

The chair Idris sat on was out of place in the surrounds of the forest. It was an executive office leather chair on wheels and he sat in it as if addressing a corporate meeting. His top commanders- 'comrades' as he liked to call them - sat on various items in front of him: some on tree logs while others on plastic chairs and upturned metal buckets.

They all sat in the main communal hall which, was simply a concrete floor and a two-foot wall to keep rodents out. It was a work in progress with dried elephant grass blades and twines to fully roof the hall. So far only half of the roof had been done.

The man standing in front of him was fat-filled when he came to them and to everyone's surprise survived the initiations. Just past his nineteenth birthday, the boy was now all muscle, more than six-foot tall, with a fanatical dedication to their cause and a brutality to match the devil himself.

He gladly bore the name he was given by peers, *The Father of Devils*. He even had followers who liked to call themselves *The Devils*. Idris knew the boy was a threat to his rule and would have ended the boy's miserable life the first time he had shown disrespect, but Idris stayed his plans. *Never get rid of a useful donkey*, his father had always said.

Right now, the boy was telling those gathered that the mission Idris was about to effect was not sanctioned by Allah. How the boy came up with that was beyond him. Either way, he was willing to let the boy talk, he intended to deal with the boys' insubordination after the success of his mission.

So he listened, nodding as if finding reason to what the boy said. Like a game of chess, he gave away pieces, letting The Father of Devils play his hand.

After what Idris deemed was a respectable ranting time slot, he cleared his throat and asked, "so just to be clear, you propose that we do what, exactly?"

"We have been sanctioned by Allah to create his caliphate on this soil." The boy yelled. "We should do so and not play games with our enemies!"

Idris sat forward. Using a much calmer voice he asked. "Please, do tell us, where will you get the resources to create a caliphate?"

"Allah has already provided. Look around you." The boy turned his back on Idris and faced the gathered crowd. He spread his hands as if embracing every one of them. "We have the beginning of the end for the infidels. We spread like wildfire, we will sweep through their lands and consume them as we flow through. Those who embrace the true ways of the prophet shall become our people. Those that refuse shall be crushed!" The boy punctuated the end of the sentence with a slam of his fist in an open palm.

"And what do you think I am doing?" Idris rose from his chair and stepped towards the boy. "Our ammunitions are running low, our guns are jamming and the next shipment from across the border is late. Don't you think it is wise to replenish our supplies first?" Without waiting for a reply, he faced the gathered. "Comrades, I have led you with tactics and superior intellect. Do you not think that once we are fully supplied, we shall consume this land?" Some of the men nodded in agreement. The boy tried to speak but Idris placed his hands on the boy's shoulder, interrupting him. "Our brother is desperate to begin the work of Allah, I understand that. Which is why we attack tomorrow!"

The men's shout of war was cut short as the boy interrupted. "You waste our men and limited resources on this!" Silence greeted his outburst. "Replenish the ranks, take all they own. Take their daughters and turn them to brides of destiny. Take over their puny villages and create the caliphate of Allah, it is our destiny!"

Idris punched him. He had put all his strength in the punch and the result showed. The boy stumbled to the floor, using his hands for balance. The boy made to attack but more than half of the gathered men belonged to Idris. The boy straightened and spat out a tooth.

Idris walked up to him and said, "we are on the same page, you idiot. To conquer you need the tools!"

"Who needs the tools when Allah has provided?" The boy brushed past Idris, stopped as he was close and whispered. "If you fail, I shall be the judging hand of your destiny."

As the boy walked off, joined by a few others, Idris realised he had made a mistake. He should have killed the boy.

***

The night of the attack was moonless. The gathered warriors stood in silence as pickup trucks were prepared. The only semblance of a uniform was the colour of the garments they wore, black. Even their faces were painted with a black concoction made of charcoal and plant roots, this left the whites of their eyes floating like orbs of light in the darkness. The younger boys were armed with rusty AK-47s and pistols. The armaments of the older men were in much better condition and some even wore body armour.

The first of the pickup trucks came through and the younger boys clambered into the back trays in silence. As the last truck drove past his position, Idris noticed The Father of Devils and four men standing aside.

"We will guard the camp!" The Father of Devils called out. Idris nodded and climbed into the last truck.

***

The predominant religion in the region was Islam. This meant the only place one could purchase and consume alcohol for miles was at the mammy market. This was situated just past the entrance to the Nigerian Infantry Division 7 (NID7) barracks, an all army barracks that currently housed about two-hundred soldiers. The mammy market was just past the first entrance and in addition to alcohol, the market catered for general goods for the resident army and staff.

At just past seven pm on a Saturday night, the market was already packed with civilians and soldiers in trade and social engagements. It was a thriving marketplace where general goods for the resident army and staff were sold, including all the pleasures and grief of a warm flesh.

On the other side of the barracks and almost directly opposite the market was another entrance. This was guarded, with civilian access strictly prohibited. It was the entry point that seven pickup trucks from the Sambisa rolled up to.

Idris climbed out of the last truck wearing Nigerian army fatigues and army issued boots. He unshouldered his AK-47 and left it on the car seat. He also removed his Glock 17 from a shoulder holster, clicked off the safety catch and held the gun behind his lower back. He walked towards the security gate eyes scanning around for any signs of trouble. *Never trust a man you pay to commit a crime*; his dead father had always said just after giving a bribe.

The first thing that gave him pause was the number of guards at the gate. He expected one but counted two. He stopped in front of them and greeted them in Hausa. The guard he knew gestured at the man next to him and said. "He already knows, I shared half with him. Bring your boys through." Idris nodded and returned to his men. His first lieutenant was waiting next to the first pickup truck.

52

"Line up the new recruits from the first four trucks, tonight is their destiny." He walked to the last three trucks containing his prized fighters. They were already out and ready, the anticipation of the fight shining in their eyes. "We line up behind them as support. Once through, we head straight for the Armoury." He turned to one of his men. "Do you have the remaining grenades?"

"Brought six, four are at the camp just in case."

Idris nodded. "Move out!" he barked into a hand-held radio.

The first line of fighters, with an average age of eleven, moved towards the security gate. Flowing through their blood was a cocktail of drugs including the potent *Captagon*. Even in light of what they were about to do, their faces were calm with a detached, serene look, not an ounce of fear in their eyes.

As they closed in on the gate, the guards aimed their weapons and opened fire. The gate squealed open and soldiers poured through from the sides, shooting at the young fighters.

Like zombies and without any thoughts of self-preservation, the young fighters returned fire.

When the gunshots started, civilians at the market were alarmed. The soldiers within their midst, numbering about thirty, told them to remain calm. It was a training exercise they suggested, nothing to fear.

Life at the market continued.

***

The Father of Devils and four of his Devils looked on.

Idris and his fighters had recovered somewhat, taking defensive positions behind their trucks and in drainage channels on the side of the road. It was a stalemate. The soldiers were pinned at the entrance and Idris and his men could not retreat any further. The floor was littered with the dead from both sides and no clear winner in sight.

"Did I not warn Idris, the idiot?" The Father of Devils did not wait for a response. "Come let's find the

Armoury." He and his men crawled to the barrack walls away from the fighting.

3.

When Alihu was dropped off at the Sambisa forest by Sani almost seven months before, he was a very angry young man. The reality of where he was hit him when he was tracking his way back to the camp, surrounded by sounds that touched senses he had never felt before. If he died in the forest his body would never be found, he would die a failure, something his father seemed certain of. He persevered, stumbled through the thick forest, waved his machete at a persistent hyena and even lost his water bottle to a gang of red monkeys. By the time he got to the communal hall he was a different man with one goal, a total submission to Islam.

During his training, while listening to the teachings of the camp's Imam, he did not question the deviation of the teachings from what he was brought up with as a child. In his mind this was the true way of the prophet. He became a vicious Jihadi machine never needing drugs to embrace the brutality of terror.

By the fifth month, during the raid of a small hamlet in the outskirts of the Sambisa forest, he was found in a room with the headless corpses of the family that lived within. Infidels he called them, spitting on the bodies, a look of pure indifference on his blood-soaked face.

His brutality did not end there that night. As a lesson on whose law reigned, he raped the daughter of the chief before the eyes of everyone including her father, then for good measure, stoned her to death for adultery.

Before being beheaded, the chief named him. The *Father of Devils*. In the eyes of the revered who looked on, the name stuck.

Whenever a judgment was required, Alihu was called upon to pass it. He had two weapons, the machete he used to judge was called *Hukumchi,* Judgment, and his fighting one he named *Fansa*, Redemption. It was not long before he gathered men around him who worshipped his very essence.

***

Alihu and his followers stood behind the ten-foot barrack fence, trying to find a way in. The sound of gunfire at the gate still pierced the evening night. And they ignored it.

One of the men tapped his shoulder and pointed at a small metal door and moved to it. As expected, it was locked from within. Alihu attached a silencer to his pistol and fired into the door locks. Two of his men slowly pushed the door open and stepped into the barracks.

The door opened into the back wall of two structures. From the pane-less windows, they could see a group of chairs in a line facing a blackboard. Although the rooms were empty, Alihu gestured for his men to remain low. He recalled the map Idris had shown them days ago. The Armoury was not far off.

He pointed at the right end of the structure. The first man peeped around and gave the all clear. They moved in.

Despite the sounds of chaos, the area they came to was devoid of any activity. Ahead was a maintenance workshop for the army division. Carcasses of trucks, cars and vans in different stages of dismantle, were strewn like dying beasts. He and his four fighters used these as cover, slipping silently from one shadow to the next.

At the edge of the workshop they paused, eyes fixed ahead. Across a small road was their target, a building almost the size of the one they were leaning against. But while the workshop was open plan, the armoury was built like a prison. Alihu noted the concrete walls with small rectangular windows too high for anyone to climb to and too small for even a child to fit through.

Their hiding place was directly in front of the Armoury entrance and a group of soldiers were loading boxes into a pickup truck. Alihu counted six men. The closest had his back to them as he leaned on the driver's door for support. Two men carried boxes down to the back of the

55

truck and the last three stood at the entry, weapons held at their sides.

Alihu raised his pistol and shot the soldier at the driver's door in the back of the head. He released *Fansa* from the harness on his back and with a roar he attacked. His men recovered quicker than the soldiers and started firing.

By the time Alihu was past the driver's door, the two soldiers carrying the boxes were on the floor dying from bullet wounds. The three at the entry already had their guns up and were firing at Alihu.

The account of Alihu's men later was a work of legend. Alihu, like the angel of Allah, ran towards the men with no fear. Their bullets were turned away and he hacked into them, harvesting their souls, sacrifices to their cause.

In truth, fear or the ridiculous nature of a madman running at them with a machete may have affected the soldiers' aim. It was even more plausible that they had limited visibility. Regardless, they were butchered with a look of surprise on their faces. Limbs hacked by the frenzy of a berserker.

By the time Alihu's men got to the Armoury entrance, they had the look of those who had witnessed a miracle.

Panting and covered in blood, Alihu barked at them. "By Allah! Fill the bags quickly. Mine first with launchers and bullets bring it. Then yours. Quickly!"

The men obeyed and Alihu scanned the area. Their encounter was not yet known but they needed to hurry. His chest still heaved from the rage and his blade *Fansa* called out to him, beckoning for more bloodshed.

"Hurry!" he called into the armoury. One of his men returned with a long duffel bag and dropped it next to his feet. He picked it up, ignoring the twenty-kilogram weight of it.

After a minute he yelled, "You have thirty seconds!"

In twenty-five his men returned, bags full. One carried two bags across his back. Alihu grabbed two grenades hanging off his belt.

"Wait at the fence door. I will be with you soon".

***

Idris prayed for a way out; his men had to retreat and soon. The soldiers had unlimited supplies of ammunition and fighters. He did not and was already running short of both. Cursing at the dead body of the soldier that betrayed him, he lifted his head from the drain and fired a volley of shots towards the soldier's prone form. He needed a lifeline. As if in answers to his prayers, an explosion rocked the grounds behind the gate. There was a pause of gunfire from the soldiers.

"Throw the remaining grenades!" Idris yelled.

Five seconds later a well thrown grenade exploded in front of the gate. "Retreat to the last trucks!" He was already running for the trucks.

***

At the first explosion, the market crowd turned to the soldiers within their midst. Seeing a confused look on their faces the crowd questioned.

The second explosion broke them. There was chaos in the Mammy market as exits and covers were sought.

***

Of the forty or so fighters Idris came with, only about fifteen were now capable of fighting. The rest were wounded or dying. And as the remaining trucks crashed through the Sambisa, dead bodies were flung out of trucks.

Some lucky non-human inhabitants of the Sambisa were to spend the next few weeks on full stomachs.

4.

Idris walked into the camp first barking orders for a retreat to the second camp. Few knew the location he had prepared, a forward thought for moments such as this.

He scanned the camp site and saw Alihu sitting on a tree trunk in the main communal hall. Alihu had a machete leaning on one leg and a smile on his lips. The perceptive ones would have noted the blade was *Hukumchi*. Idris for his part overlooked it.

"Your timing was impeccable brother! How many weapons did you get?"

Alihu's response was ungodly. He rushed forward and kicked Idris in the chest. Idris staggered backwards, tripping over the small wall of the hall. Raising his right hand for balance, he watched in awe as it was hacked from the wrist. He reached with his left, which was also hacked, this time from the elbow. Arms bleeding, he stood with a dumb look on his face. Alihu kicked him, a kick like one was stepping on a fly and Idris crashed to the floor still in shock. He never truly recovered enough to understand what was happening as Hukumchi ate through his flesh like a butcher's carving blade.

***

Some say history is written by the victorious and in the case of the incident at the NID7 barrack, history was simply a poorly manipulated tale of events.

Citizens woke up to the news of how insurgents attacked the military; surprisingly, during a training exercise. Who they were or what they stood for was never stated. The tale told was that the army had viciously fought back, chasing the criminals all the way to their hideout in the Sambisa. There, they were met with a weak opposition of unskilled and poorly equipped fighters. The remaining fighters and their leader were quickly dispatched and their camp was dismantled. This was the Army's story and pictures and videos were sent to various news outlets depicting this view of events.

The truth on the other hand, like most histories fraught with inconsistencies, was substantially different. The army had not been able to chase after Idris until dawn. Due to the attackers' rapid retreat with no attention to stealth, it was easy to trace their way to the camp, occasionally stopping to take pictures of bodies in stages of consumption by carnivores and scavengers.

Arriving at the camp, save for what was left of Idris, it was totally void of human life. The army commander ordered the camp searched, telling his men to take whatever valuables they found. What was left behind was blown up.

*****

Alihu stared at the tiny screen of the portable TV. His anger growing with each telling of the tale. He took a deep breath to calm his nerves and closed his eyes to subdue the rage within him. His thoughts were on what should have been. He envisaged a different news feed. One with his face splattered over screens around the world, a tale of the brutality that befell infidels, the creation of the caliphate of Allah. A place with true values of life and void of the corruption of western atrocities.

If only Idris had listened.

He did not dwell on this thought for long, he believed that his slain brothers were a sacrifice to Allah. A sacrifice that had produced true leadership, he intended to return the favour to the one true *God.*

*****

Sani watched the news in the comfort of his six-bedroom, two-storey, well-secured home in Abuja. Unlike his brother, Garuba, who had decided to remain connected to family roots by living in Madagali. Sani preferred the infrastructure available in the nation's capital, where power and water were *almost* not a luxury. He was more disappointed than angry at what he saw on television. The overall plan had been foiled by the difficulty in getting their consignment from Libya and he understood what Idris had tried to achieve. It had been a good plan: weapons from the army base would have begun a momentum, introducing the country to the new caliphate and an incapable Nigerian army. Most importantly, by the time the army had effected a response, Idris and his men would have been restocked with far more superior weapons.

Unfortunately, the ever-porous nature of the Libyan border was getting more difficult to exploit and Sani had to overcome this with enormous bribes. Finally, their consignment had started its way to its final destination. If Idris had waited for a month, he would have had all he needed for the next phase of their plan.

Idris had chosen to improvise and now he was dead. Sani had to deal with the uncertainty of Alihu's leadership. *Was it a good thing?* In a way, he was proud of the boy. Alihu had embraced the brainwashing of the Imam quicker than anyone else, taking what was asked of him as the only true doctrine.

The other side of it, Sani thought to himself, was control. Alihu no more believed in orders from his superiors. The boy now believed *he* was the hand of Allah and only Allah told him what to do. Sani himself did not doubt Allah but, *when last did the one true God speak and men listened?*

Sani sighed. He knew he now had to visit the new camp to gauge Alihu's state of mind. His brother would not object to the killing of a son, but Sani hoped it did not amount to that. To build and expand they first needed someone like Alihu. He did not need to order Alihu around, all he needed to do was guide the boy. After all, a caliphate to Allah was exactly what the plan was. *Right?*

He picked up his mobile phone to make plans for his trip to Madagali and then the Sambisa. After speaking with Alihu, he would have to at least stay in Madagali until things improved. He disliked being that close to the action but had no choice. Their investors would have no doubt seen the news and if he was not seen as doing something they may well pull out. An unacceptable thought, as in the order of things he stood to be the scapegoat and what became of that scapegoat was not something he wanted to find out.

His brother answered at the third ring.

***

The old *Dambé* trainer knew the news was not the full story. His investigation of the burnt camp was proof enough. The insurgents, as the media was now calling them, had not been defeated but moved deeper into the Sambisa. *Wounded? Yes. Defeated? Far from it.*

60

The location of the new camp would soon be known to him.

The Old Man casually walked through the forest. He did not need a map or a GPS device to know the way and tracked through the dense foliage until he came to a well-known local footpath. His destination was the hamlet it led to. He adjusted the pack on his back, checked his caftan for his concealed weapons and set off on the half-day walk.

5.

Olu was still not sure how to take the news. The moment he heard it, he had contacted Folami at the Madagali police station. Although a team of officers never got to the Sambisa, Folami had assured Olu it was now all over.

Also, the grandmother he was worried about had suddenly returned. She had found her grandson, alive and healthy and had decided to work with him. Now both of them were supporting the family from the Sambisa and it seemed their fortunes had improved. All seemed well but he still was not sure if all *really* was well. The stories he had heard about these insurgents meant they had been planning this for a very long time. *Could they really be gone?* If the world had not heard the last of the insurgents, their survival would soon be known.

Olu gathered his study materials from his desk and stood up. He looked around the office. It was not big or fancy. The walls were covered in a fading polka dot wallpaper and there was only one window with a view of students' classrooms. Two desks sat in the office, the other belonged to a geography teacher who was currently on maternity leave. He was glad for the privacy and solitude. He stepped out of his sanctuary and locked the door.

A student in the class he was about to take approached him and asked if he needed assistance. She was the current class prefect. He remembered her. It was only a few months ago he had asked her mother about the camp in the Sambisa. They both began the short walk to the classroom.

"Do you think the insurgents are really defeated?" she asked after some idle chat.

Olu laughed. "Sorry, you just voiced what I have been thinking about all day. Frankly I don't believe so, but time will tell."

She sighed dropping her shoulders.

"What is the matter?" he asked.

"In two months' time after we complete our last exams, I am getting married. I want my wedding to be a time of joy. Not with the news of mad people beheading people like *akwiya*." Goat.

"Congratulations." Olu stopped and placed his hands on her shoulder, a smile lit his face. "A wedding is about you and your husband-to-be. No matter what happens around you, enjoy that day."

***

Mama Ajiya, as she was now fondly known in the Sambisa had done exactly what she told Olu she would.

When next the recruit officers came to her village, she had insisted, wailed when she was refused and threatened when she was harassed. Eventually the officers had yielded. One of them made a call on his mobile phone.

"You will come with us. Know that we will not return for three weeks and we leave now."

She had no choice, in her heart she knew this was the only opportunity she would ever have to locate her grandson and she had to take it.

Three years before a series of unfortunate incidents had changed her life. Her son-in-law had gone first from tuberculosis leaving her daughter to care for a boy and two girls. A year later her still-grieving daughter fell ill with malaria and died. In her ageing years she was to be a mother again. A trying physical exercise for her fifty-plus-year-old body. Emotionally it was also difficult. Many nights, grief almost crushed her sad heart but the children needed her and she took strength from that knowledge; she was all they had left. Luckily, the boy was old enough to assist more than he required her care. The girls were a different story, the eldest was seven while the youngest was just four years old.

Luckily for her, before being carted away by the recruiters with a promise of finding her grandson, she had noticed her neighbour's son, too young to be recruited, running towards them on an errand. She had stopped him.

"Please my son, when you return home, tell Zainab that I have gone to look for my grandson. If I do not return soon, I shall send a message to her." The boy had nodded and ran off.

Zainab had been heaven sent. She had been with them for a year now, helping with tasks she and her grandson could not. The younger girls had also warmed to her and now saw in Zainab the elder sister they had never had. She was grateful to Zainab and showed her appreciation by sending her to an afternoon Islamic girl's school.

She had been absent two months now and was comforted to know her family were in good hands. She had seen them twice and sent money more times ensuring they were financially better off.

***

Mama Ajiya, now part of the citizens of the Sambisa was one of the few allowed to leave the forest sanctuary for neighbouring hamlets.

During her visits to hamlets, she was normally accompanied by two guards but eventually she had become trustworthy enough to be allowed to handpick her minder and even the number she needed.

For today's trip she had selected a young man she knew had taken a fancy to a girl in the hamlet. While he was busy, she intended to visit a friend.

***

The old *Dambé* trainer sat on a mat in a small hut. The walls were blackened by cooking smoke and the raffia roof still had the smell of wood and kerosene smoke. Below the only window in the room was an old cooking pit with dead coals. The Old Man, after acquiring the hut from a farmer, had never used it as he preferred to cook in the open air at the front of his hut.

One of the first things he had done before using the hut was to install a proper door, to stop the smoke from drifting in and to secure the hut while he was away. He had paid more for the door and bolts than he had for the hut.

The previous owner, unlike some in the hamlet, did not like the fighters from the Sambisa. He openly objected to the local chief's pact with them. Ignoring the fact that, had the pact not been made, the hamlet would simply have no longer existed. Selling the hut and his few belongings, the owner left. Some believed he had not made it far and his remains lay somewhere in the Sambisa.

There was a knock on the door and the Old Man rose to open it. He was expecting an important guest.

Mama Ajiya stood in the late evening sunlight, a bag in one hand and a sad smile on her face. He let her in and locked the door behind her. When he turned to her, she fell into his arms, tears already streaming down her weathered cheeks.

Their re-union was not always a mixed feeling of joy and sadness. The Old Man knew she had just seen a lot of evil. Most of the boys she cooked for at the camp were among the dead in the mass grave the army had dug.

He remembered the first time they met. She had spent a night of sorrow in the Sambisa. Her heart-wrenching sobs calling out to him from his hiding place as he watched the camp.

He instantly knew why.

In the middle of the camp was a pole and staked on top of it was the decomposing head of a young boy. He had been hiding long enough to know it was placed there as a warning to any who considered running away. From the condition of the head, it must have been there for weeks.

Early the next morning, the woman had left the camp
for a stream close by. He had followed, weary of the look on
her face. When they got to the stream, his fears were
confirmed. She intended to end her pain.

From his concealed spot, he had asked. "Do you not
have others to live for?" He knew the question had reached
her. Slowly she turned to his voice. He stepped out of the
bushes. "Do not waste the life you now have. It is a gift."

"You are not one of them." It was not a question.

"No, I aim to destroy them." She had laughed then.
Although filled with sadness, it was a good laugh. He smiled.
"Okay, I intend to try."

Her laugh became a smile. "Come let us talk. I do not
wish to be found out, especially in the presence of a crazy old
man."

He led her into the forest until they came to a
secluded spot he was happy with. There he had convinced
her to return to the camp and seek employment as a cook. He
had overheard some fighters complaining about the food and
he was sure she could do better. He urged her to gain their
trust, be his eyes and ears. He then went on to expand on
how valuable any information she shared would be. She had
listened quietly, her face expressionless.

When he had finished, she took a moment to think
on it. Tears escaped her already tired eyes and the Old Man
delicately brushed them off. Eventually, she agreed, saying
she would tell their leader he had just killed the only
breadwinner in her family. She would suggest preparing a
meal and if they liked it, would ask for double the payment
her grandson had been given. If they wished her to perform
more tasks, she would ask for more payment.

The Old Man had been elated by her response and
their conversation had turned to each other's lives and the
dreams and the losses of years past. As the sun rose to its
zenith, she had stood up to return to the camp.

She had hugged him then, telling him she looked
forward to their next meet.

They had met in secret several times after that, forming a friendship that both never expected to ever have again. Eventually, the relationship surprised them both by becoming more.

***

They lay on the mat in each other's arms. Mama Ajiya had her back to the Old Man. She could feel his warm breath on the back of her neck and the rise of his chest on her lower back. His presence made her feel safe and she shifted into him, enjoying the feel of his skin and the protection of his arms around her chest. She traced his weathered skin with her fingers. His skin was old, but she knew there was strength in his limbs.

A child outside laughed, bringing her back to her surroundings. She missed the sounds she now heard: everyday people going around their business, the sound of grain being beaten, the groan of wood as it was cut for firewood, the chatter of domestic animals. She missed it all.

Tears she was unaware of dropped to the Old Man's arm. He felt them and lifted his lips to her ears.

"You or I are not to blame," he said. She understood; he thought her tears were for the boys killed during the NID7 attack. Images of their faces flooded her thoughts, she had fed them before they were taken from her like her grandson, gone for a belief she now knew was false. She had sent him to his death. It was her fault.

"If they had taken the weapons quietly, with your help, they would have been caught red handed." He propped himself up with his elbow. "Think about that! They would have been forced to give up their leaders!"

"We would have stopped it," Mama Ajiya said.

"No, the army already knew what they wanted to do." He turned her face to his and wiped her tears. "The army saw them as an enemy. You can't blame yourself for what they chose to do. You just cannot."

She nodded and got up to dress. He lay on the mat looking up at her. Her minder would still be busy and the

66

supplies she needed would already be in the pickup truck they came with. There was no rush.

"Alihu is now the leader and I fear all hope of destroying them without much bloodshed has been lost." She finished dressing and sat opposite him. "I fear the evil in him."

"Yes, he truly is a mad man. He believes in his cause. A mad belief." The Old Man also dressed. "Are you sure the power will not calm him down? Responsibility does some surprising things to some."

She laughed, it was a hysterical laugh. "That young man believes that he was given this responsibility by Allah. He feels it in his bones. He thinks... No! He *knows* that it is his right!" She paused, reining her emotions back in. In a much quieter voice, she added. "He will be a tyrant that exercises his right because he believes it is for the greater good."

After a while, the Old Man said. "But we know he is the devil."

"No," Mama Ajiya said shaking her head. "He is the father of the devil." She walked to the door. "Forget this talk. I will continue to earn his trust no matter what it takes. Let me enjoy my moment of freedom."

"You are a free woman, Ajiya. You can leave when you want..."

"And lose the only ear in the camp?" Again, she shook her head. "I will stay."

"Then I shall protect you with my life." He hugged her. "We will prevail."

"We and what army?" she asked with a smile. She nuzzled his neck with her face. "I brought some food for you. Come let's eat, you have made me very hungry."

6.

Ike turned around to the sound of his name. A smile lit his face as he saw who had called. Boni was a good friend, Ike

67

would have loved to call him a best friend but such a label could not be used with Boni.

Boni was currently the leader of the university's Black Axe Confraternity. Bonds of family and best friends were not attachments an *Aye* brother had with none members. Regardless, his closeness to Ike still puzzled students and brothers alike.

"Igbo Mann-nu," Boni said navigating his way to Ike.

Ike was sitting on the edge of the roof of an uncompleted building. The building was supposed to be additional student accommodation but the unfortunate spirit of corruption already marked its fate, the project was bound to never be completed. Shrubs, grasses and rodents now called it home.

Some of the scaffolding was left when construction stopped three years ago and it was one of this Boni had used to climb to the roof.

Boni found out a long time ago that it was a favourite spot for Ike. His friend always came here to clear his head, think of home and have fond thoughts of his wife to be, Fatima.

"My Man, *how far?*" Ike replied. He stood up from the roofs edge. Boni came close and they shook hands and bumped shoulders. "I thought you were travelling?"

"Still am, just waiting for some of my brothers to get ready." Boni replied.

They both sat on the roof's edge, taking in the view past the university grounds and into the adjoining farmland and lush rainforest beyond. A silence grew, it was not an uncomfortable one. Sometimes when Boni joined Ike on the roof, they talked, other times they just sat in silence. For Boni it was a moment of peace, a time to shut out his world. Ike knew the life his friend lived was against his ideals but their relationship had started before Boni became Don.

They both had started their studies together and had met just before the matriculation ceremony. Ike had been standing in front of the school's registration office looking lost. Boni had walked out of the office, saw the look on Ike's face and had asked what was wrong. Ike was missing some documents he had left at home and the registration officer was refusing to give him his formal acceptance letter. Boni had retreated into the office. A few minutes later, he walked out with Ike's letter. His response to Ike's surprised look was still a recollection of humour between them.

"Don't mind that idiot. He hates Igbos. I told him to return the money my father sent him and he changed his mind," Boni had said.

After the ceremony, Ike had offered to buy drinks as a repayment for Boni's help. Copious amount of alcohol and marijuana were consumed and with a head that felt like it was used as *Dundun,* Ike had staggered to the motor park for the trip back to Madagali.

A few weeks later, when courses were due to start, Ike had returned. Boni looked him up and from that point on they became inseparable. Ike never really understood why Boni took a shine to him, it was glaringly obvious that their family background and up-bringing were totally different.

Ike came from a middle-class family that required him, from the age of eleven to work during school holidays, contributing his wages and time to the family business. His father's fortunes had only improved recently when the investment of transporting goods directly from Aba to Maiduguri proved lucrative.

Boni on the other hand, had seen several countries by the time he was eleven. His family was in the oil business and an average life was never in his books. This became apparent on Ike's first night back when Boni had taken him out on a pub crawl in a new Peugeot 406. It was one of several cars Boni owned during their years in university.

By the second semester, Ike moved into Boni's four-bedroom house. Boni refused rent, so Ike felt housework was the least he could do to show his appreciation. Although he took the role of caretaker, their friendship was never in doubt and both men treated each other as equals. This friendship continued to grow until the end of the first year when an incident forced Ike to move out. Morality was at the forefront of his decision.

Ike knew his history well, especially that of the early 70s, when various organisations formed in universities across Africa. All started as political movements that fought against oppression of blacks in countries such as South Africa. The tools employed to fight were mostly organised peaceful demonstrations or minor civil disobedience activities. These organisations, often referred to as cults, had unique constitutions, rules and guidelines. New members were initiated in secretive ceremonies that often reflected the cultural beliefs of founding members.

By the late 80s and 90s, cults soon spiralled into violent machines of change. Politicians and power brokers saw in confraternities an opportunity to increase their power through intimidation and control. Most cult leaders for their part embraced the change with open arms. Organisations such as The Neo Black Movement became the Black Axe Confraternity and others formed from rogue factions of existing groups. Soon the quest for supremacy spawned violent activities to claim territory.

Increasing their numbers to army regiment proportions, cults were able to spread fear and hate across all Nigerian universities. Worse, various methods were employed to remain above the law. One way was to ensure law enforcement stakeholders were bribed or blackmailed. Another much cheaper option was to initiate the sons of the rich and or powerful.

Boni, simply by the fortunes of his family, was always going to be a target. By his first year he had no choice. Life suddenly became exceedingly difficult for him. Many occasions, on campus or on night outs, he was accosted by cult members who relieved him of his designer accessories such as wristwatches and shoes. He soon realised that, if he wanted peace, he needed the protection of a confraternity.

Ike remembered Boni's revelation like it was yesterday. He had tried to persuade his friend not to join and informed him of all the atrocities that confraternities had wrought. It was useless. Deep down, Boni wanted the power, fame and fear that came with the status of a confraternity member.

Come their second year on campus, Boni was flying the colours of Black Axe, one of the most notorious of confraternities that existed. By the end of their third year, Boni was the State's chapter leader. How this came to pass, was a story for another time.

***

"Difficult runs?" Ike asked. He did not usually ask about Boni's activities, in fact he made an effort to keep that aspect of their lives separate. Sometimes though, Boni needed to talk about it.

"Only difficult because we have to deal with *Tingos*," Boni replied.

Ike knew the term, it referred to a rival cult group called *Airlords*. "Is money involved?"

"The only reason I would be dealing with them," Boni replied.

"And I assume you are the supplier of a product?" Ike asked. He knew Boni was into the local arms trade, another activity of which he did not approve but left his opinion to himself.

"Yes, we are," Boni replied.

"Easy, if this is your first trade, ask for 100% payment and give them the best products they have ordered. Make it about 60% of total delivery. After a few days, deliver the rest." While Boni was considering this, Ike added, "Tell them next shipment will be 100% pay, 100% delivery. You can even add conditions like if the product is used against your brothers, it will be the end of the deal."

Boni laughed. "I did not say what type of product; how can they use it against us?"

71

"I didn't say you did," Ike replied with a straight face, but not being able to hold it for long, he joined in the laughter.

"I know you don't approve," Boni began. "But in all honesty, I think it is better to be in organised crime and not a petty crime business or tool for politicians."

"Crime is crime," Ike replied.

"Come now, you should know certain things are necessary evils. In those cases, such evils should be managed by honest and business-minded people like me."

Ike laughed again. "Business minded I agree, Honest? Well…"

"Oh yes! An honest crook you can trust because his wares are his business. A dishonest one? Dishonesty *is* what he sells," Boni replied.

"And I am the Igbo man?" Ike laughed.

They sat in silence once again until Boni had to go. "I will see you in Madagali at the wedding."

"*I beg be* careful," Ike said. "I will give you a call once I'm back home."

"Be safe," Boni replied.

Ike watched him leave. Thinking back on the activities of Black Axe since Boni took over, he now understood what Boni was trying to achieve. In his own way, he was trying to turn the branch into a lucrative business with profit at its core. If successful, members were bound to gain financially and improve their lifestyle. This in turn would make them value their lives more. Simply put, instead of an organisation of thugs, his friend was building a company.

Of course, as the key driver, if Boni left the confraternity he would still be valuable to all. A good exit strategy considering most leaders retired in body bags.

7.

Mama Ajiya could feel the excitement building in her veins. The previous day, Alihu had asked her to prepare a special meal for a guest. And from Alihu's demeanour, she knew this person was someone he wanted to impress. No, someone he *needed* to impress. Her hope was that this special guest, if not the leader of Alihu's cause was someone close to the top. Exposing the head could bring an end to the carnage.

Alihu now controlled over two-hundred fighters and as a show of strength, he had ensured his fighters were ready for the visit. They stood in rows dressed in army fatigues. Their faces were covered with turbans, wrapped around their heads only exposing their eyes. Most held assault rifles such as AK-47s, while others clutched grenade launchers and the occasional sniper rifle.

Mama Ajiya was impressed; the fighters did look formidable. Anyone who met them in such a way would feel Alihu's power over the faceless men, who were ready to follow orders to the very end. Moments like these forced her to pray for hope. Alihu was not only dangerous but an inspiration to many.

As they waited for the guest, she and her helpers stood behind Alihu. Unlike his men, he was dressed in a white caftan that reached his ankles. The cuffs of the caftan and the single breast pocket were embroidered with gold coloured threads sewn into patterns of circles and spirals. On his feet, he wore an expensive looking pair of brown sandals and on his head, he wore the Hausa styled traditional beret.

She knew Alihu enough to tell he was getting restless. If they had to wait much longer, pacing would follow. Alihu was not known for his patience. Tension thickened the air around the gathered, several expecting an explosion of rage at any moment.

Like an answer to multiple silent prayers, the fighters in front of them saluted to a man who then arrived. They opened a path that led directly to Alihu and she craned her neck to see the visitor.

Mama Ajiya's heart sank. The man walking towards them did not look like a leader. His attire was simple and his face showed some exposure to a hard-working life. He was flanked by two veiled figures wearing a white caftan similar to Alihu's but without the embroidery.

She did not know what to make of the figures walking at the man's sides. Petite, feminine and the graceful way they moved made her think; pleasure girls.

Alihu stood proud with his hands held behind his back. The man approached, a smile breaking on his face. He stretched out his hands. Alihu bowed deeply, then stepped into the man's embrace. Both held the embrace for a few moments, then broke apart as the man gently pushed Alihu back and looked at him as if admiring a trophy.

"You inspire us all," the man said to Alihu.

"It is the will of Allah, uncle Sani."

***

Already she hated the man.

He had waited for his companions to taste the food they were provided. Waited after some deliberations, which he covered with idle talk and then finally started eating her food.

"I fear you may have upset our mother," Alihu said to Sani.

Was her anger that obvious? After months of experience with Alihu she had hoped her true countenance was always well masked.

Sani looked up from the ram meat he held in his hands and looked at her. She bowed her head for fear of the man reading more from her face.

"My apologies, mother. An old habit of mine, please do not take offence."

"You will find no deceit here, uncle. Mama Ajiya, has proven herself to be a mother to us all." Alihu beckoned her forward. "She came to us with doubt in her heart. Now she cares for us. Soon she will have more helpers to train in the true ways of Allah."

She stepped forward, her heart beating in her chest. This was the first she had heard of Alihu's plans for her. She knew she had been gaining his trust but not to what extent.

She had cared for Alihu's men, treating them like the boys there were. In some cases, she even berated Alihu when his action affected her sphere of influence. She simply did what any woman her age would. And like all boys in isolation, she had filled the space they all longed for. Even Alihu had started calling her mother, an endearment she previously had ignored but would heed from now.

This did not change anything, she still hated him and his devilish ways. If given the chance, she still would slit his throat and walk into the sunset without a care in the world.

"I thank you for your dedication and hope you are rewarded appropriately," Sani said to her.

"Our leader continues to take care of all my needs. He provides Allah's blessings," she responded, her head still bowed.

One of Sani's companions adjusted her veil and she caught a glimpse of a face. She held her reaction in check and the look on Sani and Alihu's face betrayed nothing. The face she saw, although delicately painted was that of a young boy.

"He inspires us all," Sani said and she stepped back to her spot.

Alihu had chosen to receive his guests in his personal tent. It was a three-room, high quality out-door canvas tent. Her back was to two rooms that Alihu used as private quarters. She and the guest were in the third room he used to receive special guests or plan attacks. A waist-high table usually stood at the middle of the room but had been replaced with a low one for eating, set on a Persian rug. Hard pillows were used as a seat, Alihu on one side and Sani on the other flanked by his companions. One, she still was not even sure was a he or she.

The man was an abomination. She   felt uncomfortable in the room and asked if she was needed. Alihu waved her away and she gladly left.

One of her helpers, a boy too young to be a fighter stood at the tent's entrance. In a loud voice, she instructed the boy to ensure the needs of those within were well taken care of.

***

Sani had to admit the food was good. It was the fiery ram pepper soup he loved to eat every time he visited the region. Slow-cooked with spices and tomato. He normally had the delicacy with several chilled bottles of stout to counter the heat but accepted the sacrifice. Alcohol was frowned upon in Islam and he did not want to be a bad example. He was only here for a night; some of the pleasures of life could wait.

He turned to the veiled figure to his right and asked for his bag. He took it and produced several bundles wrapped in plastic and gave them to Alihu.

"The money you asked for. It is all there."

"Thank you, uncle. It will be put to good use."

"So," Sani began. "How is my favourite nephew? Is leadership treating you well?"

"Allah rewards me with strength for I am now a changed man. I see now my destiny and embrace it," Alihu replied. He washed his hands in a bowl placed on the floor next to the table and stood. He took the money and walked into his private quarters.

Sani waited for his return. Unconsciously, he stroked the legs of one of his companions, his other hand he used to pick meat from his teeth. The other companion leaned forward to pour water in a cup. If Mama Ajiya was present, she would have noticed this companion was female. Young, with no makeup, but still female.

Alihu returned and sat across from them. If he noticed his uncle's caress of the boy next to him, he showed no sign.

"How is my father?" Alihu asked.

"He now sings your praises, claiming his blood has made you who you are." He noticed the rage in Alihu's eyes and smiled inwardly. A reaction he had hoped for.

"He sees me as nothing. Now Allah has made me what I am, he claims it?"

"Do not worry, all know you are who you are because of what you are now and not what you were under his embrace. He is a proud man, humour him," Sani said with a smile on his face. "What next?"

Alihu calmed himself and also smiled. Sani felt shivers in his spine as he looked upon the smile. *This boy has surely gone mad.*

"What comes next is the beginning of the end for the infidels!" Alihu began to explain. Sani approved, it was a good plan. He inwardly vowed to be far away from Madagali when it was executed. Still, he continued to listen.

***

The following morning, Mama Ajiya watched as Sani and his entourage left. She now knew the man's name. The Old Man will be happy with the news.

8.

Fatima walked between rows of bunk beds. She made a mental note of the occupants of the beds. As a senior prefect, a roll-call was her duty. Her dormitory room was on the ground floor of one of three student accommodation structures at her all girls' college. The room was big enough to accommodate sixteen bunk beds, eight on each side with spaces in-between for dressers. Luckily this was the senior's room and not all bunks were occupied, making this one of the less crowded rooms.

It was just a few minutes to lights out, at which point only candles and desk lamps were allowed for another hour. Due to lack of electricity, the former was more reliable. But with the full exam season not yet over, most students would be taking advantage of the extra hour to study.

She glanced outside. The moon's silvery light shone on the grassy field just behind the windows. There was once a fence beyond the fields, but it now lay in ruins. Beyond this was land farmed by teachers and their families. In a way, the corn and cassava farms created a secure perimeter beyond the school grounds and bordering the farms was the beginning of a thick undergrowth not many ventured into.

She came to her corner and closed the remaining glass louvres between her and her neighbour's bunk. She sat on her bed, looked at the books on her pillow and sighed. She really did not feel like reading anymore. The girl on the bunk in front of her looked up from her studies.

"What is wrong, Fatima?" she asked.

Ene was a childhood friend, they had even started school on the same day. Among all her friends, Ene was also one of the few she felt comfortable with.

"I just can't wait for this to end," she replied. "Study, study and more study!"

Ene laughed. "You have not failed a subject since you got here. Don't start now." She sat up and with a concerned look, asked, "What is really the matter? Bad dreams still?"

Fatima nodded. She had been having terrible dreams of late. Waking up in a scream or covered in her own sweat. Ene and some of her other friends had attributed this to the anxiety of a wedding but Fatima was not so sure. *Are these what Westerners called wedding blues?*

"Just clear your head and have happy thoughts of your very handsome man and you will be fine," Ene added.

Fatima smiled. Yes, thoughts of Ike always seemed to calm her. She missed him now more than ever and could not wait to see him.

Once again she sighed and picked up her books. A siren went off, signalling lights out. She removed a candle from under her pillow and succeeded in sparking it to life just before the lights blinked out.

***

Fatima could feel her eye lids getting heavy. She blew the candle out and placed it on the floor next to her books. Ene was already fast asleep and she prayed for a sound sleep herself. She fell into beckoning pillows. Taking Ene's advice, she thought of Ike.

She remembered the first time she had met him. Church had just finished and her mother was having her usual chat session with peers. Fatima sat on some blocks under a tree, waiting. Ike had walked to her, a sly smile on his lips.

"I see the most beautiful girl on the planet."

"I see another sweet-tongued Igbo boy," she had replied.

He had laughed, taking a seat next to her. "If you don't mind I will wait here with you for my mother as well."

She moved slightly away from him.

"I don't bite," he added.

"I don't think you do. I might though," she said.

Again, he had laughed. "My name is Ikechukwu, but please call me Ike."

"I'm Fatima," she replied. "You are Aunty Ngozi's son in university. When did you get back?"

"Yesterday." Then he added, "I see you already know who I am. Let me see if I can repay the favour." He glanced to the sky and continued. "You are Hassan's sister and that is your mother over there."

"True, did the sky tell you that?" She laughed. "How was uni? I hope to go too one day."

Ike had then proceeded to tell her about campus life, the subjects available and how important it was to have a degree. She had listened, vowing to complete her own studies.

"I want to see you again," Ike had said when she made to stand. "Please."

She did not know why, but she had told him she would be at the market the following day to collect her mother's grain profits. They could meet after and if he wanted, he could walk her home.

She had spent the whole night thinking of seeing him again, brooding on what she would wear and how she looked. Eventually as the time came close she had rushed to the market. Even then she cogitated at the uncertainty that she did not look her best.

Ike was not at the grain stall and she felt disappointed. *Did she think a university boy wanted anything to do with a secondary school girl?* A Hausa one at that? She tried to brush away more thoughts of him to discourage more feelings of disappointment.

After collecting her mother's money, she had stepped out of the stall and to her heart's joy, Ike was waiting. She smiled at him and his face lit up. He told her she looked beautiful and she told him he smelt of food. He laughed at that and they began the trip back to her house.

It was the longest walk she had ever made home from the market. It was self-inflicted, of course, and with the sole purpose of enjoying every moment of Ike's company.

They had met regularly after that in the two weeks of holiday Ike had left and he made the effort to see her most evenings. On the day before he had to go, they had their first kiss.

Slowly, sleep claimed her. In a way, Ene was right. She did have good dreams of Ike and for a few hours, she slept well.

***

There is a belief in a particular hour when dark forces are the strongest. The belief further stipulates that; this extra strength is gained from a momentarily and circular closeness of the world of the living to that of the dead. Consider a continuous timeline for both the living and dead and a closeness that fluctuates in a side-by-side parallel run. During these moments, the spiritual powers of the dead meant the timeline of the living stood no chance.

Due to the nature of time itself, like seasons, timelines had buffers, a period like spring before summer or autumn before winter, a moment when one timeline at its greatest strength, may transcend or bump into the other.

For Fatima, her peaceful sleep ended at about three am.

She was in a forest and it was dark. The only light that seeped through was the moonlight between leaves. In most instances the moonlight would have been a blessing but as the trees moved, the shadows filled her with dread.

Then she heard it. Ike's voice calling out to her.

"Fatima! Please help me." It was not a shout or a scream. It was a cry for help from someone who had lost all hope. "Fatima… Please."

She looked around. Where was the voice coming from?

"Help me! Fatima!" Right ahead! She ran into the forest, all thoughts of fear forgotten.

Leaves, branches, twines, all came at her but she brushed them off. She found him lying on the floor. A branch was on his chest and another on his legs. "Help me."

She screamed as she realised his throat had been slashed. He reached out for her with both arms and she ran forward to him, but each step she took increased the distance between them. She stopped. *How is this possible?* She tried again and again. Finally, out of frustration she jumped.

She fell onto a dark soft rock. It was black like obsidian but the surface felt like soft clay. She could hear voices around her. Moans of agony, none high pitched but low moans that made her feel the pain more than hear it.

She lifted her face from the floor, looked up and once again screamed.

In front of her was the bald head of a man or woman coming out of the rock. The rest of the body was buried in the rock, it opened its mouth and added its low moan to the others. She shuffled backwards, her legs in front of her and arms behind her, taking her away from the thing in the ground as fast as she could. She hit a wall and arms dripping with blood reached out around her, as if seeking an embrace.

This time in both timelines she screamed.

She turned around to see what was behind her. A wall of the same black obsidian stood behind her. Human-like creatures extended out of it. Their faces were trapped, sometimes coming to the surface with a silent scream, but never breaking fully out of the wall. Their arms were free and moved about seeking something to hold on to. Their legs were trapped, like their heads.

Remembering the head in the rock, she turned around and this time the room she was in came into focus. It was a cave and body parts were strewn over the floor, all still alive. There was a pattern to them and as she looked closer, they formed into a pile in the middle of the room. At the peak of the body parts stood a throne that was somehow made of still moving and wriggling body parts stood. A man-like creature sat in it and when she looked up to its face, she realised it was not human.

Where a mouth was supposed to be was a wide grin of rows of shark-like teeth. The nose was like that of a gorilla with nostrils blowing plumes of steam. Red eyes with unnaturally large bird-like black pupils pierced her and the intensity of the creature's gaze caused tears to flow from her own eyes.

"Faaatima." It was like a whisper of death itself. *"Faaatiiimmmaaa.* I..."

***

"I told you I would come for you."

She woke to the dark eyes of Alihu staring down at her, a smile on his face almost like that of the creature that had just haunted her dreams.

This was by far a worse nightmare. She screamed and lashed out with her right hand and her fingers dug into the left side of Alihu's face. He pulled backwards, but her nails had already bitten and dragged two gashes from his ear to his lower cheek. She threw her legs off the bed and pivoted around and kicked him in the chest as he was staggering backwards.

Ene was staring at her with wide eyes. "RUN!" Fatima yelled. She was already at the window. She jumped

82

out, smashing into louvers and onto the wet floor beyond. Ene was right behind her and they both ran for the bushes.

As they got to the end of the field, she turned to Ene. "We must separate. If one of us gets caught, the other can tell who came." Ene nodded, selected a destination and ran into the bushes.

Fatima, turned to see Alihu who seemed to have recovered, climbing out of the broken window. The wound on the side of his face was bleeding and he grinned at her.

"You are mine!" he yelled.

She ran.

She prayed to wake up, tears running down her eyes, she cried to the sky. *Please, Allah, this cannot be! No! Please! Jesus, help me.*

She glanced down at her form. She was still wearing her white nightgown. Underneath this was a pair of short tights and a tank top. As she ran, leaves and branches whipped into her body, cutting into the gown's light material. The pain she felt was physical, it was real. This was not a dream. She ran faster.

As she got further into the forest, she pulled the night gown over her head and threw it over a branch. She continued to run, hoping the act would give her more time to get further away from the monster chasing her.

Like an illusion, a dream came to her. The forest she now ran in looked familiar and she expected to hear Ike's voice calling out. She expected to stumble upon his broken form at any moment. But instead, her right leg fell into a rabbit hole and her momentum twisted her ankle. She yelled and fell forward, seeing a tree stump in her path, she twisted to avoid it. She fell backwards, slamming into the ground and smacking her head on a rock.

The blackness that engulfed her was a merciful respite.

***

Ike woke up with a start. He looked outside and realised it was still dark. He glanced at his phone's screen. It was just after four am. He turned into his pillow and sleep took him once again.

***

Rekia's eyes flicked open. A feeling of isolation overwhelmed her. Her beating heart made her feel as if she had just woken from a nightmare.

She glanced at her bedside clock, it was just after four am, an hour before she normally got out of bed. Sleep would not come and it seemed that her day would start earlier than normal. She dressed slowly, unable to shake the feeling that something terrible had happened.

9.

It was not yet sunrise and Olu was already exhausted.

Most of the dormitories were on fire and teachers and villagers ran back and forth with buckets of water trying to fight the flames. The chaos of the night was overwhelming. Students who had escaped the blaze gathered on the fields, dazed and in shock, where they were being treated on the fields in front of the burning buildings. Girls screaming and yelling lay on the floor crying out in several languages. No one really knew the extent of the damage. How many were wounded, missing or dead? Olu could not say. All he knew was hours had passed and he still saw chaos around him.

They got lucky, the home education teacher was also a nurse. He had grabbed supplies from the emergency cabinet in the principal's office, already knowing it was never going to be enough. Some of the girls had cuts on their backs that suspiciously looked like machete wounds that could fester. As the nurse worked, assisted by several teachers, he had quickly dialled the local hospital.

When the ambulance arrived, several wounded girls already lay on grey blankets strewn over the grass fields, their cries adding to the night's sombre soundtrack.

Olu had pushed aside the cries and moans, searching the unharmed for senior students he recognised and organised them into groups. The girls not harmed were set to

84

various tasks while the younger girls and those immobilised by shock were kept on a section of the field. In terms of security, they only had two police officers and were waiting for the major police force from Madagali to arrive. Hopefully, the attackers were far gone and would not return, today or ever.

A senior student stood next to a group of seated girls taking a roll call. It was then he remembered Fatima. He walked to the student and asked after her. The girl pointed to another group girls. He walked to them fearing the worst.

"Is this Fatima's dorm? Have you seen her?" he asked the exhausted girl.

She nodded. After a few seconds she recalled he had asked two questions. She replied. "No Sir, she was the first to alert us and jumped out of the window. Ene, her friend followed after her." The girl paused, remembering the hell she just escaped. "A big fighter jumped out after them. Shouting her name."

This shocked Olu. "What! Fatima knew the fighter?"

"Yes sir, some of us do." She looked at another girl sitting on the grass, who turned away from her gaze. "He looked different, but it was Alihu Garuba her neighbour."

Olu could not believe it. If one of the fighters was known, surely there was a chance of retribution.

"Did he catch her?" he asked. It sounded like a stupid question but he still hoped.

"We do not know. She and Ene ran into the bushes behind our dorm." She pointed to the rear of one of the only structures not torched by the attackers.

Olu ran to the unofficial command centre erected on one edge of the field. The school principal was leaning over papers and talking frantically to teachers around him. He definitely did not want to be in the man's shoes right now. He addressed the man who looked up with bloodshot eyes. Olu could not tell if the redness was from smoke or exhaustion. Besides, God knew how he looked to the man.

"We need to search the forest behind the dorms," he said.

"Yes!" one of the local police officers yelled. "Some of the girls ran into it and were chased by the criminals, they may still be alive and hiding!"

Olu ignored the term the man used. *Criminals? Bah!* They all knew who the fighters were and none wished to voice it. "I need some of you to come with me. We will spread out and walk through the forest until we get to the road on the other side." Some of the teachers stood up, picking up various items they came with for protection. Olu noticed one man even had a pistol. "I don't believe the *fanatics* are still around."

"Better to be sure than not, eh?" the man with the pistol responded.

Teachers and villagers walked to the edge of the forest. They glanced at each other and headed into the trees. Olu chose the path in front of Fatima's window and stepped into the forest. Dawn was close, he sure would appreciate the light.

***

The road on the other side of the forest was not a major highway or state road. It led to more remote maize farms and a smaller village. It was an untarred and dusty road, filled with corrugations that spanned its full width. Sections of the road were only just becoming passable for buses and cars as the rains dried up. Weeks ago, tractors, motorbikes and bicycles were the only means of transport across it.

To get to the road, Olu and his team of searchers would have to walk for an hour.
Halfway through, he had found a white nightgown hanging off a tree branch, dashing his hopes that he had found Fatima. A flash of terror went through him.

Girls had been found in shock, some hiding under tree trunks and dense bushes. A dead girl had also been found, an angry gash on her neck showing all how she was killed. The teacher to Olu's right yelled out to Allah and he knew the man had stumbled upon something. He ran to the man's voice, praying for some good news. He came into a wide clearing surrounded by small trees. A girl about Fatima's age lay on the forest floor panting and staring into the stars. Her mouth was bloody and its sides were caked with already drying blood. Her form was covered in tattered remains of a wrapper that had been ripped to expose her naked flesh. As Olu stepped closer, his nose wrinkled and he knew the dried starchy liquid on her breast and stomach were remnants of a grave ordeal.

Pooled blood from the girl's sides led behind him and he turned to follow its path. A man sat on the forest ground with his back leaning on a tree. His head was slumped and no sound of life came from his body. His pants, probably the reason for his fall were gathered around his ankles. His groin was an ocean of blood, staining the ground around him. Olu turned back to the girl and noticed a bloody mangled flesh on the forest ground near her head.

Realisation hit home. The girl had bitten off the man's manhood, spiting it out after she ripped it off him. He could not imagine what she had thought and the defiance that preluded the act.

Looking at her he could tell she had been attacked by several people. The man on the floor had probably been the last, the one supposed to kill her once his cowardly act was complete.

"This man is not Nigerian." It was the teacher who had found the girl. He had used a stick to lift the dead man's face.

"What?" Olu asked moving closer to the dead man.

"I used to trade in Gubio, this man is definitely *Nigerien*."

Olu shook his head, the ramifications of what the man said only added to the chaos of the night. *A foreign fighter in Nigeria?*

The man called out to volunteers following their search party. The girl was still alive, but Olu knew the horrors of the night still filled her as she stared into the stars. The people coming would do as much as they could for the girl's wounds, but he knew psychological recovery, if at all, would be a long time away.

He cursed and turned to continue his search. By the time he got to the road, he had found nothing. The sun was up and life around him had woken, oblivious to events of the previous night. He closed his eyes and focused on the sounds, taking solace from Mother Nature's arrogance.

A horn brought him back and he opened his eyes to a colleague astride a Chinese made 150cc motorbike. Olu hopped on and the bike sped back to the school.

The school was a hive of activity. Students were being wheeled into the back of several waiting ambulances and cars. News had travelled fast, locally at least, as Olu identified several parents in the crowd. The army had also arrived and he recalled their last take on the attack at the barracks. *What will they say about this one now?*

He hopped off the bike before it rolled to a stop, thanked the rider and ran to some of his younger colleagues standing together. These were a group of junior teachers just out of university. They were obliged to train in schools around Nigeria for nine months as national service before they were able to look for jobs. Seeing them already on their phones, he knew he had made a good decision.

"We must tell the truth of what happened here before the army changes things," he said once he was within their midst.

"Be factual, leave nothing out except sensitive things that may identify victims."

"True, it will be bad if a sister or brother sees the victimised body of their siblings." one of the teachers said.

"What is your name?" Olu asked the teacher.

"Ada, I teach history," she replied, frantically tapping her phone's screen.

"Ada, I also have some more information and I want you to spread it." He glanced around. "I am sure between you all we would have social media covered."

He told them about the foreign fighters and that some of the fighters were local boys. Finally, to cement how gruesome the attack was, he told them about the defiant girl found under the stars.

When he left them, Ada was still tapping on her phone, tears ran down her cheeks. He prayed her words would reflect her grief.

***

The security guard at Turaki's residence chuckled to himself. The cleaners sweeping the compound seemed upset, showing their emotion by frantically attacking the grounds under the trees. Soon he would have to remind them that they needed to sprinkle more water on the ground to reduce the dust.

Like the young ones of today, he let them suffer the rising dust they made. *Yes, it may punish others, but who first?* He had overheard them complaining of being woken up earlier than normal. He chuckled again. *Ah, to be young with minimal worries.*

Rushing feet approached the gate and he turned, reaching for his bow leaning on the wall next to him. There was a bang on the gate and he jumped out of his chair.

"*Wanda shi ne a?*" He yelled. *Who is there?*

A young girl's voice responded, incoherent and banging frantically. Behind him the cleaners stopped, one of the Turaki wives was at the door of the main house with a worried look on her face. He turned back to the gate and peered through the peeping hole.

The girl looked dishevelled, her clothes and body were covered in scratches and her face was the only clean part not covered in dirt and what looked like dried blood. He recognised her and started unlocking the gate, although it was not due to be unlocked for another hour.

The girl continued to yell and bang on the gate. Normally he would yell at such insolence but the look on the girl's face scared him and he began to murmur a silent prayer. Finally, the padlock accepted one of the keys he carried and the gate swung open. The girl flew in, not even acknowledging him. He turned to watch her and she ran straight into the arms of a woman from the house, already half way to the gate.

The woman tried to calm the girl, whispering in her ears, telling her it was okay. The girl tried to stop crying and her cheeks puffed with the effort of breathing. She wiped her face and looked into the woman's eyes.

"She was taken…" the girl sobbed.

Rekia instantly knew who Ene referred to. "No," she whispered too low for any around her to hear. "No." This was much louder.

"They came in the night, burning, raping and killing…" The girl sobbed again. "Most of us they took but Fatima helped me escape."

"Who! Who took my daughter?" Rekia asked, her voice already betraying the hysteria overcoming her.

"He looked different, but it was Alihu Garuba." Looking into Rekia's eyes and seeing pain broke Ene again. She began to sob. In broken breaths she added. "I… ran… all… wanted was… her"

Rekia stood in shock and Ene stood up with an uncomfortable look. "Go to your parents." Rekia gently pushed Ene. "They will worry for you. GO!" Ene nodded, tears still streaming from her eyes. She ran to the gate.

Rekia wailed. The sound of her anguish carried and woke the rest of the house. She turned and ran straight to her husband. He met her at the door to his quarters. One arm struggling into a shirt and the other on the phone. When he saw her, he dropped the phone.

"No," was all he said. A surprised look on his face.

Rekia flew into his arms, sobbing. "They took my daughter!" She wailed banging her hands into his chest.

"The attack I just heard was at Fatima's school?" He held her, a bewildered look on his face.

Hearing Fatima's name, Rekia wailed, falling to the floor. "Garuba's son was with them!"

Hassan and Musa were already there, Musa ran to Rekia, holding her. She clutched at him and sobbed into his chest. Usman picked up his phone and turned to Hassan.

"Did you hear that? We MUST be certain! You..."

"I AM!" Rekia yelled. "Ene just left! She was covered in scratches and blood! She saw him take her!"

Usman ran back into his room. After a few minutes he returned carrying an inherited *Long Dane* gun. From the way his father was holding the gun, Hassan knew the gun was already loaded.

"Organise the family. Take only the most valuable of items. Head to the town border and wait for my instructions," Usman said to Hasan. He was already walking past his gathered family, heading to the main sitting room.

"Father, I must go with you!" Hassan said, pacing to catch up with his father.

"Listen to me, boy!" Usman turned to Hassan. Seeing his family staring at him with distress in their eyes, he softened. "I need to go to Garuba's house. He must know what is going on. Now, I don't know how deep he is in all this but I suspect very." He paused and looked at every one of them. "You all need to be strong for each other."

Rekia ran to him. He lifted the gun above her head for fear of setting it off. She clutched his chest, then fell to his legs. She held him back, pleading, begging. At that moment his other wives entered. Seeing the gun and Rekia, they too joined in the despair.

Hassan grabbed at his phone. It had been ringing non-stop since he walked into the chaos. *The Old Man*. The call would have to wait.

"Hassan!" Usman boomed. In the past, absolute silence would have followed his outburst. Today, the cries increased. "You must take the family. Now! I intend to meet up with you all. But I have to see what has become of

Fatima." This quietened them somewhat. "I know his son wanted my daughter so I know she is alive. NOW! GO!"

This sent everyone in motion, clearing the room. Rekia still held on to her husband's legs. Slowly, also in tears, her sister-wives plied her fingers away, whispering to her, telling her it was okay and imploring on her to go get her valuables. Finally, she relented and followed them out of the room.

Musa made to follow but Usman called him back. "Musa, my son." Musa used his sleeves to brush the tears out of his eyes and turned to his father. "We all have our strengths. Do not feel that because you do not know it now, you do not have one." His father touched one of his shoulders. "I have a task for you. It is very important."

"I will do it father." Musa replied, clutching on to his father's hand.

"I know you will. Take my motorbike and go to the police station. The name of the head officer there is Mr. Folami. Tell him what has happened and let him know that I want his presence at Garuba's house." His father paused, then added. "Once you have told him, join your brother."

His father did something Musa could not recall ever happening. He knelt down, holding the gun to his side; which was almost at Musa's height and hugged him. Musa returned the hug for a moment, the pride of showing no tears was forgotten and he cried.

Father and son held each other.

His father pushed him back and looked up at him. "Now hurry."

Musa bolted out of the door with new found determination in every step.

10.

The Turaki family evacuation convoy was modest. The lead vehicle was a pickup truck with the back tray filled with clothes and soft items stuffed into bags and boxes. Behind this, was a van, its cargo space taken over by more family valuables. Another van followed, full of mothers, their young and helpers. Everyone held onto each other praying while the van pierced the chaotic Madagali streets. Two more cars followed, carrying more people with Hassan's car covering the rear.

The drive through Madagali was hectic. It seemed news had reached the town and everyone was heading out. When Hassan approached the town's border, he picked up his phone and dialled the Old Man.

"WHAT?!"

The car screeched to a halt. Horns and tires protesting behind them. "They are coming here?" He yelled back into the phone. One hand still holding the phone to his ear, he started indicating trying for a possible U-turn. As he turned to see behind him, his gaze fell on his passengers.

Faces showed absolute fear and he realised, back was not a direction they wished for. His heart went to them as he engaged first gear and sped forward.

***

Without the constraints of family, Usman walked towards Garuba's house in a rage. Two men stood at the gate, guns at their sides. As Usman approached, they made to lift their weapons. He already had his up and he moved the barrel between them.

Most Dane guns used for the West Africa slave trade were flintlock systems, but after inheriting the weapon from his grandfather, Usman's father modified the gun to a cap-lock system. Pointing at the security guards was now a more formidable, single barrel filled with black powder and shots forged for bringing down boars.

"One of you will kill me and one of you will die. Choose quickly or drop your weapons." The men looked at each other then dropped their weapons. "RUN!" he yelled at them and they bolted towards the town. Usman stepped into the gate calling out to Garuba.

Garuba was already waiting with a pistol in his hands pointing directly at Usman as he stormed into the compound.

"Ah my brother, you come to my house armed. Are we at war?" Garuba said a smile on his face.

"If there is war, it is your hands that will be stained with it," Usman replied gun raised and eyes scanning the compound.

"Probably, it will stain my pockets with money more though." Garuba took a step to the side, his gun still pointing at Usman's chest.

"I do not care for you schemes. Your son has taken my daughter. I want her back." Usman said taking steps closer to Garuba.

"Ah, so you risk death for your daughter's favour?" Garuba shook his head. "Well I do not have her, like you said, my son does."

"He is your responsibility as much as she is mine. You of all people should know it is not right to take what belongs to others without recompense or choice!"

Garuba laughed. "I, of all people?" He laughed again. "I always take what I want no matter whose ox is gored!" Both hands went to the pistol. "My son has your daughter; she belongs to him. You can leave here now with your life as a gift for her hand, or she will learn of her father's death!"

Usman could not believe what he was hearing. *Had Garuba gone mad?* The man had always been an arrogant fool, personally and professionally. *Had he now lost all humanity to greed?*

Usman aimed his gun. "Then my daughter and your son will lose fathers today."

The men stared at each other. Garuba glanced behind Usman, smiling, he lowered his weapon. Usman refused the urge to turn and kept his gun on Garuba. Two forms came into view, walking to Garuba's side. Usman's heart dropped.

Folami had an arm around Musa's neck, his elbow just under the boy's tear-stricken face. In the other hand he held a pistol similar to the one Garuba held.

"So you are part of this?" Usman asked. Folami shrugged his shoulders.

Garuba laughed. "You should see your face, my brother!" He looked at father and son. "Tell me, do you wish to die with your son too?" Folami raised his gun to Usman. "Make your choice now. Last chance!" Garuba added, the mirth lost from his face.

Musa who had been struggling in Folami's grip looked up at his father. His father looked back, eyes moist, he stared at his son for what seemed like eternity, nodded then smiled.

Musa heaved his head backwards and then forwards. As he came forwards, he took a chunk of Folami's flesh in his teeth and bit down, hard. Folami screamed in pain and dropped his gun. The gun hit the floor, firing a bullet into Usman's left thigh.

Garuba was already lifting his pistol to Usman's chest but Usman fired first. Smoke enveloped his head as the single barrel modified Dane went off.

Garuba was pushed backwards with the force of several lead shots slamming into his left shoulder and chest. As he fell backwards, he managed to pull his trigger. His bullet shot forward and pierced between Usman's eyes, it was a lucky shot.

For Usman, death was instant. Garuba on the other hand would take longer to die.

***

Musa ignored what his brain registered as his father fell. He slammed both elbows behind him, satisfied when he heard Folami grunt in pain, *or was it shock?* He turned to run for the gate but two men were already rushing in brandishing AK-47s.

Musa made another turn and ran to Garuba's main house. He went straight for the servant's access through a side door leading to the kitchen. He had been in the house a long time ago and knew his way around. He only had to make it to the rear gate.

Folami was not far behind. Clutching his bleeding hand, he fired shots after Musa. Uncaring who or what got hit by his salvos. As he navigated his way through the servant's corridors, he shouted at anyone he met, pointing his gun in their faces.

"Where is Musa Turaki?" A lady old enough to be his mother pointed to a room. He went straight for it kicking the door open and stormed in, gun raised.

A girl, about Musa's age pointed at the window on the far wall of the room. Cotton blinds still shaking, told Folami of Musa's exit. He ran to the window and looked out, the boy was gone. He cursed and turned to the girl. "Go get someone to help your *Oga!* He has been shot!"

The girl stared at him, frightened and shocked. She nodded and ran out of the room.

Folami furrowed his brows, trying to remember. He knew he had seen the girl in Garuba's house several times but something nagged at him. He had also seen her somewhere else.

He stepped into the sun and walked towards Garuba. It came to him then, like an epiphany. She also worked at the Igbo woman's restaurant at the motor park.

When he saw the amount of blood Garuba had lost, the thought of Ngozi's minion was forgotten.

***

The light that creeped into the tent told her she had woken at the break of dawn.

She tried to lift her head but fell backwards, the pain was almost unbearable. Head throbbing, she managed to lift it, holding back the urge to throw up as a wave of nausea hit her. She moved her legs and cried out as the pain from her ankle almost made her pass out. Glancing at her foot, she noticed it was not only swollen like a melon but was also chained to a stake in the floor. Her other leg was fine, and the anklet Ike had given her reflected some of the sun rays.

"Ah, so you are awake?"

The night came back to Fatima. For a moment she forgot her pain and stared at Alihu. He had an evil smile on his face as he walked towards her.

96

"While you were asleep, I have introduced the world to *Jama'atu Ahlis Sunna Lidda'awati wal-Jihad!*"

In her head, she silently translated the Arabic name. Alihu had really lost his head, she laughed at him.

"Oh! You think it is funny?" He stopped before her chained feet. "The world knows of us. And your sisters are the first brides of the Caliphate!"

If the devil smiled, Alihu's was more frightening.

He nudged her swollen ankle, sending a wave of pain through her body. "Where is your dog eater now?" he asked, the smile turning into an evil laugh.

She spat on his face but the satisfaction of the blob of saliva hitting him was short lived. Alihu took a step forward and back-handed her. The slap flung her backwards, her head feeling as if it was in a twirling spin. She hit the floor, her gaze a widening of circles, waves and bright lights.

"Don't worry, I do not intend to fuck a wounded dog." He wiped the saliva from his face. Staring down at her, he added. "I shall wait until you are on all fours." He laughed again and leaned forward. The gash she gave him earlier in the night made him look even more evil.

"I go now to take our first prize. Madagali." He grabbed her neck and brought her face closer. "And I will destroy everything you hold dear until you are left alone in this world." Bringing her even closer, he added, "with me." He pushed her back to the floor.

Blissful darkness was already approaching. She heard him, her brain even registered his intent, but she accepted the darkness instead.

***

Folami stepped closer to his former boss. Although the man was still breathing, life had almost left his eyes. Several women and children surrounded Garuba's dying form. A young woman cradled his head crying and Folami recognised her as Garuba's youngest wife. He walked to them and crouched down to go through the man's pockets. He was still owed a last instalment and he was not leaving without it.

Shocked by his actions, Garuba's youngest wife reached for his arms. Folami pushed her away and continued his search until he found what he was looking for.

"You will never enjoy that money!" Garuba's youngest wife spat at him.

Folami shot her in the face and left the compound.

Outside and leaning on the wall was Usman's motorbike. He hopped on and rode straight home. Knowing what was coming, his family was already gone two weeks back. Their welfare was the last thing on his mind. Arriving at his deserted house, Folami threw the bike to the floor and ran inside. His destination was the buried safe under his bed and within it, the rest of his cash.

Proceeds of greed sorted and with a turban covering his face, only exposing his eyes, he stepped outside and ignored Usman's motorbike. Someone was bound to recognise it and he was not ready to give any explanations. He flagged a passing motorbike and without arguing about the transport price, asked to be taken to the town's southern boundary.

11

Situated at the junction between a federal and state government road, the Madagali town boundary was already becoming a community in its own right. On one side of the road leading from Madagali, makeshift tents made out of canvas and bamboo poles were already being constructed. The tents were to be a temporary solution for the flux of people trying to leave the town and surrounding villages.

Some people already had a destination in mind, others just plain wanted out. For those heading to places like Lagos and Port Harcourt, an early morning taxi or bus was the only option. Those with business on their minds flocked to the boundary willing to transport people away; for a price of course.

With alacrity, other business ventures also popped up within the community. Hawkers who previously manned the junction selling seasonal products such as roasted corn and peanuts now walked amongst the desperate selling items such as phone recharge cards and clean water sealed in clear plastic bags.

Several eating *bukas* had also emerged to feed the hungry. Women and children stood over frying pots and pans while customers sat on low benches waiting for whatever was being served. Quality was not really an issue, quantity was. After all, most customers intended to be gone by morning.

The community was protected from both sides by makeshift roadblocks of overturned burnt out cars and manning the roadblocks were former Madagali police officers and locals. Every car entering Madagali was searched and the occupants questioned. The guards at the roadblocks did not approve of going back into the town, but they understood why some would.

In both directions, people passed through the junction. Some stayed but most, fearing for their lives or not willing to risk it, left.

***

Hassan looked around. It was not yet mid-day and the junction had already taken a life of its own. He was glad to know that the rest of his family were already on their way to Abuja. He had refused to continue on with them, telling his mother and Rekia that he intended to wait for his father and Musa.

Another reason, which he did not mention, was the Old Man. Hassan cursed himself for not listening to all the man had been preaching.

He heard a commotion and turned around. People surrounded what looked like a drum and were yelling at something sitting on it. He ran to it just as he saw the Old Man hopping off a motorbike.

Hassan pushed past the people around the drum to see Alihu's face on the screen of a laptop. Alihu was wearing army fatigues and was surrounded by an army of men wearing ski-masks. Hassan had come in mid speech and turned to ask the person next to him what was going on but what Alihu said next silenced him.

"And now like a fire sanctioned by Allah, we shall clear this land of sin!" The camera turned to a group of girls sitting on a forest floor. "These are the brides of Allah and they shall be a vessel for the righteous…"

Hassan refused to hear anymore. "I will kill him," he murmured to himself. "I will kill him." It was becoming a shout. He turned around, facing Madagali, facing the Old Man. "I will… kill… HIM!!!" He tried to run but someone held his arm. "Let me GO!" without knowing who it was, he lashed out with his palm. It connected and the pressure on his arm released. He tried to take another step but more arms held him back.

Punching, kicking and screaming, Hassan tried to escape the flood of arms. Somehow, with two men holding him back, he still got to the Old Man.

"Tell them to let me GO!" Hassan yelled.

"Do you know where to go?" the Old Man asked calmly. "Because if you do, please let me know."

"I will find that bastard in whatever hole he has crawled into!"

"My apologies Hassan, but I will not allow you to go and get killed."

The Old Man was fast. Faster than any Hassan had seen or fought with. Before Hassan could react, the Old Man was already behind him with one arm around his neck. He felt the other hand behind his head and slowly his vision began to darken, he fainted.

***

While the commotion was going on with Hassan. A lone figure wearing a turban stepped into a bus bounded for Abuja. No one recognised him but it was the former Madagali police chief, Folami.

As Hassan fell to the floor, the conductor of the bus turned back to his passengers. Seeing he had an extra one, he collected the man's fare and shut the door. That was their last passenger and this was his last trip. From what he heard from the video, he doubted any notion of profit would entice him back to Madagali.

***

Somehow, Garuba managed to stay alive to see his son walk into the family compound.

Alihu stepped up to his fallen father and squatted next to his dying form, he ignored the dead woman who held his father.

His father's breath was a gurgle with each expel of air and was accompanied by frothing blood around his lips. It was a nasty way to die, drowning in your own blood, Alihu thought to himself.

His father's wives and relatives still surrounded the bloody form on the ground and their muffled cries filled the air as they tried in vain to comfort him.

Alihu waved them away and stared into his father's eyes.

"It is a good thing that you lived to see a man return," he said, brushing some of the blood from Garuba's lips. It was then he noticed Usman lying on the floor not far off with an angry bullet hole between his eyes.

"I see the bride price negotiations did not go well. Ah well, she was already mine." He turned to the security guards who were stationed at the gate. "What happened?"

They tried to speak at the same time but he lifted a hand, stopping their bauble. "It doesn't matter; you have failed me. I will deal with you later."

He withdrew a knife strapped to one of his boots. "As you are welcomed by Allah, know that you leave behind a stronger man and a true believer."

He slit his father's throat and held him until life's light finally escaped his eyes.

The shock of the act silenced the gathered. Alihu wiped the blade on his father's caftan and stood up. He addressed them. "I now rule this house and soon this town. Eventually, we will have the caliphate of a true god. The only

101

GOD!" He gestured to the gate. "Those of you not willing to be under my rule, leave."

Nobody made to move and he turned to the main house. "I will be in my father's quarters, prepare a bath for me and bring some food." Alihu did not intend to stay here long but while he did, he would enjoy the luxuries.

***

She woke to a wet cloth cleaning her face. She tried to rise and fend off the attack but a firm hand pushed her down. She realized she was now lying on a soft mat. Thinking she had been freed, she tried to move her legs but the pain reminded her she was still chained.

"Shh… lie back." A soothing voice said to her. "You will only make your pain worse."

Fatima allowed her body to be pushed back into the mat. She even had a pillow placed under her head and she took advantage of the comfort.

Delicate fingers continued to wipe her face and her neck. Her pain forgotten, she slowly began to fall asleep. As sleep engulfed her, a thanks to Allah passed her lips.

***

Like in every society, Alihu's words found acceptance in the hearts of many Madagali citizens. When it was clear the Jihadist had power behind them, citizens turned against each other. Christians or those perceived as such were dragged to the streets and slaughtered. Houses and businesses were looted, vandalized and in some cases burnt down.

By night fall, Madagali was in the hands of the Jihadist and black flags with words in Arabic flew on the town's tallest peaks.

More than two hundred men stood in his compound waiting for his arrival. He looked at them and when he smiled the gathered men gave a loud roar, raising their guns and firing shots into the darkening sky.

"*Allah-Hu-Akbar!*"

"*Allah-Hu-Akbar!*"

102

Alihu allowed the shouts to go on for a while then he raised his hands and the men fell silent.

"Today is the beginning of the end for the enemies of Allah!" The men roared again. After a while, he raised his hands. "We have secured this town and we will secure others. We will create the promise land here! On earth!" Another roar. "Now, remember your teachings and enjoy the spoils of your labour."

As the men moved on, Alihu called out to one of his lieutenants. "Suleiman! Take fifty men and secure the northern gates. I believe we have lost the south, no point in losing both." Alihu turned back to his quarters.

***

Alihu opened the door to what was once his father's private room and a woman lay on the king-sized bed waiting for him. So, she had accepted his invitation after all. He smiled.

"There you are," she purred. "I hope your performance today will be better than the first time."

When he was thirteen, his father had married a Fulani girl, who was a few months younger than himself. Unfortunately for her, she had not been able to have any children and his father had grown bored with her and married another, one who now lay with half her face missing next to his body. His father's Fulani wife was also the first girl he ever had sex with. Well sort of, as it was not a performance he was proud of.

The woman on the bed smiled and threw off the sheet covering her body. She was naked underneath, her light brown skin glistering in oils that smelled of pine and spices. She slowly turned over showing her back to Alihu.

"When you saw my buttocks all those years ago, you couldn't even fuck me properly," she giggled. "You spilled your seed before you were even inside me." She turned around and slowly moved her legs apart. "Now show me you have become a man!"

Alihu went to her, he was primal and so was she.

***

As evening fell on the second day, the boundary community realised the full extent of what was happening in Madagali. People who escaped told of a madness that spread with the coming of the Jihadists. Neighbours were killing neighbours and friends were settling old scores.

Possessed with psychotic crowd ideology, attackers had no qualms with destruction and in some cases, death. As night fell, the numbers of those fleeing the town increased, an exodus of people carrying only what they could and memories of all they once knew.

When some within their numbers decided to stay and help, the problem of accommodation and welfare became apparent.

During the past era of Nigeria's fully functional rail network, trains passed through the Madagali Junction, stopping to load and off-load people, goods and animals. The stop was a four-decade old abandoned train station that sat just off the main road.

Considering the current state of the rail network, Hassan was sure the government would have no problems if he used the abandoned building. The structure was cleaned out and for a time the problem of accommodation was solved.

The previous night, Hassan asked for more volunteers to build zinc shacks and fill sand bags. The first of the shacks to be built were for security persons manning the roadblocks.

Situated far enough from the road, security personnel could provide support to the roadblock if it came under fire.

Luckily for him and those who were now called the 'inner circle', a transport company donated one of its buses. The engine required replacing and the company opted to donate the vehicle rather than send a replacement engine. Hassan and three others now used it as accommodation and a place to host sensitive meetings.

He sat in the Mercedes-Benz Luxury Line bus staring into nothing. It was pretty much cemented that most of the locals now looked up to him for guidance. He was not sure why the promotion but suspected the Old Man had something to do with it. He sighed and moved to the exit, he had work to do.

So far, the army had not responded. The closest barracks had not fully recovered from the last attacks and worse, the barracks were on the northern side of the town. The information they were getting was slowly proving the Old Man's theory. The northern border was in the hands of the Jihadist.

Hassan thought of the enigma that was the Old Man. He still was not any wise to who or what the Old Man was. More often, the mystery had become where the Old Man was. Seemingly appearing out of thin air, the Old Man was always at hand and able to provide valuable input or intelligence.

The Old Man was the first to suggest forgetting about the army or expecting any help from them. Hassan remembered how the Old Man had taken him aside and pointed out the importance of marshalling a vigilante; of ex-police and local fighters. It was a sound idea and the border's security force was formed from locals who had something worth fighting for and so would take their tasks seriously.

The numbers of those willing to fight came to Hassan every morning. He had to assess them to determine if they were even capable of holding a gun or machete. Most could not and the rage of what they had lost was the only driving force behind their decision to fight. Such rage he could not trust, as seeing a person's head hacked off was bound to quite promptly wash away any feeling of anger. He only needed people who could fight with the determination to live coming from the need to exercise as much vengeance as possible.

Right now, among all his problems the most pressing was convincing some of his comrades that attacking Madagali was foolish. The argument was already on the way in the train station and he needed to end it before a division destroyed the little community they had created.

Hassan walked to the entrance, his walk of confidence was a direct opposite to the turmoil brewing beneath the smokescreen. The Old Man stood next to the steps to the main entrance waiting for him. Again Hassan wondered where the man had been.

"*Kana lafiya?*" the Old Man asked. *How are you?*

"Don't ask," Hassan responded.

The Old Man laughed. "Only a leader knows the pain of leadership." Before Hassan could respond, the Old Man added. "The jihadists have over five hundred men in Madagali."

Hassan's foot paused on the second step. "That many? Where did they come from?"

"Some from the forest, others from the town itself." The Old Man had not moved. "I must go. If you attack the town, you will take losses you cannot recover from. The progress you now hinder will be achieved," the Old Man said.

"Where are you going?" Hassan asked, ignoring the thousand questions the Old Man's statement raised.

"To look for your sister and brother." The Old Man replied and turned, leaving Hassan on the steps.

Hassan sighed. He pushed away thoughts of Fatima and Musa. Climbing the last few steps, he was happy to note that two former police officers sat behind sand bags protecting the entrance. He nodded at them and stepped into the building.

Typically, the conversation was loud, the opposing parties raising their voice in the belief that the loudest always had the way. They stood opposite each other yelling and screaming, an activity Hassan noticed had not yet turned to blows; at least of a physical nature.

The table between the debating parties was located in the room that Hassan guessed had been the main waiting room for the train station. There was no other furniture in the room and the plainness of the room added to the post-apocalyptic look of the block exposed walls that surrounded the room.

A window opened on to the entrance he had just walked through but was barricaded with wood and zinc sheets. Another window on the opposite wall opened to the rear of the building. It was bare of any barricades as it faced the protected part of the building and he could see several faces watching the exchange in silence.

Hassan folded his arms and stood apart watching the argument. After a few more shouts, one of the men pushing for an attack on Madagali noticed him and called out.

"Hassan! Tell this young man that we must attack now while the Jihadist are drunk!"

A hush descended on the room, even those beyond the window seemed to be standing extremely still, waiting for his next words.

"It depends," Hassan replied. "Can we attack over five hundred men?"

Even those pushing for the attack gasped then fell silent. The man who asked the question stared at him wide eyed.

"Five hundred in a few days?" The man was dumbfounded. One of his comrades tried to continue the debate but the man silenced him. "Five hundred?" He whispered the question to himself. "That is a lot of fighters."

"Yes, it is," Hassan replied. "That is why I believe we should strengthen the border to stop them in their tracks."

"And leave our land, houses to those bastards?" someone asked.

"They have more superior weapons and have been training for months!" Hassan yelled. "Do you honestly believe we can win or do you want to fight to quickly end the feeling of loss?"

Hassan thought he had pushed too far; was this the moment that ended his leadership of the locals? It was not. The first to leave were those watching from the window, Hassan's argument was sound. Only fools fought in battles they knew were lost. The rest of the gathered murmured and dispersed, nodding at Hassan as they walked past him to the exit.

A man in his late thirties walked to Hassan and placed his left hand on Hassan's shoulder. "*You talk am well,* brother."

The man's name was Jibril. Once an opponent of Hassan's in Dambé, their friendship had flourished outside the ring. Although Jibril had won his last fight, his opponent had left him with a broken leg. Unable to fight any more, he had settled to training with Hassan and the Old Man.

"I simply *talk true,*" Hassan said.

"Yeah, that probably saved some lives," Jibril replied. "I was close to telling them to go fight if *na wetin them want.*"

"We cannot afford to lose any able-bodied man, Jibril. You know that," Hassan said.

"I know." Jibril said. "I was tired of hearing women dressed as men shout that is all."

They both laughed and headed for the exit. There still was more work to do.

***

"You must not allow them to know who you are." Ngozi's minion said to him. Her name was Joy. "It is not safe to leave this place yet." She adjusted the head-tie on his head. "Once it is, we will help you escape."

Musa allowed her to continue to adjust his costume. His red eyes were painted around the edges and his lips had a tiny film of gloss applied to them. Like a zombie, he left her to her actions.

He was still in shock. Once Folami had left, she had come looking for him under the only bed in the room. He was not ashamed to admit that when she peeked under the bed, he was holding on to his knees sobbing. He had seen his father die and it had broken his heart.

Joy had tried to console him, crawling under the bed to hold him as he cried into her caftan. She had held him close as his body convulsed in grief. Her name was called, and she had to leave him. She told him she would be back as soon

108

as she could and brushed her forehead on his before crawling out from under the bed.

Her consolation had helped and he remembered thinking of escaping the hell he found himself in; out the window and straight for the border. Before he could put any of his plans into play, Joy had returned with an elderly woman in tow.

Fear had set in then, almost forcing him to bolt for the window. But the look in the woman's eyes was that of pity and his tears had threatened to return, all thoughts of escape forgotten.

He had succeeded in holding the tears back and the woman and Joy dragged him from underneath the bed.

"Be still young man, for although you have seen horrors, you were man enough to survive them. You are a true fighter," the woman had said, a stern look on her withered face.

Not trusting words, he had nodded and stared at both of them. They looked at him for a while, studying his face and limbs.

"I see what you mean," the woman had said to Joy. "With a little bit of powder and some *eye pencil* he can pass as a *yarinya* and no one would know."

"See! I told you! It will work!" Joy's glee had almost brought a smile to his face. "I have the clothes here."

Without any complaints or objections, he had stood there while they stripped him and dressed him in a female caftan.

Now he sat on the bed while Joy worked on his face. The old lady stood behind her and watched as the last dab of powder was applied to his face. When Joy was done, the old woman stood back and looked at him, then at Joy. Their smile was infectious; this time, Musa could not help but smile with them.

"You look a lot prettier than most women I know," the woman said.

Normally he would have taken offence to such a comment but her face was pure honesty and he smiled at her. "Thank you very much ma…"

"What are you doing Mama Amina?" A voice said from the room's doorway.

Joy and Mama Amina turned to face the lady standing at the door. She was slim, with light brown skin and dark smooth hair tied in two buns on her head. She wore a navy-blue caftan with yellow cuffs and a black wrap draped over her shoulders. Her cheeks had the distinct traditional marks of the Fulani.

Musa did not know her, but the woman looked like someone with power in the household. She stared at Musa for a few seconds then turned to Amina.

"Joy's cousin escaped from the fight in town and we are just consoling her." Amina responded.

"I see," the lady replied, staring at Musa again.

"Mama Amina was just helping me stop her from crying." Joy said. "Her Father was killed by a stray bullet," she added.

The lady nodded, stared at Musa again and then left the room.

Once she was far away for Joy, she giggled and said to Musa under her breath. "At least you are prettier than her."

The woman who Musa now knew was called Mama Amina laughed. "Her true colour now shows. What else sleeps with a dog if not a bitch?"

Joy had to cover her mouth to stifle her laughter. When she saw the surprised look on Musa's face, she said to him. "She was one of my uncle's forgotten wives. Now she shares Alihu's bed and thinks she runs the house."

12

Chief Chibuike Amadi was fortunate enough to have secured a three-acre plot of land on a newly released prime reserve located at the outskirts of Aba. Considering Aba was probably the biggest metropolis of the Igbo kingdom, being able to acquire the land was more than luck alone. Not only was the acquisition expensive, one had to ensure the land was developed as quickly as possible. Stories were rampant of investors losing part or all of their land to scams because it sat vacant after purchase.

Ike's Father had taken no chances. Once he obtained the plot, he fenced it with a ten-foot tall, two-foot wide brick wall. For good measure, barbed steel wires were attached to the top of the fence in a spiral formation to discourage trespassing. A few months later, he divided the plot in two. Construction then took a more leisurely pace and his dream was completed after two years.

Built into the forward-facing fence wall were two main gates. The one on the left, a massive industrial steel type gate sitting on rails with round steel wheels led to the commercial wing. An 18-wheeler truck could drive in or reverse out comfortably with no qualms. This was the heart of his transportation business covering loading, unloading and maintenance of trucks.

The gate on the right was quite different. Although also made of steel, it was stylishly welded into patterns of the family crest and sprayed in red, black and yellow. It opened to a stoned driveway, lined with manicured beds of hibiscus and bougainvillea. At the end of the driveway was a two-storey, seven-bedroom mansion with a top floor balcony just high enough to see into the commercial side.

Mainly painted in white with red beams around the window and doors, the main house managed to look both simple and bold.

Ike paced under the arched doorway to the main entrance. He glanced at the watch on his left wrist and then at his phone in his right hand.

Just wait for us there. We are fine and on our way. His father had said *Fine? Nobody was hurt? Dead? Was there any financial loss and most of all, was there any news of Fatima?*

The wait was killing him.

When the news broke, he was on his way to Madagali and only stopped at their family home to stock up on cash and other resources. Out of respect for his father, he agreed to wait for them before continuing his trip, but the way things now stood, he was close to breaking his word.

"*Oga!* They are here!" the security man yelled, running to open the gate.

Ike rushed down the steps as cars drove into the compound. The first car drove straight for the rear of the building. Ike ignored it, the car probably contained important items that needed to be unloaded quickly and away from prying eyes.

His mother was in the second car and she climbed out of the Acura SUV crying. His father followed consoling her. She saw Ike and ran to him.

Ike caught her in his arms a baffled look on his face. His father calmed him with an open palm and tried to untangle his wife from his bemused son.

"It's okay Ngozi…" Ike's father said to his wife, he turned to his son and said. "She just found out the church has been burnt down and the pastor killed."

"What the hell!" was all Ike managed.

His mother, tears still streaming from her face berated him for his language. Ike walked to his father.

"Father, what is going on?"

"Son, calm down…"

"Don't tell me to calm down." Ike interrupted. "The pastor was killed? How?"

"My son that is not something to discus in public." Ike's father placed his hands on his son's shoulder. "Let's take this inside." They followed the rest of the family into the house.

***

What do you say to a person who tells you your life has just ended? You stand there with a dumbfounded look on your face and wonder if the person had lost their mind.

A similar look registered on Ike's face as he listened to his father's stories. Had Madagali, a town of his birth, a town with no thought for religion or tribe really become that terrible?

And his bride to be, where was she?

The exhaustion of grief and the journey had finally caught up with his mother. She had excused herself from his father's study and left for her room. She hugged Ike, burying her face in his neck for a few moments before finally leaving.

For the first time in Ike's life, his father's study which was designed to intimidate some and impress others held no fascination for him. Always when he walked in, the massive mahogany desk that sat atop a thick rug in the *centre* of the room was unnatural.

His anger was still there, seething beneath the surface as he tried to fathom what was going on. More so as he remembered his friends and neighbours. From what he was hearing, some had lost their lives while others had simply vanished.

The days after the chaos were still few and he felt for those families waiting for news of loved ones.

The words from his father were both devastating and depressing. And realising he was still standing, hands placed on his father's impressive desk and leaning forward as if interrogating, he sat down on the closest chair.

"What of the Turaki's? My Fatima, what of her?" he asked.

Chibuike's tale had been general, occasionally telling of what had befallen landmarks, shops, acquaintances and friends. The tale was frightening enough already and Ike was now not sure if he really wanted to know the answer to his questions.

"Get me a drink, my son."

Chibuike stood and walked to one side of the room that was reserved for group conversations and meetings. Four comfortable sofa chairs were set around a low carved table made out of a tree trunk. The *iroko* tree had been growing on the land when he bought it. Rather than destroy the almost 200-year-old tree, he employed a skilled wood carver to make as many products from it as possible.

The table was one of the best of such works. Carved into the base of the table was a village scene that depicted women cooking and men farming.

Ike walked to a mini bar and prepared two doubles of London dry gin soaked in roots for his father and himself. He sat down opposite his father and sipped his drink. He smacked his lips and suppressed a shiver. The bitter taste of the roots and the gin combination was definitely an acquired taste. He took another sip, surprisingly in no rush to hear his father's tale.

When the tale finished a few minutes later, his glass was empty. He could not recall finishing the drink. He got up to walk to the bar and his father gestured with his own glass for another drink. Ike could see how much strain the telling of the tale had affected him. His father now looked deflated, as if a huge burden had fallen off his already heavy shoulders.

Ike was numb from what he just heard and poured the drinks in silence. Fatima was with a monster and he had no way of reaching her. He looked down at his eternity pendant and tears threatened to reach his eyes but he willed them away; weakness was never a friend of his. He gave his father his drink and sat down.

After a few more sips, he looked up. "You know I must go for her."

"I was worried you would say that," Chibuike replied, then taking a sip that almost drained the glass. "Did you not hear what I have said about Madagali?"

"I did father and I understand if you try to stop me" Ike emphasised 'try'. "But I do not know which will be more difficult to live with. A life without her or knowing I did not go for her."

"She is alive, Ike. This in itself is a blessing. Her father is dead, Musa is missing, or worse, and Hassan leads the vigilante. She will be saved eventually."

Ike calmed himself, stopping a retort. "Alihu is a spoiled brat who always had his way. He will kill her before anyone takes her away from him. To him she is a trophy and I have to save her."

This time Chibuike lost it. "Are you not listening? These guys are monsters! He will kill you! She was taken because of you! His hatred for you! US! Igbos, Christians!"

Ike stared at his father then stood up.

"Where do you think you are going young man?" It was a shout.

Ike turned to face his father. "I understand your worry father, I really do. You fear to lose your only son, especially after all you have built." Ike opened his arms gesturing around. "But…" Ike took a breath in to calm his nerves. "Fatima is my foundation; my beginning and she will be my end. She once asked me if I would always love her and I said I would, no matter what. It is a promise I intend to keep, father."

"I forbid you to go!" Chibuike yelled, standing up from his chair.

Before Ike could respond, a voice called out from behind both men.

"*De-de…*"

It was his mother. She often used the term for her husband. A term of endearment that always calmed him.

"Think on your actions for we may lose a son," Chibuike made to interrupt but she calmed him with a wave. "Then ask yourself, if it was me, would you come for me."

This time Chibuike fell silent and sat back into the sofa. For the first time in his life, Ike heard his father sob. His mother walked past him to his father and took the sobbing man in her arms. The sight broke his heart.

"I will be in my room." He turned, then added, "I won't think of leaving until tomorrow."

He left his parents in each other's arms.

***

115

Ike woke to a cloudy morning. The first rain for the season had decided to fall during the night, washing away the accumulated dirt and grime of the *Harmattan* season. He opened his window, took in the fresh air and filled his lungs. Before expelling the air, he savoured the smell of moisture. Soon flying ants would fill the air and the stomachs of those who saw them as a seasonal delicacy.

His bags were packed the previous night and his money belt was leaning on a sofa in his room. He walked to the shower. When the burst of cold water from the shower head hit his skin, he sighed.

His father invested in a water bore system to counter the erratic national supply system to their property, an investment Ike was grateful for as not many in the whole city would be standing under a working shower head as he did now.

His thoughts, like his disturbed dreams, went back to Fatima. He was blind to her situation and needed more information. For this, he would have to locate Hassan.

His father had mentioned Hassan's rise to leadership and Ike was grateful for the knowledge. At least he knew where to start.

Finished with the shower, he dressed, grabbed his bags and without a backwards glance left the room.

He was still in two minds as to which car to take. The Mercedes-Benz E300 popularly known as v-boot, or his graduation present, a Toyota Corona. The Benz, although more reliable would draw eyes to him. The Corona was newer, faster in a sprint and much nimbler. It was also slightly higher with less kerb weight. The perfect credentials for a getaway car.

When he got to the lobby, his parents were already waiting. He greeted them, hugging his mother and then his father. The emotional night they would have had was only slightly visible in their eyes as they stood watching him.

"Please don't worry too much. I really do value the life God has given me. I also value the care you have provided. It was not always like this for us and I too remember the hard work we all had to put in. Know that I intend to live long enough to make you proud."

Chibuike nodded and said. "I expect nothing more from you, Ikechukwu. You will go with God's guidance."

"Let us pray," Ngozi said and took her husband and son's right hands in each of hers. "Father in heaven, we stand before you today with thanks as well as worry in our hearts. We thank you for the love you have provided us and the life you have blessed us with. But we also worry that our son has chosen a path that we have no control over nor wish to stop." His mother paused, sighed then continued. "Like a father to us all, you know this decision is borne of love and regardless of its difficulty, you will protect him. We pray for your guidance and will forever be grateful for your love. Please bring him and his betrothed back to us. In your name and the name of your son Jesus Christ. Amen."

"Amen," both men chorused.

"I have prepared some meals for you in the kitchen and placed them in the cooler, I will go get it," Ngozi said releasing their hands.

Chibuike turned to Ike. "The Corona has been checked, fuelled and is ready to go. There are two Gerry cans in the boot, which should carry you a long way. Come to the study, I have something for you."

Chibuike walked to his desk and pulled out a small shoulder bag that could be worn under a shirt. He gave it to Ike, who opened it and gasped.

"Carry it with you at all times. There is fifty-thousand naira in there and a pistol that has never been fired so check it first. It should be okay as it is new."

Ike opened the pistol shaped leather pouch and pulled out the Glock. It was a silver model with brown wooden grip that felt comfortable.

"Never point it at something you do not wish to kill." Chibuike said

Hearing footsteps coming to the door, Ike quickly replaced the pistol in its pouch and zipped the bag close. He stepped around the desk and hugged his father.

"Be careful, my son, as we live in trying times. Already some of the Hausa businesses have been burnt down and most are leaving town. MOPOL are everywhere and you know how trigger happy those idiots always are."

Ike knew Nigeria's military police were a trigger-happy lot and needed no excuse to gun down those deemed a threat. This was a warning he already knew to heed.

His mother entered the study. She glanced at the bag Ike clutched and if she knew its contents, she did not show it. "The day is getting bright; you should leave now."

Ike thanked God for his parent's strength and hugged them one last time. The car's engine was already running and his bags were behind the passenger seat. He climbed in, took a breath then closed his eyes for a short prayer for journey mercies. His looked into the rear-view mirror and turned to wave at his parents.

He drove out of the gate and faced the main road.

Although the roads were already busy, he drove like the ex-government convoy driver that taught him how to drive. He left the car in second gear and used the engine's sweet spot to slip in and out of cars. Finding tight spaces between traffic and then speeding off when space opened up in front of him.

The Japanese car was in its element as it powered through lanes, the 2.0i engine revved in glee as he worked the clutch pedal and gears. Fifteen minutes later, he was out of the city and already speeding through the major national highway.

"Fatima, I am coming for you."

***

Sani had mourned his brother by first crying in solitude and then getting drunk.

Garuba had always been a pillar to him, dragging him into trouble and also saving him from it even when he caused it himself. The shock of the death had immobilized him. He never thought on ever losing his brother. *The man was immortal, was he not?*

Finally, he had dragged himself out of his drunken stupor he laid in and began preparations for his journey to Madagali.

The news of his brother's death was followed by Alihu's video of introduction. Subsequent videos of the liberation of Madagali had also been released and Sani knew their investors would be placated by the control they saw. All that was now required for their goal was a strong guiding arm in the beginning of the caliphate. A job that was reserved for his brother's shoes but one he now had to fill.

He knew he could not go into Madagali from the south as a vigilante force was blocking the border. His only option was the north from Maiduguri which was now secured by Alihu's men. He had chosen two Landcruisers, the first full of his security team and the second for himself.

He sat at the back flanked by two of his companions and another security detail in front next to the driver. They had made good time and were now approaching the northern border. In a couple of hours, he hoped to be in Madagali.

***

Dressed in full combat army gear, Terfa held the submachine gun to his sides. He admitted he did look formidable and was sure people would be frightened by the look. However, considering he did not have any confidence in his gun or the bulletproof vest that covered his chest, it was all face service.

As long as he could remember, he always wanted to be in the army. Hailing from Benue state and growing up with movies such as Rambo and Commando, he found it easy to join the army.

Unfortunately for him, the first few years dispelled any romantic notion that a soldier was immortal. Stints with ECOMOG such as the activities in Mali and Liberia showed him the bitter side of war. He had come out of these with a

119

few scars and the drive to be a soldier fighting for what was right.

Now that a war was brewing in his own country, he could not help but feel that he and his comrades had already lost. Information on the armament of the Jihadist had already reached his post. Worse, there was also news that some of the fighters were from neighbouring countries such as Niger and Chad.

He glanced at the gun on his side. He was not even sure what model it was. It looked like it had been made of bits from different guns, patched together as a quick fix with no hope for a replacement unit. He thumbed the safety off and had to use two fingers to switch it back on. He cursed to himself; the bloody thing would need oiling again.

For the second day he considered deserting to the southern border were he could be of more help to the vigilantes. The thought of standing barely five kilometres from a much superior force was disconcerting and was bound to end with his death. Training the vigilantes on the other hand would be a better cause to die for.

Two government spec Toyota Landcruisers approached his road block. Putting his game face on, Terfa flagged them down.

***

Before leaving Abuja, Sani made sure a high-ranking army officer sat in the passenger seat of his first vehicle. As they got to the checkpoint, a soldier flagged them down and upon seeing the officer, saluted.

He had also made sure that all his security personnel were dressed in standard issue army uniforms. Until this point, this and the formidable cars had ensured an uninterrupted drive across numerous checkpoints.

All of it, with the exception of protocol to salute superior officers, did not seem to impress the checkpoint soldier. After a short discussion with the senior officer, the soldier was told to proceed to Sani's vehicle. When the man got close, his driver powered down the window and the warm air that blew in made Sani instantly appreciated his car's air-conditioner.

"Get me Yakubu," Sani barked at the soldier.

The soldier paused for a few seconds and looked into the car. Intelligent eyes marked Sani's companions and the guns that his security detail carried. The soldier turned to the roadblock and called out to a colleague.

Internally, Sani laughed at the soldier. The man did not know that their commandant was in his pocket and the only reason the roadblock had not been overrun was that it acted as a lookout for his cause.

Shortly the commandant came to them, saluted and waved them on with no comment.

***

Terfa watched the cars drive past the roadblock. He stood next to his commander waiting for an answer to his silent question. The man turned to him.

"Good work officer, those men may be able to bring peace to the region before all this gets out of hand." The man then added, "back to your post."

As the man walked away, Terfa resisted the urge to shoot him in the back of the head. The uncertainty of his gun actually working was one of the reasons that stilled his thumb.

He sighed, calming his fraying nerves. Unbeknown to the man, he had spent a long time in Madagali and knew the faces of all its prominent citizens. The owner of the face in the car was one he knew quite well. He made his decision. Tonight he would use the back roads into Madagali and then find his way to the southern border.

13

The Old Man crouched in the bushes. His old knees protested from the flexed position and he rubbed them for comfort. *I am really too old for this shit*, he said to himself.

The house he was watching was heavily lit and guarded. Although the main power was cut to Madagali, a diesel generator growled powering the main house and the security lights around its perimeter.

Satisfied with what he saw, he slowly stood up but remained stooped. He looked around the darkness and strained his ears for a few seconds. He gathered his knapsack and like a crab moved away from the house.

A few meters behind him, two men rose from the ground and slowly followed the Old Man.

***

About a thousand kilometres from the troubles of Madagali, and very close to Lagos, a Peugeot 505 wagon slammed into a porthole.

The driver tried to control the pre-destined slide but eventually gave up. The car rolled, spilling people and items through its breaking windows and one opened door. After what felt like an eternity to those still within, two massive trees immobilized the car's momentum.

Soon after, another public transport vehicle came to the scene of the accident. Passengers spilled out to help, knowing how critical the first few moments of an accident were for the survival of victims.

One man was still stuck in the car, silent and his head slumped on his chest. Upon closer inspection by volunteers, they realised there was not much they could do for the man. A tree branch had pierced the side window of the car and passed through his lungs and heart. There was no point moving the man or the branch.

It was not a particularly fast or slow death. On the contrary, it was just right. A slow enough death for the man to feel the excruciating pain, but also fast enough that shock had set in few moments before total darkness. His dying eyes seemed to contemplate crimes of a by-gone life before finally winking out.

By the time the ambulance arrived, the man remained the only fatality. Search to his body for identification only ended up with wads of cash and no identity papers or documents. For fear of the dead, the money was returned to the body and its valuable placed on its chest. Shaking their collective heads in sadness, some of the gathered put the body into the ambulance.

"*Chei!* A bit sad not being able to take all that money with you to the grave! Or even give your family!" the driver of the 505 managed to say as the ambulance drove away.

Those standing around him silently agreed.

Although no one was any wiser to the identity of the man, an onlooker noticed the man's shoes were standard police issue boots; those worn by high-ranking officers. He would know because as a junior police officer he had polished a few boots in his day.

This information he kept to himself, it was someone else's problem.

***

The Old Man waited behind the burnt-out hut for his mole. Once again, he glanced into the bushes behind him. The sense of unease that he was being watched was heavy on his soul. Not seeing any movement, he turned back to the hut.

After a few minutes, a man in his late forties approached the hut from the road behind it. The Old Man fell to his knees and hooted like an owl. The man stopped in his tracks and then scratched his head with his left hand.

The Old Man held his breath, his body tensing in anticipation for flight or fight. The standing man then repeated the head scratching motion, only this time he used his right hand. The Old Man relaxed, it was the all clear sign.

"Sani just arrived." The man whispered. "He came with two cars, his Yan Daudus and a bunch of security people."

"What of Alihu?" The Old Man asked.

"He leaves in two days for his fortress in the forest, Sani will remain in Madagali, hold the town and control the expansion of the Caliphate."

"That is wise. The forest is easier to protect and it's very difficult to restrict their movement in and out of the border."

123

"Correct. In addition, since they own all the surrounding villages, no one gets close without them knowing." The man then added, "Anything else?"

"Yes, what of Fatima and Musa?" It was a question he had to ask.

"Musa escaped after his father was killed. They looked for him for a while but could not find him. Nobody really knows where he is," the man whispered back.

"And Fatima?"

"She is in the Sambisa." The man glanced back to where he had come from.

The Old Man could tell the man was impatient to return to his post. "Alihu is keeping her as a trophy. Even though he has taken one of his father's wives, he still keeps her for himself."

"I see," The Old Man said. Feeling for the man's impatience, he told the man to return to his post.

He watched his spy walk back into the streets while he remained squatting behind the burnt out hut. The nagging feeling instantly returned.

A sound came to him. It was low and most people would have missed it but not the Old Man. He knew the sound of feet carefully stepping on dry grass. It seemed the person hiding was also good enough to know when they had been detected as the sound stopped.

A shadow rose from a hiding spot behind bushes and the Old Man realised his mistake. Mistakes, they were two of them. Two AK-47s pointed at his head. He remained crouched.

"Ah so you are not just a silly old man always appearing like a coincidence?" one of the men said.

The accent was instantly obvious to the Old Man. The man who spoke was either not a Nigerian or would have spent a long time in northern Africa, probably Libya.

"Please don't kill me!" The Old Man said, putting on the mask of fright. It was a good mask. It transformed him from an old Dambé fighter to an aging old man. "I sell information that is all. Please!"

The soldier who spoke laughed and began to walk to the Old Man his gun still raised. "Do you, now?" He said, still coming closer.

It was exactly what the Old Man wanted. As the fighter got close enough, using his bent knees as a spring, the Old Man jumped forward and brushed the nozzle of the gun aside. A shot rang out, but the Old Man was already past the gun. He jabbed his left knuckles forward into the man's sternum. Satisfied with the cracking sound he heard, he shifted his body in front of the already falling fighter in an effort to block any shot the dead man's companion would think of firing.

The Old Man needed not bother. A figure ran from the bushes behind the second fighter and the moonlight reflected on a blade as it slashed into the side of the man's neck. The figure twisted the blade, then pulled it out, oblivious to the spray of blood that gushed out of the already dead man's neck. The figure then guided the falling man to the floor and turned to the Old Man.

"Are you okay old man?"

He did not know the voice, but his saviour moved like a soldier. "Yes, I'm fine. Thank you my, son."

"Are you with the vigilante?"

The Old Man looked into the man's eyes and made a decision. "Yes, I am" He said.

"Good," The soldier said.

He wiped the blade on the dead man's clothes, glanced at it confirming the cleanliness and then wiped it one more time for good measure. "You must take me to them urgently."

"Why?" the Old Man asked.

"That is only for the ears of their leaders," the man replied.

"Well," The Old Man said standing up and moving to the bushes. "You are looking at a set of those ears."

The Old Man led the way as they scouted around the town avoiding security patrols and makeshift spotlights. His guess was that in a months' time and without any outside influence, Madagali would be fully locked down by the jihadists. The town was already taken; it was the expansion of the Jihadists that worried him.

If Hassan could stop the southern advance, the only option left to the Jihadists would be a northern expansion towards Maiduguri, a major city that would surely be a more difficult choice.

While moving silently through the bushes, the Old Man was glad for the company. Especially considering the man moving next to him was almost as skilled as he was in stealth. Not once did he have to worry for his companion's safety and the ease of the task was a welcome opportunity. Allowing him to learn more of the enemy, moving closer to eavesdrop and investigate structures.

When they could, they continued their conversation in hushed tones and only falling silent when foreign sounds accosted their ears. These conversations allowed the Old Man to know a little bit more about the man next to him. More skilled than the average soldier, a patriotic one too and most importantly with several combat campaign experiences, the man may just prove to be a valuable asset.

After a bit more crawling and scampering they came to the southern edge of Madagali. This was by far the most dangerous part of the journey.

Most recently, the Madagali main gate to the south was simply symbolic. A concrete arc stood on the double carriageway that led into the town. A welcome sign that usually hung from the peak of the arc was now covered with a black cloth with Arabic written on it.

Expecting an attack from the vigilantes beyond, the Jihadists had fortified the roads beneath the arc with sand bags and barbed wire barricades. As a further deterrent, a sand bunker was set on one side of the road leading into the town and mounted inside it was a 7.62 PKM, one of Mother Russia's potent contribution to the wars of men.

There was no fence but for years, a thick row of Melina trees flourished and now extended out from the support pillars on both sides of the gate. The trees continued like a flora fence to form a thick growth around the outer edges of the town. This the Jihadists used to their advantage, patrolling it with the efficiencies gained from living in the Sambisa.

The Russian-made gun was a confronting surprise to Terfa. The stories they had heard about the Jihadists, although worrying was not half of what he was seeing. The brutality was definitely evident from all the burnt houses and mass graves he saw. What made him shiver to his core was their superiority in training and gear. No matter what the brass in Aso Rock thought, the Nigerian army in its present state stood no chance.

Another surprise for Terfa was the man he was creeping with. Not only was the old man good at what he did, he also acted like he had been in the army. Not just an officer but one who led men in battle, battles Terfa felt were from an entirely different era. The man knew what to look for as well as having a much sharper mind than those his age.

Terfa followed through the thick forest wall, happy to be led considering the old man seemed to find paths regardless of the trees and bushes surrounding them.

Suddenly the old man crouched and shuffled his fingers on the forest soil. Silently he searched for something. Finding it, he glanced around and then lifted.

A section of the forest floor opened up as if leading into a basement trap door. He gestured for Terfa to enter then followed behind closing the false floor.

"I learnt that from the Viet Cong," the Old Man said. "Just keep crawling you will be fine."

They moved in the dark under the forest, the air becoming murkier as they delved deeper. There seemed to be no end to the tunnel and at one point, the hole became so tight Terfa had to crawl on his stomach to fit. Luckily, after a few more meters, the hole expanded, and the air became fresher. The tunnel eventually opened up into an exit in a washout made by water erosion years past.

Terfa turned to look at the exit, if one ventured into the washout, they would still need to look close enough to realize the little hole was actually a tunnel entry.

"I have been preparing for this for a long time," the Old man said in a quiet voice.

"This would have taken you forever!" Terfa exclaimed. "You must have known of the threat; why did you not tell someone?"

The Old Man looked at him for a moment then asked, "If it is as easy as telling someone, why are you here?" It was a good question and it stopped Terfa from asking more.

The Old Man did have a point, what good would it have made? Even now, the men at the top did not know what to do or even where to start.

Once outside the washout, they did not get far. A group of men with red bandanas covering their faces surrounded them.

***

Fatima had still not said a word to Mama Ajiya. She allowed the woman to clean her and even feed her, but she stared at the woman with pure hatred in her eyes.

For her part, Mama Ajiya ignored the hostility in silence. This infuriated Fatima more as she felt the old woman appreciated the silence.

"He comes back tonight, and I will pray to Allah for strength for you. Just remember that no matter what happens, you will always be who you are now and what you choose to be in the future."

Before Fatima could respond, Mama Ajiya got up from the tent floor. She collected the basin of water she had used to clean Fatima, gathered the damp towels and left the tent, zipping the flap as she left.

Fatima glanced at the cup the woman had left on the floor next to her. She picked it up and sniffed its contents. It smelt of Dongonyaro tree leaves and peeled barks. She lifted the cup and drank its contents not stopping until the cup was drained. After a few minutes, the world around her began to spin and she fell back onto the tent floor.

***

Now that Alihu had been gone for hours, Musa felt comfortable enough to move around the house. Still dressed as a girl wearing a hijab, Joy and Amina were the only two people who knew who he really was.

He stepped out of the room in which he had spent most of his time during Alihu's visit and started walking to the kitchen. He turned a corner to a corridor and almost bolted back the way he came.

Walking from the other end was the new matriarch of the house, Garuba's Fulani wife. Musa calmed his nerves and continued to walk down the corridor. As he came close to her, he softened his voice and greeted her. Without replying to his greeting, she grabbed his elbow and pulled him to herself.

"Don't think I do not know who you are. *Kaji?*" She dragged him closer. "Know that as you walk these corridors, you are at my mercy." She released his hands and turned away, continuing as if nothing had transpired between them. It would be a year later before Musa told anyone of the encounter.

***

For the second time in her life, Fatima woke to a nightmare.

She was lifted bodily from the ground with her hair. Not knowing what was going on, she had screamed. Lashing out with her fingers and kicking into the air. It was then she realised her foot was no more shackled.

Alihu twisted her arms behind her and turned her around.

"I see my bitch has not lost her fighting spirit," he whispered into her ears.

129

The feeling of his breath on her neck sent shivers down her spine and he laughed, feeling her fright through his arms wrapped around her. His fumbling with his pants made her realise what he was about to do.

She snapped her head backwards and the back of her head slammed into his face. He released her staggering backwards holding his nose.

She looked around for something to fight back with but Alihu was already rushing at her. She tried to punch his bleeding face, but he swatted her hand away and punched her in the chest. She doubled forward, all air escaping her lungs. Alihu followed with a slap to the side of her face and the force of it sent her sprawling to the floor.

He was on her in an instant. He jabbed one knee in her thigh, making her scream and move the leg in pain. It was what he wanted, and his knee fell between her crouch. He slapped her again and continued to do so several times. He forced his other knee between her legs and forcefully spread her legs. He continued to fumble with his caftan pants, trying to unknot the lace with one hand.

Fatima lost the will to fight. She cried as he kicked his pants off. He ripped the wrapper covering her body and tore off her underpants. Already hard, he tried to penetrate her. Fatima tried to move her hips away, denying him access to her. In rage, he elbowed her between her chest and the pain shot through her ribcage.

Her pains suddenly became bearable and she leaned forward and bit down on the first flesh to come between her jaws. It was Alihu's left nipple and he howled in pain. He jabbed his thumb in her cheek, pushing his finger inward until she let go. He grabbed her neck with one hand and squeezed. With his other hand he guided himself and thrusted his hips into her.

"So that dog eater has already had you!" Alihu yelled, thrusting harder and harder. "No matter, you are mine now."

He still held her neck in his hand and she slowly started blacking out from lack of oxygen. As her eyes began to close, he released her neck and she quickly sucked in air, every breath she took was like a gift.

He was lost in his brutality, grunting like an animal and slamming his hips into her prone form.

Fatima stepped away from her body, watching him from afar, as he slapped and then choked her continuously. She locked the pain away, separating herself from the ordeal. Slowly her body and her mind could not take any more punishment and darkness finally consumed her.

Book III: Redemption

132

Kadiatu lay on her back staring at the ceiling fan as it spun around circulating the humid air in her private quarters. Her blank, almost serene demeanour did not betray the feelings of rage within her.

She had come from nothing.

Like most Fulani, her father had started life as a cattle herder. Guiding cattle along historical paths from the north-east of Nigeria all the way to the south-east. It was a year long journey, crossing various states and ethnic groups and usually through isolated, remote parts of the country.

After three years and a swell of cattle to almost two-hundred head, her father decided to change his route to pass through Plateau State in central Nigeria.

As fate would have it, he arrived with his herd during a tribal skirmish between the Fulani and Berom natives of the region. Villagers saw his flock and without hesitation, attacked.

Unprepared for a retaliation, he made the decision to retreat, setting a bush fire as a distraction, allowing him and surviving family members to escape north.

Her father lost half of his family and most of his cattle to the violence. His only consolation was the carnage the bushfire caused. It had spread through the village, burning most of it and its occupants to embers.

Her father, who was now survived by two wives and no means to care for eight children, had returned to Potiskum a broken man. A few months later, he was found hanging from a tree on his farmland.

Kadiatu was only thirteen at his death and watched as her sisters were married off one after the other. Soon it was her turn and she accepted the burden of her faith. In truth, she was more than happy to be leaving her broken family.

The match of her mate was in honour of her father, as some saw him as a Martyr for the fire that destroyed the Berom village. Her husband-to-be wanted to continue her fathers' legacy, expecting strong and brave boys from her womb.

Unfortunately, as is the case with most unreported physiological traumas, constant sex for a thirteen-year old girl had the potential to cause unrepairable damage, not just mentally but also physically.

By the time she turned fourteen, she had had two miscarriages and at fifteen, the prognosis that was she was never going to have a child. Soon her husband moved on and she became no different to a concubine.

Internally, she hated her husband. On numerous occasions, she stared at him with murder in her eyes as he rode her like an epileptic dog on heat. Spent, he slumped on her and was soon fast asleep. His dead weight was often a struggle for her young limbs to push away and the nauseating smell of his sweat was a disgusting reminder of her worth to the man.

After a while, she realised the power of her sex and used it to gain favours from him, performing acts on him that none of his other wives could or wanted to do, acts she knew he always wished for but too shamed to ask of his perfect wives. From her though, he was more than willing to accept.

Favourable treatment from him soon followed and the fact of it manifested into feelings of hostility from some of her sister-wives. She did not care. Where were they when she had to taste his foul fluids? They had their children and she saw no problem in having the luxuries her sexual prowess fetched.

Although her husband was dead more than a year now, she was able to hold on to power within his household. His son had taken over and she put her skills to play. She, more than any knew the weakness of men and her husband's son was one she knew all too well.

For the boy, she became an object of fascination: a girl the same age as him, his father's new wife. His fascination soon became lust and when his father had gone away for a long trip, he fell to his lustful desires.

Although slightly older than her, he was new to sex. She instantly knew what he wanted as he grabbed her from behind, ripping her wrapper from her body. She remembered giggling as he shuddered, spilling his seed after only thrusting into her a few times.

After the act, the shame kept him away, but she continued to tease him with her body for years. She even recalled several times she purposely met him in the family bathroom and undressed in front of him just to observe his need of her.

He never physically touched her after his poor performance. She on the other hand had no qualms at all. Even now, she could recall a time when he was under the moonlight, brooding over one selfish reason or the other. She had fallen to the soft soil next to him and used her fingers to relive him of his hard need.

Having power over him was not difficult, she knew his weakness and she played him like a string.

Unfortunately, her power was now being threatened by the news of a woman kept in the Sambisa. She did not mind other women, but this one was months away from giving birth to his first child. Like Deja vu all over again, it seemed childlessness was going to be her downfall.

She needed to act and quickly.

She continued to stare at the ceiling fan for a few more minutes then came to a decision. She got up from the bed, startling her young helpers who sat on the floor in front of her bed playing games.

"Stay here and wait for me." She said to them and walked out of the room.

***

Ike stood watching the arms dealer count the money in the bag while Terfa carefully inspected the goods. The goods in this case were two wooden crates filled with guns, ammunition and explosives. All items were set among dried grass straws to stop them knocking into each other.

135

One of the crates was a two-meter-long box that contained several pistols and fifty M16A2 rifles. The second crate was much longer and contained two propelled grenade launchers ammunition and several types of explosives.

General Terfa, as he was now fondly called, stepped back with a look of satisfaction over his face. In his hands, he held two pistols and spare magazines.

"Not much, but enough to cause some damage and *bestow some serious nyash trashing*," he said to Ike and gave him one of the pistols.

"*For the amount of money we just pay, I hope say we go do pass to trash buttocks*," Ike replied.

He took the pistol and expertly checked its mechanism. Satisfied with the gun, he loaded the magazine and placed the gun in a shoulder holster under his monkey jacket.

They lifted the boxes and carefully placed them on thick blankets in the back of a HiAce van. Ike moved to the driver's door and Terfa went for the passenger's side.

They were in Ikom, a south-eastern town close to the Cameroonian border and had several hours to travel back to Madagali. Ike would once again have to call on his fast driving skill as there would be no stopping, save for toilet breaks and meal restocks.

Terfa was also wearing a Nigerian army uniform with the hope that the official garb would deter police roadblocks.

***

Ike always appreciated Bordertown when he saw it from afar.

The name had stuck when lost for a formal name, Okada taxis had needed a way to identify the place. The Madagali border had become the border and then finally, Bordertown.

Now a community on its own, Bordertown had a population of fifteen hundred people. However, of that number, a thousand were fighters with five hundred of them personally trained by Terfa.

In terms of military affairs, General Terfa became the pride of the community. His drive to train the fighters well inspired many and several army officers deserted their posts to join Madagali's fighting force.

Terfa gave the willing army deserters different roles within the fighting force. Some became leaders of fifty fighters while others joined the main security force guarding the roads that led in and out of Madagali.

Ike was waved through the security post without affair and as he sped past the streets, he recalled the first time he drove into Bordertown. His blood had been boiling and his eyes screamed out for blue murder.

***

Hassan had stared at him with a shocked look. He had embraced the boy who was supposed to be his brother-in-law and they clutched each other trying to contain their emotions. After a while he had pushed Hassan back.

"You are well?" he had asked.

"We thank God for everything," Hassan had said stepping back with a smile.

The smile had instantly reminded him of Fatima's and his legs almost gave way from under him. Hassan had stepped forward and held him by the shoulders.

"Two days ago, we found out that Alihu did not bring her to Madagali." Hassan had turned him around and led him out of the train station. "He has her in the Sambisa and returned there with most of his men yesterday."

Hassan then went on to give him a firsthand account of what transpired since the fall of Madagali.

The news was by far more depressing than what he had heard from his parents. It was also more confronting now because he could see the effects of the war all around him.

Only a few hours in the community and it was near impossible to look around and see people not affected by the violence, directly or indirectly.

Hassan told him of the assistance they gained from old police and army officers, giving them the ability to create the impasse that now existed between the vigilantes and the jihadists.

The enemy could not move south and they could not move north.

"What of Musa?" he had asked.

"I honestly don't know if it is good or bad that we have not heard of him," Hassan replied.

They arrived at the unofficial start of the vigilante line behind the five-kilometre buffer zone that now existed between enemies. Burnt cars and auto parts mixed with barbed wire fences marked the safe line.

Several fighters patrolled the line and he noticed that some camped out in the window of trucks that had their cabins filled with sand bags. On a closer look, the fighters sitting behind the bags were pointing their guns at the Madagali gate.

"He has to be alive somewhere in there otherwise Alihu would willingly exploit his capture or death to spite you," he said to Hassan.

"That is what the Old Man says…"

"Old man?"

Hassan laughed. "Remember my Dambé trainer?" When Ike nodded, Hassan continued. "He is such a valuable asset. He can move around in Madagali in ways no one has ever been able to."

They stood looking at Madagali's gate and their thoughts went to remembering everything that once made the town their home.

"I wish to go for her," he said breaking the silence.

"And risk everything we can achieve?" a voice said behind them.

"Old man, still sneaking around?" Hassan asked.

"I do not sneak around; you boys just chose not to listen." The Old Man stepped forward to shake hands. "Do I have to tie you down like I did to Hassan when he wanted to go save his own sister and brother?”

He looked at Hassan with a raised eyebrow and Hassan laughed.

“The Old Man had to put me in a sleeper hold when I found out what Alihu was up to. He saved my life, because if I had gone there, I surely would have been killed before setting eyes on that demon...”

“...Father of Devils” the Old Man interrupted.

“That is what Alihu is called by his men,” Hassan replied in response to the confused look. “The Alihu we know is now a monster on a whole different level.”

A shot rang out and Hassan and the Old Man squatted. Hassan pulled Ike down to the ground. “He even took one of his father’s wives as his own.”

“You are fucking kidding?”

“Nope,” the Old Man said. “Worse, he has an army of five hundred or more fighters. All armed to their blockos with far superior weapons.”

“Yes.” Hassan added, “So superior that the only reason we are not wiped out is because our position gives us the advantage of reducing their numbers if they attack.”

“Superior weapons? Where did they get them?”

“We are looking into it,” the Old Man said. “Just recently we found out that Sani, Alihu’s uncle arrived at Madagali. For all intents and purposes, he does seem to be the financer.”

“Or at least the banker.” Hassan added.

“And the Sambisa?” Ike asked, also taking the cue to stand back up as Hassan and the Old Man were now doing. “Can we not attack their position there?”

“Not a chance,” Hassan replied. “The forest is heavily patrolled and they own it. There is no way several fighters could go in there without Alihu knowing. Sending fighters there would be a death sentence”

“Worse,” Hassan continued, “the villages around the Sambisa also act as lookouts for the Jihadists. I am afraid any foray into the forest means we have to either enter from the Cameroonian side or redeem the villages around it first."

Recalling his geography, he understood what the Old Man meant.

"So we stand back and do nothing?" He had immediately regretted his statement. These were men who had been in the grind far longer than he had and here he was questioning their actions. Hassan had not only aged physically, but also now looked like someone with too much on his shoulders. It was an unfair comment to make. "I am sorry," He said. "I just wish I could do something."

"And you will. We have a soldier with us who deserted the army to come and help. You will be part of the first batch of fighters he will train." Hassan replied, turning back to Bordertown. "Don't worry, you will like him."

And like him Ike did.

Terfa trained him well, teaching him and fifty others how to care for a gun, operate it and use it to kill efficiently. Terfa also took to calling him Igbo Manu, a term that reminded him of his long-time friend Boni.

Boni also ended up being a great asset to Bordertown, visiting a few times and bringing much needed funds and assets such as laptops and satellite phones. His contacts had also provided armoury, with the largest cache so far sitting in the back of the van.

Money was always an issue and Ike put his business management skills into play. First task was to create a miniature tax system for those who did business within the community. Secondly, a teacher from Fatima's school had joined them a few months back with colleagues of his and they used social media to bring in donations from around the world.

Despite the trickle of cash, it was still not enough, Ike recalled several missions of smash, and grab against the jihadist convoys coming from the forest to Madagali. The first mission was when he first took a life. He shuddered remembering the incident and brushed images of the ordeal away.

***

Ike drove the van straight to the back of the train station so they could unload the crates away from prying eyes. The mission was clouded in secrecy for fear of given away the biggest cache of arms they could afford and now they were safely in Bordertown, he did not want to lose the advantage.

Hassan stood outside the rear entry of the building and called out a greeting to them as they stepped out of the van. Seeing him, Terfa gave the thumbs up gesture and Hassan barked orders at some men standing behind him.

The men instantly knew what to do. They rushed to the van, grabbed the crates and were already inside the building before Ike had grabbed his own bags out of the van.

"Everything went well, I presume?" Hassan asked.

"Yes, we even got a few extra grenades because of Boni."

"Great!" Hassan responded. "There is no time to waste. The information we have is that the convoy will get to Madagali early tomorrow morning."

A faction of fanatics from Kano had sworn allegiance to the Jihadists in Madagali. They had stupidly broadcast their trip to Madagali on social media sites, claiming to be bringing arms and men to the fight.

The plan was to ambush them before they got to the Northern border, escape with as many arms as possible and destroy what could not be taken.

This was a much bigger operation than they were used to and only twenty men were going to try to make it work. Hassan wanted to go, but Terfa and Ike urged him to re-consider. There was no chance of the fight continuing if something happened to Hassan. Eventually he too saw the truth to their words and relented.

The Old Man was going and would lead them through back roads with two pickup trucks. The plan was to

141

leave tonight, drive in the dark without lights and meet up with the convoy a few kilometres to Madagali.

Two things were based on the success of the mission: surprise and speed.

***

Terfa squatted behind a thick bush and glanced at his watch, he cursed at the time. He was late to get to the rendezvous point and there was no sign of the convoy or Ike's truck. All that welcomed him and four fighters was the deafening sound of crickets. Unsure of what to expect, his truck was parked behind him in overgrown bushes.

A flat tire was the culprit for their lateness and since they needed the truck, the only option was to send a team ahead while they dealt with it. Even with a moon almost full, it had still been a difficult and time-consuming task. He still felt the urge to empty a whole bullet clip into the damn pick-up truck.

The difficulty now was which direction to take. He could head towards the Madagali border to catch up with Ike and his men, or he could drive away from the border just in case the convoy was late and Ike had gone that way.

He did not have long to wait before he heard sounds of a car. He strained his ears and tried to ignore the crickets, No not car, cars…

Terfa made a decision. He would wait until the cars passed through. If it was the convoy, he would follow behind and attack at the last minute with the hope Ike was in front. The only other plausible reason for Ike's absence would be that the convoy defeated some very good fighters. Either way it could just be the five of them left to finish the job.

A few minutes later, Terfa knew he made the right call. The convoy did not look like it had been in any skirmish, which meant that Ike and the Old Man were somewhere in front.

He counted two station wagons and three Mercedes 911 trucks. Two of the trucks were full of people while the

142

truck in the middle seemed to contain goods. This was the one to steal.

After the convoy passed their hiding spot, he waited for a few heart beats and gestured for one of his men to bring the pickup truck forward. Not bothering to climb into the passenger's side, he jumped onto the back open tray.

Their headlights were still switched off so it would be a while before the cars ahead realised there was an additional engine sound coming from their rear.

He tried to think like the Old Man or Ike. If there were in front, they would know that only a limited window was available to attack the convoy before it got to Madagali.

The station wagons were in front of the trucks, a stupid idea Terfa thought to himself, but one he intended to exploit. There would be no warning before the attack on the first vehicle, so he and his crew had to act quickly to disarm the last truck of fighters.

The convoy came to a sharp bend in the road and the station wagons went first. The first truck began its own turn but its rear wheels suddenly exploded, lifting the back of the truck in the air. The force of the explosion upturned the vehicle and it fell on its head.

It was a gift of pure luck that worked in their favour, trapping the Jihadists in the rear of the truck and reducing the number of men to fight.

Shots could be heard further around the bend and he knew the men in the station wagons were being engaged by his colleagues. He did not hesitate and opened fire on the last truck. His men took the hint and started shooting at the tires of the truck as well.

When the rear tires gave way, the truck skidded then screeched to a sudden stop. They were able to pin the Jihadist down with a barrage of shots.

He ordered his driver to move the pickup truck to the side of the road so they could see a better view of the action in front and also if they needed to make a quick getaway.

One of his men threw a grenade at the side of the truck and it exploded, almost tipping the truck over. Jihadist who were climbing out of the truck from the side facing away from their attack were flung into the bushes beyond.

The fight would surely be heard by the people at the Madagali border by now and Terfa did not want to have to fight his former colleagues. He prayed for a quick operation.

***

Ike glanced backwards and thanked whatever gods of war that existed for granting Terfa the ability to foresee the Old Man's improvised plans.

The rear truck full of fighters that could turn the tides on the battle were pinned down. Secondly, the first truck was on its head which meant the jihadists in the back were on top of each other and trapped.

Time was short and they needed to hijack the ammunitions truck quickly.

Pointing his assault rifle forward and his eye looking through the barrel aim, Ike ran to the truck. He fired shots into the driver's side with no thought for the man driving or his passengers.

A few months ago, he would have hesitated, but he was under no illusion that they were now at war. Kill or be killed.

He ran, stooped and slammed his back into the side of the truck, just behind the passenger door. The Old Man was also running towards his position. Without subtlety, the Old Man fired shots into the passenger door. Ike was hoping to open the door slowly and then fire if anyone was still alive. Nevertheless, he had to admit to himself, the Old Man's method was probably the safest.

The Old Man yanked the door to the passenger side open and jumped in. Ike followed him in, coming face to face with two dead bodies pelted with bullets.

These they pushed out and the Old Man took the driver's seat. Luckily the truck's engine was still running. The Old Man engaged gear and punched the vehicle's horn twice.

Revving the trusted Mercedes straight six diesel engine, the Old Man performed an earth crunching U-turn and headed away from Madagali.

The rest of the Jihadists were still pinned down by Terfa when the ammunitions truck sped past him with the Old Man driving. Coming close behind was the pickup truck Ike had driven. And as it too sped past, Terfa banged his fist on the roof of their pickup truck. The driver did not need telling twice and he made a turn following the path of the vehicles gone ahead.

They were soon past the rendezvous point and turned into the bushes, aiming for the hidden roads back to Bordertown.

2

Fatima held the stick with both hands behind her right shoulder. She stepped forward with her left foot and swung the stick. It connected with the man's back and he yelped in pain and rolled off the young girl. In an instant, he was on his feet, an angry blade in his right grip.

When he saw Fatima standing with the stick he paused. Some of the men who had gathered around the act left while others stood in silence, watching.

"If you rape every girl that comes here do you think you will still have someone left to cook and wash for you?" She dropped the stick to the ground. "Or maybe you wish to wear a dress and help with the food and washing?"

"She is my property!" the man screamed at her. "She belongs to me!"

"Is that right?" Fatima replied, moving to the girl lying on the ground.

The look on the girl's face worried Fatima, it was that of disconnection. Worse, when others would plead or fight the girl had laid there immobile as if she was insensible to what was around her.

"You are part of the team that attacked Madagali are you not?" she asked the man.

"Redeemed! We redeemed Madagali from infidels!"

145

"Does that make it yours then?" She asked the man.

She squatted next to the girl on the ground and tried to cover her nakedness. The task was pointless as the man had ripped every garment the poor girl was wearing. Mama Ajiya stepped forward and handed Fatima a wrapper. Fatima accepted it and voiced her thanks.

"I found her! She is mine!" The man said stepping forward.

"In that case…" Fatima said standing up to face the man. "I now claim her for one who will work the kitchens."

"You have no right over me, you bitch!"

A hush fell on the scene. She could barely take the insult from Alihu and she knew what men called her behind her back. There goes the Sheikh's bitch.

The baby in her womb kicked violently, almost doubling her over but she stood her ground expressing no discomfort.

"You will die tonight," she said to the man.

She pulled the girl to her feet. Luckily, the girl responded and Fatima dragged her away. She walked to her tent followed by Mama Ajiya. Once the flap was dropped behind her, she walked to her bed and began to sob.

"You should have let me kill this child, it is evil!" she said to Mama Ajiya. "Look at what it made me commit to."

"My daughter, you cannot blame your child for the need for justice." Mama Ajiya moving to her. "If it is really your son putting thoughts in your head, then he is not the devil as you name him."

"He is the devil and I would never take a man's life," Fatima said, somewhat getting control of herself.

"The man disrespected you in front of many. You responded with a claim on his life. If he does not die by tomorrow, you will lose all the respect you have gained."

"I do not need respect from animals!" Fatima cried out.

"I heard a wise saying once. To be successful with animals, one must treat them… like animals. Only then would you be a successful handler," Mama Ajiya responded.

She briefly held Fatima on her shoulders and turned to the girl Fatima had just saved from a terrible ordeal.

"What is your name?" Mama Ajiya asked the girl.

The girl remained mute, staring at the floor. "Are you dumb?" She asked the girl. Again, silence.

"My sister, do not worry you are safe here." Fatima said to the girl.

Still, the girl remained silent.

"Have you had something to eat?" Fatima tried again.

This time there was a reaction. The girl looked at Fatima, then at Mama Ajiya. She returned to staring at the ground but shook her head. No.

Mama Ajiya nodded to a girl standing at the tent's entry. The helper took the cue and left to bring some food. She moved to the girl and gently pushed her down to the floor to sit. Like a child, the girl complied giving no objections.

Two girls walked into the tent with a bucket big enough for the girl to fit in. As Mama Ajiya made to guide the girl to the bucket, she violently brushed Mama Ajiya's hands away and moved backwards.

"You do not wish to wash the stench of that animal off your body?" she asked the girl. She responded with another headshake. No.

Fatima watched the exchange in silence. Mama Ajiya did not force the girl, rather she asked the helpers to take the bucket away. She moved to where Fatima sat and joined her. Both women looked at the girl.

"I have seen this before," Mama Ajiya said to Fatima. "The child is still in shock; I pray to Allah that she recovers from it. Otherwise she will be useless to us all."

Fatima sighed and laid backwards on the mattress. "She was from one of the villages close to Chibok. Alihu's men are violent creatures; only God knows what evil the poor girl has seen."

Fatima moved further into the mattress, creating space at its front. She gestured for the girl to come forward. She obeyed, moving silently to Fatima.

"Until you decide to speak to us, I shall call you *Kurum Daya*." Silent One.

Again, no verbal response, which Fatima ignored and tapped the bed. Without any shyness, Kurum Daya climbed onto the bed and squatted next to Fatima.

Mama Ajiya smiled at Fatima who returned the smile. She knew Fatima thought the smile was for the success of the act, but for her it was the fact that the abused was now becoming the healer.

What Kurum Daya did next surprised them even more, wiping the smile off their faces.

The girl placed her left ear on Fatima's stomach as if listening to the baby's heartbeat. In Shock, Fatima looked down at the scene with her mouth wide open and her hands wide.

Moments later, the girl was fast asleep and Fatima pulled her backwards into the bed.

Quietly, she struggled with the weight of her baby and tried to get up from the mattress. As her child grew, the act of getting up from a mattress placed on the floor was getting more difficult. Mama Ajiya stepped in to help her, also silently cursing the low mattress.

As they got close to the tent's exit, Mama Ajiya said to her. "Someone close to her must have been with child."

All Fatima could do was nod in agreement. Instinctively, her hand went to her stomach but her child was silent, as if it too had also fallen asleep.

***

A pain like a tug in her stomach woke her up with a start. This was not the first time her child woke her in the middle of the night and she was quite confident it would not be the last.

Sometimes she remained still, rubbing her stomach to calm the restless child and if that failed, her only option was to walk around for a bit. Curiously, those walks usually ended with something fascinating.

Fatima did not need to strain her ears too much to hear the soft snore coming from Mama Ajiya. Once her pregnancy started showing, the old woman had insisted on sharing Fatima's tent. Initially she said it was to keep Alihu at bay, but Fatima knew it was because of the closeness they now shared.

She glanced at the spot behind Mama Ajiya and her heart skipped a beat. The space where Kurum Daya was supposed to be was empty. One of her assistants who slept next to the tent entry was, like Mama Ajiya, also sound asleep.

Fatima silently rose from her mattress, using her hands to push her form upwards. As she moved to Mama Ajiya to wake her up, the sound of the old woman's snore changed. Fatima knew the woman had just woken up but still pretended to be sleeping.

"It is me Fatima," she said to the lying form.

Mama Ajiya's eyes flew open. "You okay? Everything okay?"

Fatima pointed at the spot on the mattress. Turing to look behind her, Mama Ajiya expected to see Kurum Daya but was also shocked by the empty space. She turned to look at Fatima, a question written all over her face.

Fatima opened her palms to indicate she did not know where Kurum Daya was. A feeling of distress began to weigh on their hearts. Fatima threw a jacket over her shoulders to block the chilly night while Mama Ajiya took her sleeping gown off and wore a wrapper and a blouse. They quietly walked out of the tent, making sure not to wake the sleeping attendant next to the exit.

The moon was out and it helped to illuminate their surroundings. Fatima hoped someone would have seen Kurum Daya leave the tent but no one was around. This was

not surprising as it was just past two-thirty am and most of
the fighters and helpers were fast asleep.

"We should search that idiot's tent," Mama Ajiya
whispered. Fatima nodded and followed her as she walked
away. Dread hung over her head mimicking the dark cloud of
sand flies that followed them both.

The number of tents around them had grown in the
past few months to make way for the additional fighters and
volunteers the Jihadist recruited from their northern
expansion. Despite the increase, an effort was still made to
continue to separate the tents with trees and shrubs for
privacy and security.

Fatima followed Mama Ajiya as she walked through
paths created between tents. They came across a few night
guards who acknowledged their presence with nods. Provided
the women were not leaving the camp, the order was not to
bother them.

Finally, Mama Ajiya came to a tent located at the
periphery of the camp. The tent's flap was open and it was
pitch black inside. Mama Ajiya switched a torch on and
stepped in. Fatima followed and gasped at the scene.

The man that had insulted her earlier on was on the
bed naked; his dead eyes stared at the celling of the tent. His
neck had been slashed almost from ear to ear and his life
blood pooled around his pillow.

The smell of blood forced bile to Fatima's mouth but
she held it back. Mama Ajiya moved the beam of the
torchlight around the room and it fell on another form in the
corner of the room.

Kurum Daya was sitting down, holding her knees to
her breast while she stared at them with no emotion in her
eyes. Her whole form including her face was covered in blood
and in one hand she held the angry looking knife the dead
fighter had threatened Fatima with.

"It is okay," Fatima said to Kurum Daya. "Come."
She walked to the girl and gestured with her hand.

Still clutching the knife in her right hand, Kurum Daya allowed Fatima to lift her up with her left. Mama Ajiya stepped forward and inspected the girl. Satisfied that all the blood on her was that of the dead man, they left the tent and its grotesque scene.

Rather than head back to their tent, Mama Ajiya led them to the river behind the camp. No one saw them as they left.

Both women stripped Kurum Daya and without being prompted, the girl walked into the cold water. Without flinching and still with a passive look, she washed herself. When done she stepped out of the water, shivering but clean.

Mama Ajiya removed a layer of the wrapper she was wearing and wrapped it around the girl. Silently, all three began the trip back to Fatima's tent.

When they got back, all was as they left it, including the sleeping attendant at the door.

Kurum Daya walked to her spot on Mama Ajiya's bed, removed the wet wrapper around herself and laid down on the mat.

As Fatima took to her own bed, a voice filled the room. "I used to have a name but I am now Kurum Daya." Before Fatima could respond, Mama Ajiya replied.

"Okay, but next time before you do anything like that, take permission from Fatima first."

"Okay mama," Kurum Daya responded, turned her back to both women and was promptly fast asleep.

***

The following morning was business as usual. Even when the dead man's body was removed and wrapped in a white cloth to be buried, no one said anything. Well, at least to Fatima's face. The rumour had already taken a new head. The young girl had been initiated to take the life of the dead man, a promise Fatima had given and was now fulfilled. Suffice to say, no one ever insulted her to her face again.

***

151

Kurum Daya continued life as normal, ignoring the looks she was given by those around her. She also decided to be completely clad in black, wrapping her young form in a caftan and hijab only exposing her hands, feet and face. She almost never left Fatima's side, standing or sitting silently, not too close but also not far off.

Fatima was worried by the lack of emotion she saw in the girl's eyes or voice but was told by Mama Ajiya not to worry. Everyone healed in their own way. *Everyone*, Mama Ajiya had insisted. The statement had instantly reminded Fatima of a past not far gone and a wound still glaringly open.

Alihu had raped her constantly for a month. Sometimes every night, other times more than once. He seemed to always want to expel his rage after battle. Coming to her covered in the blood of victims he killed, judged as he called it. Every time, she had fought back, screaming and using everything she could to hurt him, to share her pain.

In a way, Fatima had been lucky because after a month of suffering, Alihu found out from Mama Ajiya that Fatima was pregnant. Mama Ajiya advised him that his actions could harm his son, his only heir. Alihu had stopped coming to her then. He even tried treating her with a little bit more respect.

Although she had been grateful to Mama Ajiya, it had still taken her a while to trust the old woman. The old woman seemed to be loved by the camp citizens and Fatima understood why. She cared for them, made sure they were fed and, in some cases, filled out the role of a mother and grandmother.

Alihu also respected her calling her 'mother' an endearment even Fatima now used for the woman.

"I like her," Kurum Daya said, bringing Fatima back from her thoughts.

Fatima glanced at the girl to see her looking at Mama Ajiya who was currently supervising the slaughtering of a goat.

How did the girl know what was on her mind? Fatima thought to herself. She must have been looking at Mama Ajiya with love in her eyes.

"Yes, I like her too," Fatima replied.

"She is a victim like us all and hides it well." Kurum Daya continued, again surprising Fatima with her placid tone.

"She once told me that; every day, the love she bestowed on those around her was love she owed to someone else."

Kurum Daya nodded as if she understood her words. *Maybe she did.*

She recalled when she first heard the statement; it was also the day Mama Ajiya found out she was pregnant.

When her period had been late, she knew why and hated herself for it. Her first child was supposed to be for Ike but now a man she hated more than the devil had violated her.

She had spent the whole night crying and thinking of ways to kill herself. She had even tried, wrapping a rope around her neck and lopping it over a pole on the tents structure. It could not hold her weight and all she gained from her effort was a bruised buttock when she hit the floor. In anger, she searched the tent looking for something to slit her wrist or throat. Finding nothing save for a metal clothes hanger, she decided to kill the child within her instead.

Mama Ajiya had found her a few hours later bleeding on the floor.

"You stupid, stupid girl!" she had said to Fatima.

She inspected Fatima, spreading her legs to check her. She left and returned with a bucket of hot water and cleaned her up. She then forced a bitter tasting brew down Fatima's throat.

Fatima had passed out then, waking a few hours in a fever.

"It is your fault for trying to kill yourself and your child." Mama Ajiya said to her. "Fortunately for you, the life of your child will not be on your hands."

She remembered bursting into tears then. She failed to kill herself and now, also failed to kill the devil in her.

"A life given by Allah is not yours to take," Mama Ajiya had said to her.

"It is a devil child!" Fatima stammered through gnashing teeth.

"Half of it may be the devil, but the other half is you." Mama Ajiya said mopping her brow with a wet cloth.

The old woman then told Fatima of her story and by the end of it, Fatima had been in tears for the woman's sake, her and all the victims of Alihu's hate.

"When will the pain stop? How can we break the cycle of hatred? By being like him?" Without waiting for an answer, Mama Ajiya had continued. "The love I show to you and all around me is the love that I owed to someone else... My grandson."

Mama Ajiya wiped her tears and sweat then gave Fatima something much sweeter to drink. As Fatima drifted to a more peaceful sleep, the old woman had said, "The child that is half of you will have a better chance of breaking the cycle. Keep it, love it and show it that there is a different view from all the pain around."

She was once again reminded of her surroundings as a hand wiped the tears on her cheeks. It was Kurum Daya.

"My mother always cried when she was pregnant with my brother," Kurum Daya said.

Fatima smiled.

***

As the sun set and the last of its rays pierced the forest leaves creating beauty above the tribulations of the camp, Alihu returned like a dog scattering resting doves. His presence was instantly felt as the camp became more subdued and fighters expressed their best behaviour.

Fatima also knew the moment he was told of the fighter's death. In fact, most of the camp knew as he exploded in a fit of rage. She turned to Kurum Daya and said to her.

"This is the moment where I test your faith and your ability to do as I say." Fatima made to stand from her annoying bed and Kurum Daya stepped forward and helped. "No matter what you see or feel, you must not react. You must promise me this."

Kurum Daya looked at Fatima, then at her pregnant stomach. She nodded and moved to a corner of the tent.

Alihu barged in with no ceremony save for his barking rage. In one hand he held Hukumchi, the other was bare but with a balled fist.

"You dare order the death of my soldier!" It was not a question and he punctuated it with a slap to her face.

Fatima did not feel the pain as her eyes were on Kurum Daya who took a step towards Alihu's back, her hand moving into her caftan. She looked into Fatima's eyes and stopped in her tracks, remembering the promise she made earlier, she turned and left the tent.

Alihu made to turn, following her gaze but Fatima spat on him, getting his attention. He raised his hand to hit her again but she stepped back and turned her back to him.

"You still act like the idiot boy with no brains. So I should allow another man insult me even when I carry your child?" Her voice was calm as she walked to her bed, struggled to stoop and eventually sitting on the mattress. "Let me guess, when your son finally comes, he will also be called a dog."

Alihu had not moved. He stood staring at her, wide eyed and his mouth slightly open. He turned to look around, as if to ask for support. After a few seconds, he shut his mouth, grunted and walked out of her tent.

Fatima clutched her cheek and allowed the tears she was holding back to finally fall. Like a flood they came forth, eventually turning into a sob that quivered her shoulders. Her child began to get restless and she placed her hand on her stomach. Like a consolation, she felt him move to her hand.

"So you are not just the devil," she said. Tears still streaming from her eyes, she chuckled.

She went to the bed and struggled, as always to lay on it. Moments later, she was asleep.

***

And woke in water.

As a child, she often followed her mother to meet her other side of the family. It was usually during a festival season, Salah or Christmas. Everyone was merry and the joy of the season was infectious.

She had learnt how to swim then. Her mother's family lived in a village not too far from a stream and when all the women went to do the washing, the children followed. To keep them occupied, they were allowed to go swimming or fishing with a hook attached to a short stick.

She remembered how to swim, but this time her limbs disobeyed her.

She fell under the water and panic kicked in.

She jumped out of the water, sucking in valuable air.

She noticed a rock face and she reached out to it.

Her fingers did not find any grip, slid downwards as she fell back into the water.

Once again, in a desperate quest for survival, she pushed herself out of the water. This time, there was a boy reaching out to her. He was standing on a rocky platform holding a pole she must have missed the last time she was up.

She grabbed his hand and he pulled her out of the water. She had no idea where he got the strength from as he was much smaller and younger than her, *maybe eleven?* Still he had pulled her out of the water, dropping her on the rock platform behind him without fuss.

She rose to look at him and he was Alihu.

Well, not Alihu *per se* but there was definitely Alihu in there.

Then the boy became Musa.

156

Hassan, she had heard of. The pain he was causing
the Jihadist was evident enough. Musa on the other hand, no
one knew of his whereabouts.

Then it was Ike.

By then the boy had moved to her to make sure she
was okay. He held her in her arms and she felt love.

A content smile lit her face…

***

Kurum Daya and Mama Ajiya watched her sleep. Worried,
they had come to see if she was okay. Finding her fast asleep
with a smile on her face was good enough for them.

Yes, her face was still tear stricken but she seemed
fine. Quietly they left for other chores, lost in thoughts of the
beauty of the smile.

3

Deep down inside Joy knew that Musa could attempt an
escape anytime he wanted. She made a promise to herself
never to stop him no matter how she felt. She was safe in the
household but he was not.

For a year now, Musa had learnt to be a female
servant in the household and he was good at it. Several times
making her forget what gender he really was. Aside from
Amina, only two other women knew who he really was.

It was vital that the first person to know was
Garuba's First wife. She demanded the respect to know
everything within the house. To their benefit, the grief of a
lost husband meant she never paid much attention as to who
exactly was the boy disguising as a girl.

Listening to Musa's tale as she sat in front of him, Joy
realized for the first time who the other woman was. Kadiatu.
The woman had accosted Musa in the corridor and
threatened him. For months he had kept this a secret, for her
not to worry he said.

For the first time since she had last worried for his
safety, she realized her biggest mistake was not to help him
escape.

***

157

She had come looking for him by request from Kadiatu. They were to attend Sani's quarters immediately. She had thought nothing of it, but after what Musa just told her, she worried for the worst.

Everyone knew Sani's appetite. He had come with several companions, male and young. Musa was exactly what he would want. They had to escape. She spun from the chair she was sitting on and rushed to the door. She checked the corridor beyond, happy with what she saw, she locked the door behind her.

"Grab some clothes and wash your face quickly." She said to Musa.

"Why should I wash my face?" he asked.

"Because they are not looking for a boy. Now! Hurry!"

Minutes later, she carried a bag with spare clothes and he carried water, dried meat and some fruits. She opened the door slowly, looked out and silently walked out. Musa was right behind her, also trying to be as quiet as possible.

Their best chance was the front of the house. It was getting to dinner and the evening meal was ready to come off the coals. Everyone would be close to the kitchens at the back of the house salivating over steaming pots.

Musa matched her pace. Quick, but not at a rush. The sun was setting and the shadows would aid their escape. It seemed the gods were on their side.

They entered the main compound and Musa was instantly reminded of a past that changed his life forever. He could almost see his father lying on the ground with a subtle trickle of blood around the bullet wound on his forehead.

Joy dragged him towards the gate, then stopped as she heard her name being called. It was coming from the back of the house, so they still had a chance of surprise. She pushed forward and they were at the gate.

"Are you Joy?" The security guard asked as he walked towards them.

They looked at each other and shook their heads. The man scowled and stood to the side letting them through. At that moment, a voice screamed her name, this time much closer. It was Kadiatu.

The security guard reached for her, thinking she was the one to catch. Musa took the opportunity to slam his body into the guard who fell backwards. He and Joy sped past.

Outside the gate, she went left and he went right, in panic they both stopped. He ran to her and they continued running.

The dense bush behind the house was the best way to lose their pursuers and soon they were crawling into elephant grass blades, shrubs and piles rubbish. Yet it seemed that their pursers followed. Musa had no idea how many were chasing them but all he knew to do was crawl and when he could, run.

***

The Old Man had just heard about Musa's dilemma but they had to be quick before the window of escape closed.

Hassan was nowhere to be found, Ike would do. The boy had impressed him several times already and he was currently their only chance.

Ike grabbed his M16A2 rifle that was leaning on a chair, jumped over the table he was eating off and bolted after the Old Man. He was not sure where they were going but he followed as best as he could. He understood the rush though; all the Old Man had said was *Musa*, a name that was bound to send him into desperate motion regardless of what he was doing. They were soon in Jihadist country, moving through burnt houses and edging closer to Garuba's house. He did not care. *Musa.*

It was turning into a dark night and the Old Man was grateful for it. He moved from shadow to shadow, gesturing at Ike to follow when it was clear and to wait when it was not. Soon they were close to a road next to the bushes behind the house.

Ike made to cross the road, but the Old Man held him back. A young girl and a boy rushed out of the grasses into the road.

*****

Musa ran as fast as he could. When they got to the road, he knew somehow that it was their only way out. Someone was waiting beyond and Musa realized who it was. Ike.

He surged forward with new found strength but a blur of an animal cutting past his path stopped his frantic dash.

*****

Ike saw the beast before Musa did and already had his weapon up. But before he could open fire, bullets peppered the ground in front of him and he ducked back into the bushes.

*****

Joy who had been running next Musa was as shocked as anyone when she realised that a She-Hyena was sprawled over her with her neck held in its dripping jaws.

"*Rika*!" A voice called out to the animal. *Hold.*

A man walked into her view. A chain was wrapped around each fist with his fingers being the only visible part of his hands. Around his chest, he also wore a chain collar similar to what the beast striding her was wearing.

The hyena stopped moving but when she tried to struggle the beast growled, stilling her.

She heard a voice. "Come out or the young girl dies." It was Sani, Musa was doomed. She began to cry.

*****

Ike and the Old Man had already left. There was no guarantee that Sani would release the young girl even if they gave themselves up. It was not worth the risk.

By the time Sani gave the proposition, they were far away enough they could barely hear him.

*****

Some of Sani's men were already close to Ike's hiding spot and Sani nodded at them. They jumped into bushes, guns raised.

The lack of gun fight told Sani what he needed to know. He turned to Musa.

"Take *that thing* to my chambers." He turned to Kadiatu. "The young girl is your problem." He turned around and left.

The hyena released Joy, licked its lips, snorted at her and followed its chained master.

***

Hassan was waiting for them. News had already reached him that a situation had forced Ike and the Old Man to rush out in a hurry. He followed them into the luxury bus he still used as his quarters and waited for their tale.

Quietly he listened, his face devoid of emotion and when they finished he said.

"Sani will not kill Musa. He will hold him as leverage."

"Yes, but you don't know the man's appetite," the Old Man replied. He told them of what he knew of Sani.

"Then we have to go get him." Ike said, standing up from his chair.

"Bad idea," the Old Man said. "We cannot storm that fortress and we do not know where they are keeping Musa. He may be dead before we even get there."

"The Old Man is right." Hassan said.

Ike could not believe his ears. "But that man is a monster!" Ike took a deep breath. "The psychological effect this man will have on Musa would be terrible!"

"You do not know what the boy has done to survive this long. Remember until today we did not know what had happened to him. It has been a year." the Old Man replied.

"Once again," Hassan said. "Old Man you speak wisdom. What do you propose?" Ike made to speak but Hassan quieted him with a wave.

161

"We propose an exchange. They give us someone in return and we do not attack."

Ike stood up. "I will send a runner under a white flag. The terms will be that no harm comes to our prisoners."

"Guests." Hassan corrected.

***

As dawn broke, Sani replied with terms. A lone figure walked out of the Madagali gate and from the gait of the person, Hassan could tell it was a woman. As she got closer, he realized who it was.

4

Sani had no time for squabbles. He was expecting some Saudi guests and everything needed to be spot on. Also, Alihu was planning a mission that would put them on the world map and the hope was that the Saudis would realise that they were dealing with dedicated men.

After the brave, *or stupid,* attack on the convoy at the northern border, He knew safety was now an issue. So, he cleared a field in front of his brother's house and made a helipad. He had already approved two test runs and there were all successful. *So, no problem there.*

The Saudis would fly straight to Madagali from Abuja. He did not mind paying for the expensive helicopter service because it isolated the rest of Nigeria from his guests, giving the impression that he was in total control. A road trip on the other hand, was long and would expose the chaos of the town's borders.

His guests were due in five days and his last task was in the Sambisa. He needed to go through Alihu's plan one last time to make sure everything was right.

He always hated the trip to the forest, as it never made sense that he would forfeit the luxuries of life he now enjoyed.

Dealing with a fight at Bordertown as it was now called, was an issue he did not want to be caught up in at this moment. *How could one show control in the midst of a war?*

He cursed his brother for dying. How much he missed him and his penchant for crisis management.

Another worrying matter, although unimportant in his mind, was Fatima's pregnancy. Would the knowledge force Hassan or Kadiatu's hand?

He hoped the exchange was enough to calm the fighters beyond Madagali's gates. Kadiatu was not as valuable as Musa, but it gave Hassan the advantage of having the only treasure Alihu shared with his father. He prayed to Allah that the gesture was enough, at least for a few weeks. In truth, after that he did not care what they did with the woman.

Musa stood in front of two of his companions. And he watched them as they appraised the boy as if seeing a product at the market.

He noticed the look of pity in one of his companion's eyes. Rotimi always had a soft spot, a failing he still tried to flesh out of the insolent boy. No matter, the boy's softness made him the best of all the rest.

He ignored the look in the boy's eyes. "Wash him and make him look presentable and pleasing to my eyes. Find beauty under that shit," he said to Rotimi.

***

Fatima knew her baby was on the way. The cramps were becoming more regular and she had the feeling that her child was ready to come out.

Mama Ajiya had just told her the best news under the sun. She could communicate with Ike, with Hassan, and best of all, Musa was alive.

The old woman had always been an enigma to her. She knew that her dedication was for those she cared for, but Fatima always wondered if there had been more to the old woman.

Did Mama Ajiya harbour one last rush to destroy everything around her? She did, and Fatima was glad of the knowledge.

The old woman was a spy, and the more Fatima thought about it, the more sense it made. There were several times that Alihu's plans had being known by the protectors of the border town. In fact, she recalled several occasions when they had to watch Alihu wield Hukumchi to judge those he felt were spies.

Alihu was up to something and those who opposed him had to be ready. It was a final push to end the madness that he was.

Her son's birth was definitely an inconvenience.

***

Hassan stared at the woman in front of him with disgust.

There was probably some respect for her in Bordertown as during the past few months she had shown some mercy. Whether for personal gain or for self-ovation, she had still shown mercy.

Some families owed their re-union to her, others the return or ability to retrieve valuables had been made possible simply by her whim. So, it was fair to say that within Bordertown, some respected her.

Not Hassan or the two men that stood next to him. Right now, they stared at her with hate or something similar in their eyes.

She faced them, back straight and head high.

"What makes Sani believe that you are valuable to us?" Hassan asked her.

She stared at him for a moment and replied. "Probably because I am in the position to know a lot of his plans."

She looked around as if looking for a more comfortable place to be. "Are you going to offer me a chair or is this how you treat guests?"

"I'm still trying to decide if you are a guest or prisoner." Hassan replied.

"That will also depend on what Musa is," Kadiatu responded. She shuffled her feet, again seemingly looking for something more comfortable.

The room they were in was one in the old train station. The refugees had repaired a few things here and

164

there, even the walls showed signs of recent plastering and paint. For her though, it was an eyesore.

"Musa is a lot more than you a thousand times," Ike replied, his patience already exhausted by her act of indifference.

"Ah, Fatima's betrothed," Kadiatu addressed him. "You are still here? Do you realise that your betrothed is about to give birth to the future ruler of the Caliphate?"

Ike stepped back, shocked. She smiled to herself, realising that this was news to him. Her mirth was short-lived. Hassan was fast, she had not even realised he had moved and yet she was on the floor, with her head reeling. She shook her head to clear her vision.

"It seems that your existence is solely so you can belittle or hurt those around you. I see now that your worth is simply by the usefulness you believe you provide to others. Worse of all, the payment is based on the worth you feel you have brought to the table." Hassan spat at her feet. He turned to the Old Man "Take her to the hut behind the Luxurious bus, give her the basics."

The Old Man obliged and led Kadiatu out. After a pause, Hassan said to Ike. "We could not confirm the news but it seems she now has."

"You kept this from me?" Ike asked, he was still in shock. Fatima's death was the worst thing that could happen; being a sex slave was next. This was third on the scale.

"Such news, my brother must be confirmed before being delivered. Like you it is news I wish were untrue."

"But even the rumour of it should be shared!" Ike replied, his voice almost a shriek. "The pain of it is not something that one must deal with alone!" Ike walked to Hassan and grabbed him by the shoulders. "You may be our rock, but you sometimes forget you are not a mountain!"

Hassan slumped into Ike's shoulders. "Imagine her pain, imagine what he must have put her through. Imagine!" Hassan let his guard down and he cried. "I promised to protect her, but yet she has been under the roof of my worst enemy for almost a year. I have failed her."

Ike held his brother, silently they both cried.

***

For the first time, Kadiatu did not feel she had outsmarted an adversary. Hassan's words had stung more than his slap. It was like he looked into her soul and saw all her flaws.

How dare he judge her!

She tried to rally her thoughts, but there was no energy to it. His words were true.

"You must have really pissed him off." It was the Old Man next to her. She had almost forgotten he was the one leading her. "I have never seen him loose his shit like that." The Old Man continued. "From the look on your face it seems like he was spot on."

"How..." She made to respond but the Old Man was faster.

"Look, I'm just an old man. But all I can say is that, when our time comes and we grow grey it is what we could but did not do, that matters."

She had not noticed that they had walked past a Mercedes-Benz Luxurious bus and were now at a zinc shack behind it. The structure was simple, a five-by-five metre box-shaped building and inside was a bed, a small table and chair.

The bed was already made, a simple job of a white bedsheet and a pillow on a threadbare mattress. She must have really pissed off Hassan, she thought to herself, to be given such a mediocre abode.

***

As they washed him, only Rotimi spoke. Musa was not paying attention to his words but some slipped through.

"Like some of us you will learn to love him." Rotimi paused to wash Musa's delicates. "Like others, you will learn to loathe him." Rotimi lifted Musa's Face to his. "Regardless, you will soon realise that there is nowhere to go. He would make you an outcast, owning your very soul."

After Musa was scrubbed clean, an oil scented of middle-eastern origin was massaged into his naked body. He had to admit that the scent was nice, it was not harsh but still had a musky smell he liked.

His hair which had been plaited for the past few months had been clean cut, leaving him bald. Sani's companions also oiled his scalp with a different oil, this one only slightly scented. To Musa, the smoothness and scent made up for the loss of hair. He even caught himself touching his scalp admiring the smoothness.

Rotimi's words intrigued him. Like most in the household, he knew of Sani's appetite. Like some, he had also wondered about Sani's companions. Surely, there was more to their obedience, their loyalty. After all what man or boy succumbed to being labelled a *Yan Daudu?*

It was new to him and he was still not sure what his situation meant or would lead. Joy, Ike were his worry.

"Where is Joy?" He asked.

"The girl you were caught with?" Rotimi asked.

Musa nodded and looked around as if expecting Joy to appear.

Rotimi leaned forward and leaned into his ear. "She lives and wants you to know she is ready to help no matter what."

Realisation on two levels hit Musa. One, Joy was still alive. The other, Rotimi disliked Sani.

***

It was a moonless night and the cramps were particularly painful tonight, she was restless. *Ike, I wish this baby was ours.* In a low voice, she began to whisper to herself.

***

I swear I have always been attracted to him. Just looking at him did things to my body. I knew that one day, I would lose all sense of abstinence to his embrace.

The day came and was unplanned. It was one of those nights Musa or Hassan helped me to sneak out. This time it was Musa and the story was we had gone to the local cinema to watch the latest Bollywood movie.

Musa did go with a veiled girl, but it was Joy. I on the other hand was with Ike.

We had just finished talking for almost an hour, his house was pretty much empty and I felt comfortable just lying on his chest and looking into his brown eyes as we spoke.

Then he kissed me with those thick Igbo lips and I kissed back. I always laughed at the white people that kissed, as I never understood the thing. But when Ike kisses me, I feel joined with him.

Like always, this kiss led to more.

One of his hands went straight for my nyash while the other held my face to him. His hand moved to my thigh and he pulled my knee towards himself. I bent my other knee next to his body and lifted myself up to sit on him. Already I could feel his hardness between my spread legs.

I was still wearing my caftan and underwear but I was already wet for him. I lifted my hips up so I could lift my caftan free to my waist and I slowly started moving my hips forwards and backwards.

I did not think it possible, but he became harder and I had to free his manhood from his shorts lest he broke the poor thing.

Then I started stroking it. We never usually often went this far but when we did, I always took the opportunity to play with him. This time as I stroked him I looked into his eyes as he growled like a wild animal.

He pulled me to him and kissed me. Then he removed my caftan and I was naked only for my underwear. He turned me over on my back and leaned over me. I must say this was one of the best experiences I have had with Ike. He always gives my whole body little kisses from the back of my ears all the way down.

It was a terrible tease but I loved it. Especially, when his tongue got to my nipples.

Walahi! I always felt a shiver running down the sides of my body. This time he lingered more, licking around one nipple while he played with the other. I realised I was unconsciously moving my hips into him. His kisses continued to go lower and when he removed my underwear, I did not even protest, lifting my legs to help him with the task.

He spread my legs and before I could even consider protesting, his tongue was on my private part. I swear, this is the sweetest thing. I cannot explain it, but it is like a wet slow massage of a very sensitive place. He continued moving his tongue around and around with me guiding him with my hips.

From nowhere, I started feeling as if I had been running. No, more like I was breathing like I was running; short, hard breaths of anticipation. Then I exploded onto his tongue, it was a beautiful release that left my whole body shaking.

I heard him leave the bed and move to one of his bags but did not really care, I was like someone who had died and gone to heaven.

He returned to the bed and this time like me, he was naked. I looked down and he was already wearing a condom.

To the question on his face, I answered by leaning forward and pulled him to me by his manhood.

"I love you Ike and all of me will forever be yours."

He kissed me then and when he replied that he loved me back, I could see the truth in his eyes.

I guided him further into me and when the head of his throbbing penis was inside me, I thrust forward. A sharp breath escaped me as he went further in. The pain was like a tear but was almost forgotten as he slid further into me. After a while, I started enjoying myself again and moved with him.

Then he started moving faster and faster, he was so big, and I was almost going to tell him to stop but he stiffened. His body was rock hard but I could feel his penis pulsate inside me. We held each other for what seemed like eternity, willing the moment never to end. I think I even cried a few times.

We did it three more times after that, one time I even refused a condom. Wanting to feel him, his skin and his seed.

Was I not scared of getting pregnant I hear you say? Well we were lucky, but even then we both wished I did, now the more so.

*****

Was it a sign of madness when one whispered to themselves? Fatima did not care, the story calmed her and she could feel sleep's warm embrace.

Ike, I wish this baby were ours. And like most nights, a dream came.

***

She was high, very high and it seemed like she was flying. Madagali was in flames beneath her, the whole town a sea of red flames and black smoke. She could hear the cry of anguish and wondered if this was a view of the first attack on the town or a new one.

"I am taking you to our loved ones." The voice was above her. "Do not fear."

She looked up and her son, who now looked like her father, was carrying her in legs like a talon of a great bird. He had great wings filled with black feathers and his wingspan was double her height.

As the wings beat the cold evening air, the sound it made was like a sound of drums. She shivered not from fear but the cold of the night.   Her son pulled her into his warm feathery chest and she was soon fast asleep.

5

Time after time, Mama Ajiya used Alihu's meetings and the need for the camp's stock replenishments to see the Old Man.

In truth, any village would do but the Old Man had secured a network of investments that gave her both the best value for her needs and an opportunity to catch up with the outside world. Right now, it was also very important that they meet.

First, she was going to insist he told Hassan and Ike that Fatima was indeed with child and any moment from now, was going to give birth. Secondly, the meeting was with Sani to discuss the next major attack. Finally, the attack was to be done to impress some visiting foreigners; most probably the real financiers.

The last bit of information almost gifted her a beheading. And even now as she stood outside Alihu's tent staring at the back of the man who just released her, she still was not sure it had not.

170

During Alihu's high-level briefings, she was the only one allowed to serve him and his generals. In time the men had gotten used to her presence and either felt she was trustworthy enough to be in their presence or too irrelevant to be considered.

***

The briefing earlier in the day started like any other. The sun had just set and the men sat around a table in the front part of the tent Alihu used for such meetings. A rechargeable lantern was the only source of light in the room and it sat on the table surrounded by maps and Alihu's inner circle.

As always, Alihu sat on the chair facing the exit with his back to his sleeping quarters. He never carried any visible weapon but Mama Ajiya was confident he was always armed. Either that or the man sitting to his right was enough protection from any possible danger.

Suleiman was Alihu's most trusted of all his followers. One of the original *Devils*, Suleiman was willing to kill and die for Alihu. A promise he once made and openly acted on the urge to do so. He was also the only one Alihu never questioned about carrying weapons to his personal tent.

She had never heard the man laugh or seen him smile. With eyes that seemed to only be black with no hint of brown in the pupils and a face carved in a perpetual frown; his presence always gave her shivers.

Some said he refused the second-in-command position Alihu offered to him only so he could perform his main task; to always protect the *Father of Devils*. Others claimed his frown was because he was sanctioned to always be a protector and not a leader. Regardless, his devotion to Alihu was completely and utterly absolute.

To Alihu's left was a much different personality all together and Alihu's number two. Abu, who hailed from Benue State in Nigeria's middle belt, also expressed his dedication to Alihu. Not in the fanatical sense of Alihu's cause but in a manner that earned him respect from all men sitting around the table.

Mama Ajiya had to admit that the man was probably her favourite general and one she found easy to deal with. He was often the voice of reason and the first to call for calm and always ready with contributions based on more brains than brawl.

He often treated her with respect and was one of the few that seemed to trust her. Maybe because she was aware of his continual love for gin and ensured his supply was constant or that he truly did think she was fully dedicated; either way, he showed trust.

Completing the circle were two other men that commanded two-hundred and fifty fighters each. In a formal military structure, they were seen as commanders of Special Forces. Stealth and explosives.

As she poured drinks around the table, she realised that even though she knew all of their sins, she would not hesitate to slit their throat if she had to.

She remembered passively glancing at the maps on the table, memorising the locations marked and listening for information without looking suspicious. In hindsight, she should have paid more attention to Suleiman watching her but she assumed it was his normal nature of looking for threats when one was close to Alihu.

Ram meat pepper soup mixed with a native kale-like vegetable was for dinner and she served this quickly knowing the men often left further important talks until their stomachs were full.

After the meal, she purposely took her time in cleaning up. Delaying the process until their conversation returned to more important matters.

At the tent's exit, she had dropped two buckets. One half filled with soapy water and the other empty. Rather than take the empty dishes, cups and spoons away as she would normally do, she made multiple trips to the table and back to the buckets.

Taking her time and using the advantage of her invisibility, she was able to determine most of the plans discussed. She recalled how she briefly stiffened when a middle-eastern nation was mentioned.

Suddenly, Suleiman was at her side, towering over her as she scrapped the remains of a plate into the empty bucket.

"Let me help you and take those to the kitchen area." He had said with no hint of his intentions.

Not wanting to raise any suspicion, she had agreed and allowed him to pick the buckets and follow her outside. A few meters from the tent, he dropped the buckets and when she turned to find out why, he rushed forward, grabbed her by the neck and slammed her back into a nearby tree.

"Tell me old woman?" he asked in his emotionless voice. "Are you a spy or do you just like hearing men talk?"

She could not answer the question as he was already crushing her windpipe. He starred into her eyes, oblivious of her struggle to release his vice like grip around her neck.

"If you lie to me, I will know," he said and released her neck just in time for her to breathe once more. It took a few moments for her to take in much needed air and she replied looking into his eyes, hoping defiance masked her fear.

"I always listen, and I will always listen because as you all plan, I…!" Her next statement was without pretence. "I… have to deal with the loss and wounds… Of body! Of Soul! That returns with my sons!" She could feel tears coming and she allowed them. "I listen only to know what to expect and to prepare if need be." She allowed herself to crumble and he let her fall, helping her to the forest floor.

He looked at her with his dead eyes and after a few moments, he turned back to the tent.

***

Without emotion and once again, as if removed from what just happened to him, Musa squatted in the bath and watched as water and blood pooled between his legs and ran into the drain.

The cocks had just sung their first morning call and his rapist oblivious of the songs was still in bed fast asleep.

173

From what sieved through his detached mind, he and
Rotimi were the only ones who seemed to be awake in Sani's
private quarters.

Rotimi sponged his body with warm soapy water,
squeezing the water on his bent back to allow the heat of the
water to soak into his skin. Scratch marks on his back stung
but Musa ignored them.

As Rotimi washed him, in a low voice he sang an old
Hausa lullaby.

> *May Allah give me a true friend whether he is small or big,*
> *Even an infant sucking at the breast, or one lying in the womb;*
> *When he comes forth, we'll be friends.*
> *Allah, give me a true friend, whether he is big or small.*

Musa simply listened, hugging his knees and allowed
the water to flow over his naked body.

Rotimi moved him forward and he allowed himself to
be pushed to his knees. A sharp pain hit his chest reminding
him of the ordeals of the previous night. But he somehow
relaxed and Rotimi slowly washed the wounds around his
sphincter.

All the while, not noticing each other's tears both
boys performed their tasks. One remembering and
understanding the pain and the other lost, his mind already
far away.

***

The morning was still new, and someone was already opening
the door to her shack. Kadiatu rose and moved to the edge of
the bed. It would only be Hassan; he alone would have the
nerve to enter without knocking or announcing.

Instead, a young girl entered carrying two buckets of
water. She looked around the room and wrinkled her nose as
if she could not believe anyone would live in such squalor.
The first bucket she placed in front of Kadiatu and the other
she led to a door at the back of the room.

By the first day she was locked up, Kadiatu realized that her prison was self-contained. Apart from the small room she was allowed to eat and sleep in, there was a back door that led to an open space about a quarter of her room.

She recalled with shock when she walked into the space and noticed the two holes on the floor. It was to be her combined toilet and bathroom, the bigger hole covered with a wooded plank was her toilet and the smaller uncovered hole was her bath drain. The space was surrounded by zinc sheets with an open roof. The sheets were tall enough that no one could see over the top and the top of the fence still left the zinc sheets exposed. No one could climb in or out without losing fingers.

The girl exited the back room and without a word, she left closing the door behind her. Kadiatu unconsciously counted two bolts been locked. Apart from the bolts, she was sure someone always guarded the door.

She looked around the room as she always did when she woke. Apart from the bed she now sat on, there was a table and a single chair. Placed on the table were cups, plates, cutlery and a rechargeable lamp.

She got up from the bed and picked up the cup, filling it with water she grabbed her toothbrush and headed to the back room. Once again cursing her luck, she undressed in the open space and began her ablution.

When she was done, she returned to the room and looked through the bag she had been allowed to bring to Bordertown. She did not expect to leave the room. She selected two wrappers and a singlet. One wrapper she tied around her hips and the singlet she wore without a brassiere. The second wrapper she left to the side; if she did have visitors, she would use it to cover her chest.

She heard footsteps at the door and this time was not sure who it would be. It could be someone with her breakfast. The door opened without ceremony and Hassan stepped into the dimly lit room. Without greeting her, he sat on the chair facing the bed.

She was lying on the bed when he walked in, her back to the wall and her left elbow holding her up. She did not move knowing full well the picture she painted.

Her lack of children was kind to her figure. Combined with her young age, she knew most men would react to a woman lying on the bed as she did. The singlet did not cover all her breasts and because she rested on her elbow, parts of it exposed most of her breast.

As she looked down at herself, she noticed with delight that only her nipples were covered and most of her perky breasts spilled out of the material. She stretched her legs arching her hips upwards showing her curves and exposing one long leg.

She looked to Hassan's eyes with a smile already playing on her lips but cut it short when she saw what registered in his eyes.

Somehow, his eyes managed to look more disgusted and disappointed at her. She refused to give up hope and exposed more of her leg, showing a thigh.

"I wish to ask you about Sani and Alihu's plans. At least the little you know of it." He paused, and then continued. "You can choose to lie to me, or you can tell me the truth. Either way I will find out." Coolly he added. "The Old Man seems to believe that there is hope for you to redeem yourself."

"I do not need to redeem myself," she was still shocked by his lack of reaction. "I simply made do with what life put in front of me. I have saved a lot of people in this small community of yours. Never have I done wrong."

"Is that so?" he asked with an arched eyebrow. "Okay just so you know how much I know of you, hear me."

He leaned back into the chair, glanced at her from head to toe and then back to her eyes. She shivered at the continued look of disgust.

"All the people you have saved were for your selfish heart. The bank manager and his family had to provide you with a document that showed all your loans were cancelled.

Only after someone in Abuja confirmed that you did not owe the bank any more, did you save the man and his family."

She shrugged her shoulders in defiance. It was a good deal if you asked her, Hassan did not.

"Your closest family members were already heading north with most of your valuables before my father was cold from your husband's bullet. You took money from some of the towns elites to secure their passage. At times increasing your price just because of greed." He leaned forward his eyes intense. "I tried to find someone you saved out of kindness, I searched Bordertown, my spies in the north, but not one person, not one soul." He lifted a finger.

She tried to speak but once again, his words stung deep. She sat up, oblivious of how much legs or breasts she exposed. She picked up her second wrapper and covered herself.

Hassan looked away to allow her adjust her attire; this was his first show of respect. When she finished, he turned to her, the look of disgust still in his eyes.

"You think you did well? Locked up in your palace you believe you are absolved of all crimes?" He shook his head. "Come, I will show you your crimes. Not Alihu's or Sani's, yours."

Hassan stood and she followed him outside. The light briefly blinded her but she kept her eyes low. Once they had adjusted, she lifted them to look around.

She realized how the citizens of Bordertown looked at her. In the eyes of some, she saw pity. In the eyes of others, she saw hatred. Only a few were indifferent to her, these ones she was sure did not know of her.

She followed Hassan through the make-shift streets of Bordertown. The growth of the place was breath-taking. The old train station had been renovated and looked something like a town hall or central house of authority. The main road that passed through the town was properly guarded and barb-wire fences blocked any access to it on each side.

On the side of carefully planned streets, zinc shacks and tents had been erected for accommodation, shops and eating cafés. There was no order to how they were placed but she noticed how clean and orderly people interacted with each other and the environment.

Hassan had really done a good job. Considering available resources, he seemed to have fared better than Alihu at the Sambisa or Sani in Madagali.

After a short walk, Hassan came to an area of the town with more residential shacks and tents. Here the people looked more hostile at here, the hatred clearly showing in their eyes. Silently she followed with her head bowed and wrapper drawn close as if to make herself smaller or invisible.

She almost walked into his back when he suddenly stopped. She stepped to the side and noticed they were in front of a shack slightly bigger than hers. There was a cooking fire in front of the main door and a woman old enough to be her mother sat on a stool minding the fire.

The woman looked up and saw Hassan, she smiled at him. Then her gaze fell on Kadiatu. The woman stood up quickly spilling the pot and its contents into the fire. Oblivious of the sizzle or her lost meal, the woman started yelling.

"YOU! Evil witch! Heartless bitch!"

Kadiatu was taken aback at the outbursts as she did not recognize the woman.

"Mother, I do not…"

"Mother? Wash your dirty mouth. I will never ever, EVER have a daughter like you!" She stepped closer, one finger pointed menacingly at Kadiatu. "YOU!"

She was now an arm length closer to Kadiatu. Hassan turned between them but did not interject.

"You ruined my daughter's life! Even after she has made your hair for three years! LOOK!" Kadiatu followed the pointing finger.

A young girl she had not noticed sat on a low stool to one side of the shack. The girl was staring into the distance, looking but unseeing. She looked closer at the girl and gasped. The girl's left foot had been cut from the ankle. The stump was bandaged and placed on a pillow.

Kadiatu stepped back. "No…"

"Yes!" the woman screamed. "Yes! You did this to her. YOU!"

"But…"

"Three days we came to your door. Asking your security guards while you lived in your palace to see us!" The finger was now back to her face. "Every time, you were busy. All we wanted was for you to intervene because one of your Sheik's…" The woman spat on the ground. "…dog wanted her as a bride!"

She turned away from Kadiatu and held on to her uncovered hair. She began crying. Again, she turned her finger back to Kadiatu. "Then at night he came for her, he beat me and took my daughter!"

A crowd gathered trying to understand what was going on. The only person not paying attention was the maimed young girl who continued to stare into unseeing darkness.

"Later someone came to ME! That my daughter was to be taught a lesson in front of their wretched court house!" And the woman suddenly fell quiet. "They cut off her foot." Tears streamed down her eyes.

"She kicked him and he wanted her to pay. A young girl, not even twelve years old. Pay? For what?" Tears flowed and the woman wept turning away.

Hassan turned Kadiatu round to leave and she was suddenly aware of a hundred eyes on her. Head bowed, she allowed Hassan to lead her away.

"I curse you. God will punish you," the woman said and went to her daughter.

Back at her shack, Kadiatu sat on the bed. She remembered the young girl, deft fingers that made the best braids. She recalled someone telling her of the visit but was too involved in her world and its games to help. It would have been simple to do, inherit the girl and her mother or send them safely to Bordertown.

Now, the young girl's hump would ride her nights until she died.

She went to Hassan and held on to him resting her head on his chest. Not like a lover or husband. Not even as a brother or sister would. She held him like someone seeking forgiveness. She cried.

For his part, Hassan held her to his chest as she cried. She confessed her deeds, baring all she thought she had done wrong. Exhausted from talking, she continued to hold him crying.

"Not everyone is beyond redemption," Hassan said.

She sniffed. "I will tell you everything I know. I am still cursed but I will not spend the rest of my days as an evil person."

Later that evening, she sat in front of Hassan, Ike and the Old Man. She told them all she knew.

Some information like the northern border being in Sani's pocket they already knew. Others like how many fighters were in the Sambisa and how goods moved in and out across the Cameroonian border, was new to them.

Ike took notes, asking questions for clarity and confirmation. By the time she had finished, it was well past midnight.

Kadiatu went back to her shack unaccompanied. Hassan's parting words where that she would no more be behind a locked door. She was free to move around, provided she did not leave Bordertown.

She was grateful for the gesture and after a very restless sleep, she woke before dawn. Her destination was the old train station. When she got there, it was already stirring in preparation for daily activities.

In the past months the building had taken on several roles because almost all roles involved visits from the public. Sanitation was now required and a team of porters and cleaners were employed for the tasks.

She went to the public toilets and without any sanction, dragged the cleaning tools from the cleaner's store room. By the time the cleaners arrived, the toilets were spotless.

No one thanked her and she did not do it for thanks. She felt she needed to do it, in her thoughts she owed much more.

From the toilets, she moved to the main grounds. Sweepers were already on duty and she grabbed a spare palm broom and helped. Some thanked her for the assistance while others ignored her.

As days passed, she continued her penance.

6

Mama Ajiya woke early for her trip to the village for supplies. She had much to do and the sooner she and her minder were on their way, the better.

For this trip she decided she would use her regular minder. The relationship with the minder and the girl at the village had finally become more. He was now a father of a boy and the girl was pregnant with his second child.

Mama Ajiya knew the man cared for the girl and planned to marry her. With downcast eyes, he told her it would be once he saved enough money from his exploits. Enough to run away as far from here as possible he claimed.

Personally, she was unsure if he deserved the redemption he sought and did not much care for his well-being either. She simply found it easier to control her activities while he was occupied.

He had not seen his family for a few months and with the pending attack, she was sure he would not miss the opportunity to do so. His time with them was bound to give her ample time to see the Old Man to express her concerns and share knowledge.

As she walked to the Hilux pickup truck they normally used, her heart dropped like a sack of shit. Suleiman stood next to the truck waiting for her. A bag and his rifle were flung over one shoulder.

"I thought I should follow you this time," he said to her. For the first time, he smiled at her and a shiver ran down her spine.

He continued. "I have relieved your regular, he did not seem happy. I wonder why?"

"Well if you really want to come don't expect any special treatment," she replied, ignoring his question. "You will carry the heavy bags and foods stuff."

She moved to the passenger door. Again he smiled at her and sat behind the wheel. He started the car and they were off.

The drive took them on a passable maintained road made by the Jihadists, created to link adjourning villages redeemed back to the Sambisa camp. The only maintenance the road saw was once every three months when a bulldozer levelled it.

During the drive, Suleiman stopped to talk to the fighters who hid in bushes guarding road blocks of upturned cars and drums. Their conversations were brief, as most fighters did not feel comfortable talking too much with a high-ranking officer. Questions were answered promptly. *All was well*, they replied.

***

After almost an hour of the back-jarring ride and multiple stops, Mama Ajiya was grateful for the welcoming sight of their destination.

As Nigerian villages go, this one was not large. The only road that could take two trucks on each side was the main road that cut through the centre of the village. Makeshift shops lined the sides, selling small provisions such as long-life milk, biscuits and drinking water. The wealth of the village was also evident. Only a few houses were made of cement and zinc roofs. The majority were of cheaper baked mud blocks and raffia roofs.

Off the main road was the main market and Suleiman turned into its narrow street. He had to slow the car down as

182

pedestrian and livestock shared the road. She directed him to one of the large buildings.

The structure was built like a warehouse and divided into two sides. One side was for bulkier goods such as sacks of grain and yams while the other was designed like a supermarket with smaller goods placed on shelves.

As she stepped out of the car, a young boy with a humped back ran to her and greeted her by prostrating on the floor.

"Ah, Saidu," she replied to his greeting. "How are you? Please get up I have an errand for you."

The boy rose with a bright smile covering his face. He was one of the lucky few who was spared recruitment by the Jihadists due to his bent back. Like him, such young men were used for errands and small jobs only.

"Go to the butcher and tell him to start preparing four rams and fifty kilos of cow." She rummaged through her bag and brought out a parcel given to her by her regular minder. "And give this to Mariah, tell her that Hudu was not able to come."

She did not notice that Suleiman had moved to her sides and he took the parcel from her hands before the boy could take it. He opened it and looked at her.

"Why is Hudu sending money to a woman?" he asked her.

"Why don't you go and ask her?" she replied nonchalantly.

Suleiman offered her another bone-chilling smile and replied. "Maybe I will." He turned to Saidu. "Saidu, come take me to Mariah. I will deliver the message from my brother."

Saidu nodded and turned to leave. "Take him there and hurry to the butchers. I don't want to waste time here." She called to his retreating back.

After they left, Mama Ajiya busied herself with supervising the loading of sacks of garri, rice and yams. Knowing she had arrived and keeping to routine, sellers of vegetables and other items also brought their wares for her to buy.

By the time the men and women had finished loading the truck, Suleiman returned. She glanced at him and noticed the sad look on his face. Not wanting to sound too interested, she told him they were done and the butchers was next.

The livestock farmers had their own market located at the other end of the village. It was a seasonal market and so the animals that now moved in makeshift pens had been primed for consumption as normal with the culling season. Some of the pens contained cattle but most of them contained smaller animals such as goats, rams and chicken.

She directed Suleiman to another building located at the rear of the livestock market. It was the only abattoir in the village, servicing wholesale buyers and consumers alike. Some of the buyers displayed their wares in front of the abattoir, calling out prime cuts and prices.

The smell of blood and flesh was strong in the air as they stepped out of the car. Flies descended on them buzzing around their heads and Mama Ajiya quickly moved into a door to the side of the abattoir.

The owner's waiting room had benches lining the walls with most taken by people waiting to transact business with him. The owner of the Abattoir was wealthy enough to have a power generator for his building so the room was cool. A fan spun in the middle circulating the late morning warmth and an insect killer zapped above the door they just stepped into.

Across from them was another door, it led to the owner's office and the back section of the abattoir. A man was standing in front of the door and when he saw them, he stepped to them with a smile on his face.

He bowed to Mama Ajiya and shook Suleiman's hands enthusiastically. By the time the man had thanked Suleiman for the liberation of the village and the promotion of proper Islamic ideals, Suleiman had relaxed to the man and was also smiling.

He led them to his office and waited for his guests to sit. He told Mama Ajiya he was expecting them and had food ready. Politely they declined and politely he insisted. He called out and a girl brought food for both of them.

When the food was placed in front of her, she gestured for the girl not to open it. She stood up and asked for the toilet. The owner jumped off his chair and insisted on showing her the way.

The toilet was located at the far end of the premises and they walked to it in silence. A wall almost as tall as the toilet block was built in front of the doors and windows for privacy. Once Mama Ajiya turned into the walls protective shadow, she turned and fell into the man's arms.

The Old Man held her in a tight embrace. After a while, he pushed her back, kissed her forehead and asked. "What the hell is he doing here?"

"I don't have much time…" She told him all she could with the short time they had. Starting with how Suleiman had caught her eavesdropping, she continued on with what she knew of the plans. A date had not been set but it was a big attack and most of Alihu's resources were to be utilised for it.

The Old Man thanked her, kissed her again and rushed back to his office and Suleiman. He did not want to add any more suspicions on Mama Ajiya.

For her part, Mama Ajiya spent a few more minutes in the toilet and then walked back to the office. Both men were laughing when she entered and she quietly sat down and ate her already cold meal.

On the way back, Mama Ajiya was surprised when Suleiman turned to her and asked.

"Why do you think Hudu keeps that woman and his children secret?"

"The Sambisa is not a place for a young family." Mama Ajiya replied without taking her eyes off the road. "When we get back, look around you. Is that a life you want for those who have fought for your cause?"

"Our cause…" Suleiman replied, but Mama Ajiya interrupted.

"My cause is to care for you all. The fight of the Caliphate is beyond me…"

"Yes, but I see your point, I have done you wrong. Your dedication is to us all and I saw something else." Suleiman paused.

I will see the downfall of you and most of the Sambisa. It was a thought alone. Mama Ajiya adjusted herself in the car's seat. "Allah will always shine the right path," she voiced.

The rest of the journey was made in silence.

***

Two days later, Alihu informed Mama Ajiya that Sani and his entourage would be visiting the following night. She simply nodded and listened to his instructions. When she was done, she asked the normal questions. How many were coming and how long were they staying.

After their discussion, Alihu paused. Not knowing what was coming she waited and directed her attention to an ant that searched the floor of his tent for sustenance. She envied the creature, wishing she was like it. A scout searching for sustenance for a hive, a sole purpose with no other care in the world.

Finally, Alihu asked, "How is she?"

"Have you asked?" Mama Ajiya replied.

"I have no time for such baits, woman. Answer the question."

Most times, Mama Ajiya said to herself. *I wish I could wring the neck of your stupid head or at least pour acid into your foul mouth.* Instead, she responded, "The child is near. She will give birth soon."

Alihu nodded. "Make sure she has everything she requires. The heir to the Caliphate must be born."

"If that is the case, why not send her to Madagali? At least the hospital there still works."

"I will see the birth of my son." Alihu replied with a hand wave. "After that she can go to Madagali. Even I tire of this forest."

He turned his back to her and Mama Ajiya knew she was dismissed. She turned and left his tent, holding back curses.

***

The Sambisa accepted the next day as it had days gone past. The birds chirped away to the dewy morning, the insects rose to the prospects of a better life and the forest dwellers moved to their various tasks. As for the humans, men cleaned weapons, women swept common areas and clothes were washed by young children.

Fatima was now almost immobile and Mama Ajiya left Kurum Daya at her side, instructing the ever-silent one to let her know of any changes.

As the sun moved to its last legs, Mama Ajiya inspected the food, happy with what was done, she left for the stream to wash.

Sani was due soon.

***

Similar to his last visit, Sani arrived with his companions. He walked into the camp as if he owned it and everything around him. Apart from his two companions, he was accompanied by two security guards. His eyes were for Alihu alone and he embraced the Father of Devils as if a lost son. Once the pleasantries were done, Alihu led Sani to his tent.

As the men stepped into the tent, Mama Ajiya realised something different with Sani's companions. They were both male. With his constant visits, she had come to the realisation that he always brought a girl. Curious as to the change, she followed the men into the tent.

She ignored their conversations and stood next to the tent exit waiting for instructions from Alihu, while also hopping to learn more about the odd companion.

In mumbled voices, Alihu told Sani of his plans. The map she had memorised and given the details to the Old Man

187

were laid bare. On numerous occasions, Sani slapped Alihu on the back.

"You have impressed me my son," Sani said. "I wish your father was alive, even if it is to see what has become of his son."

"It is the will of Allah," Alihu replied with a smile.

After the men had exhausted the discussion on their plans, Alihu finally noticed her presence.

"Go bring the beautiful meal you have prepared for us, mother." He said to her prone form next to the tent's exit.

"Let me also see the mother of the heir to the Caliphate," Sani said and got up from his chair.

Mama Ajiya shrugged her shoulders and walked out of the tent, Sani and his companions followed close behind.

***

As the cramps got worse, Fatima spent most of her days on her bed or in her tent, she barely walked far these days and the constant and persistent pain meant her temper was now always very short. Everyone around her understood this and bore the treatment like they had a chest full of war medals.

Mama Ajiya walked into Fatima's tent as quietly as she could. There was no more a pattern to Fatima's sleep as her child was now deciding the exact moment to grace the world with its presence. The expecting mother slept when she could.

"You don't have to sneak in like a thief," Fatima said from the bed.

Someone was in a mood, Mama Ajiya thought to herself. Nothing new here to see.

She sighed. "I bring guests wishing to see the Mother of Destiny." Before Fatima could respond, she continued. "Sani and his concubines."

"I don't give a shit if it is *IBB* and *Fela!* I need sleep!" was the response from the bed.

Kurum Daya, who had been mopping sweat from Fatima's brow, stepped back from the outburst. She was not angry, just shocked. She turned accusingly to Mama Ajiya.

"Ah beautiful Fatima," Sani said walking past Mama Ajiya. "I see your tongue is still as sharp as ever." He moved closer and stopped by the bed. "I bring you a gift."

"I don't want anything from you. It is tainted with *hate and greed*." Fatima replied.

"Oh, you will like this gift. Especially considering Alihu knows nothing about it." Seeing curiosity in her eyes, he smiled. "A choice that rests in your hands." Sani gestured to one of his companions and the boy stepped forward.

"Take off your veil." He addressed the boy.

Like all of Sani's companions when he visited the camp, this one was wearing a white caftan that covered most of his limbs. A white veil like a Burka hid his features and a small slit exposed eyes painted with black Lalle.

As the boy stepped closer, the dim light in the tent made his eyes more visible. Even with the make-up around the moist eyes, a memory struggled to burst through Fatima's discomfort and pain.

The boy removed his veil and exposed his face. Fatima was shocked, even her child calmed, kicked and then calmed again.

Musa and her stared at each other for a moment and then he ran to her. Unable to rise from the bed, Fatima could only stretch out her arms to receive his hug.

Siblings cried in each other's arms and for a moment, the world around them was lost. Even Sani was affected by the emotion and cleared his throat.

"I will leave him here with you until we leave tomorrow." Turning to the boy next to him, "Rotimi, come let us leave this sombre family re-union."

Mama Ajiya looked at Kurum Daya and gestured with her head to the tent's door and the girl understood.

"I will be outside the tent door if you need me," Kurum Daya said to Fatima.

Still caught up in a brother's embrace, Fatima simply nodded and Mama Ajiya led Kurum Daya out of the tent.

Her mind was racing, what was Sani's game? Did he try to appease Fatima? She doubted it, the man was evil. His actions were simply to control Fatima or at least to let her know the leverage he had over her. It was a ploy and she wished she knew its meaning.

Well, she had her own card to play. She would insist that Fatima be moved to the palace in Madagali once her child was born. They would destroy evil from both ends. She needed to see the Old Man once again and desperately.

***

Musa was leaning on her slightly and he felt a kick from her stomach. They both paused and started laughing.

"He wants to say hello," Fatima's smile lit her tear-stricken face.

Musa moved his ears to her stomach and started stroking it. Those at the palace knew Fatima had been pregnant, so he was not surprised by what he saw.

What had always bothered him was how he would react. His sister was to have Alihu's child. *Will she always have love for the child?* And as for him, *would he feel hatred?*

Now that he held her and her child in his arms, he realised the importance of it all. He too had seen pain; worse, he no longer knew who he was. Love and Peace was all he wanted now.

But first, his story.

***

Fatima was overjoyed. She had refused to accept Musa was dead and continued to hold on to hope. Hope that he had somehow escaped, hope that he was far away from all this. Hope that he was a coward and continued to hide.

All that did not matter as she held him. This was all she had ever wanted for him. To be with her no matter what. As she looked at him, she noted the changes, her heart broke as the reality of his company sunk in.

She would hear his story and she would be strong for him.

***

190

As Musa continued his story, he brushed his fingers on Fatima's stomach. It was a calming action and she relaxed, taking advantage of the reduced cramps and discomfort.

"… When I walked in, he was sitting on the bed with only a towel covering him. And I stood in front of him wearing nothing but a light silky caftan. I remember thinking I was like a goat ready to be slaughtered," He paused.

"You don't have to tell me this Musa," Fatima replied.

She knew that the story was always going to get to this point. *After all, how could he now be in Sani's grip?* She did not even know if she wanted to hear the story.

Trading places with him, she knew she did not have the will power to tell the tale of atrocities Alihu committed on her. Body and soul. If Musa wanted to tell his story, it was a brave thing to do.

"No, I wish to tell it. I have not been able to speak of this and it will help me to talk about it. I have continued to live because I spend my waking days with people who have experienced the same or worse. Rotimi has been supportive, but I fear he is the most scarred."

Again, Musa paused. This time Fatima let him gather his thoughts.

"He walked around me and I could feel his eyes on every part of my body. He did not touch me but I felt as if hot water was sprinkled on the parts of my body he looked at. I felt like crying, running away but the truth is I was curious. Was this who I was? Did I like what he liked?" Fatima made to interrupt but Musa lifted his hands from her stomach and raised the hand for silence.

"He moved to stand in front of me and said to me. 'Take the caftan off.' I ignored him and continued to look at my toes. 'Musa,' he said. And when I looked up, he hit me. A brutal slap that sent me a few steps backwards. His towel fell to the ground and I was staring at his pot-bellied nakedness. He was rock hard, and I looked from his penis to his eyes. It was then I realised that I was never going to be anything like him. He was evil. His thirst was not for boys or girls. His thirst was only sated by what he truly enjoyed-Brutality."

Tears began to form in Fatima's eyes but she wiped them off. They were Turaki, strength ran in their blood and although what he said raised her own memories, she would hear him. They were here because they survived.

"Then his madness could not be contained any more. Maybe it was the indifference he saw in my eyes or maybe the lack of fear. I don't know. But he went mad. He rushed me and ripped the caftan from my body. The bed was five steps away and he already had me naked, the silk hanging off my limbs like a beggar's."

"Face first he threw me onto the bed and jumped on me. He placed one of his hands on the side of my face and squashed me into the mattress. 'You are now mine; I own you until the day you die.' Then he used his knees to push my legs apart. I refused, knotting my foot around the other…"

Musa stopped his tale and rose to a table that had a jug of water and some cups. He looked at her and pointed at the water. She nodded and he poured both of them a cup each. He returned to her side, gave her the water. After draining his cup, he placed it on the floor and continued to rub her stomach.

"He leaned backwards and started punching me here." He showed her his lower back just above his waist. "Once, twice, three times. And with every punch, he was whispering. 'You are mine. You are mine, you are mine.' I don't know how long it went for but I began to get weak. He put one arm under my neck and pulled me back. The pain was so much I thought my back would break. Then he punched me one last time and my legs weakened. He growled like a dog just winning its first bone and moved between my legs. He fumbled for his penis and as he penetrated me, it was the first time I made a sound. I screamed."

Tears she had battled with won, and she cried. Tears were also in his eyes, but he continued.

"He raped me three times that night. Not caring I was bleeding or in pain. He raped me." He looked at her with tear-stricken eyes. "People call him Yan Daudu, but he is not. He is evil, he is a monster and it runs in their family. They are all devils."

He paused and looked at her stomach as if realising what he just implied. He tried to move his hand away but Fatima moved hers to hold it in place.

"I assure you, with the pain this boy is giving me, I have called him the devil several times." She laughed and he joined her.

If anybody walked in, they would have seen sorrow and laughter on their faces. Expressions not always made at the same time.

"But he has proved to also be my Angel. I will raise him as we have been raised. And he will have good uncles and a mother like we all have had. Most of all he will grow to know his father and the devil his father is."

"We must destroy them." Musa said after a pause.

"Yes, we will. I also have something to tell you. You know the woman that brought you here?" Fatima began to tell him of her and Mama Ajiya's plan.

In hushed tones, they talked, only pausing when Kurum Daya brought their meal. Fatima told her to join them and like a family they ate, exoneration the topic.

7

Olu was shocked by the changes of Bordertown. He returned to it once a month and each time there was always something different to see. Some people *and one could attribute it to boredom,* had taken it within their power to beautify the place. Flowers in garden beds now lined the main road. The rains had boosted the life of the plants and now they bloomed green, flowery and vibrant.

Even the old Peugeot 505 he was driving seemed happy with the newly repaired main strip. The suspension that had been groaning from the trip from Abuja sighed as he tracked his way to the main administration building. The visage of an old train station now a distant memory replaced with a newly painted façade.

Something was going on in the town and his passenger, one who had stuck to their cause since the attack on his school, asked if he knew what it was. It was then he recalled a message from Hassan. Today was General Terfa's wedding.

"Then we have brought him a terrible gift," his passenger replied.

Olu simply nodded. When her national service ended, Ada had refused to go back to Enugu. She had become one of his most valuable assets when it came to the *Social Army of Redemption*.

Olu chuckled inwardly at the name. He had coined it after a few too many jugs of palm wine to numb the pain of watching one of Alihu's now regular promotional videos. The name had stuck and while Hassan and his generals fought with weapons, he and his team fought using the tools they could: social media.

It was effective and Ada proved her worth. She regularly updated *Facebook*, *Twitter* and *YouTube*, confronting the world with their plight. And this had also brought cash and goods from around the world, providing an extra boost to their resources.

"Even in war, flowers sprout," Olu said, bringing the car to a stop in front of the old train station.

The wedding was happening in the safety of the rear of the building and guards still manned the front of the structure in case things turned sour. They knew Olu and some waved at them while others stepped closer hoping to hear of the outside world.

The Nigerian government had forced all mobile carriers to stop network and GSM services to the region. In order to stop the Jihadists from using mobile phones as detonation devices for bombs. A fair call, but it also hampered the ability to communicate efficiently or access the internet.

Some privileged citizens of Bordertown could afford satellite phones and officially, the redeemers had two phones active. One Hassan kept and the other was managed by Ike for day to day tasks. It was an expensive asset but a necessary one.

Olu accepted the welcome from his comrades and provided as much information of what was happening in Abuja as he could. Some people had moved to Ada and Olu was grateful for her professionalism. She re-iterated what they had agreed, snippets of information to boost morale only and nothing more.

After a few minutes later, they both excused themselves and walked into the building.

***

Hassan was seated at a table reserved for special guests. As the head of the ceremony, his chair faced the newly married couple.

Well-wishers had formed a circle around a cleared ground in the centre. Terfa and his newly wed sat on a chair draped in white sheets with gold embroidery. Their backs were to Hassan and beyond them was the entertainment.

A *masquerade* in the form of a ram was dancing around while a man in a wide hat and a white *Agbada* held a stick directing the masquerade's movements. Some believed that the masquerade only sensed the man and his stick, everything else was ignored. If the man lost the stick or stumbled, the masquerade could lose control and attack the people around.

As if to prove the point, the man's stick faltered and the masquerade rushed to one side heading straight for the seated guests. The man recovered quickly and rushed to its front, raising his hands and calling out words none understood.

Musicians to one side increased their tempo and the man started gesticulating with arms and stick. The masquerade moved in jerky movements to the beat and followed the man's own jerky movements away from the crowd.

195

The sounds from the musicians were a mixture of frantic drums and trumpets blaring like a drone of bees. The tune was followed by a woman singing in Tiv, the language of Terfa's tribe.

After a while, the masquerade was led out and the beats of the drums changed and the drone of cow horn trumpets became more hypnotical.

A man covered in leopard skin pants and a mask moved into the dance ground. The drumming was frantic but he moved in a slow twisting dance with shoulder and arms and an occasional leg or acrobatic movement. This was the traditional *Tsuwetsele*, cat dance. The grand finale of the dance was a performance that mimicked the cat's stalking of a prey and the final pounce. Just as it started, it was quickly over.

A group of eight dancers, four women and four men, rushed to the dance ground raising dust. While the previous dancers and musicians were from Terfa's tribe, these were different.

Although from the same state, Terfa's wife's culture could not be more different. The dancers had red and black wraps around their waist. The women had a similar wrap around their busts and all had bells around their wrists and ankles. Where the beats of previous dancers were frantic, this was erratic and the moves almost erotic.

A drummer beat a drum he sat on with vigour, wailing as his bare palms slapped into the leather. The dance was *Icha-ho* and the legs of the dancers moved to the beats of the drum, their arms, outstretched as if flying to the wails. When one would think the drummer or the dancers could not hold the performance any more the drummer pounded short beats into the drum, shoulders and buttocks moved to the rhythm then all suddenly stopped, and the cycle continued.

"I am surprised he decided to marry," Hassan whispered to Ike sitting next to him.

"I hear that his wife insisted. She claims her ancestors, *Alekwu* see a long life for our general," Ike replied.

"Amen to that," the Old Man replied from Hassan's left. He also nudged Hassan and nodded at Olu and Ada who had just stepped under the canopy that covered Hassan's table.

"He is not due for a couple more weeks," Ike replied.

He made to stand but Olu waved him down and moved to a chair to their rear. *Later*, he mouthed. Hassan nodded. Terfa deserved the respect, he thought to himself. The world and its madness could wait a little longer.

***

Kadiatu's waking mornings had continued to be all about the cleaning of toilets and sweeping of the old station grounds. The spite of those who performed the tasks with her had reduced significantly and the help was now appreciated.

The first few days had been hell, it was filled with judgmental comments and half-dressed children calling her names.

"Look at the Queen of Madagali!"

"Look at the Queen of Shit!"

She had persevered. The behaviour of the children seemed justified; to them and most around her. Even then, to her it did not come close to atonement. She continued to clean. Scrubbing grime and shit off walls and floors like it was her soul she was attempting to clean.

Her day was usually done by noon. And she usually ended it by taking two buckets of water back to her room, one for a scrub and the other a meal. She refused further assistance from people Hassan sent to bring water and food, opting to see to her own needs.

With some of the money in her possession, she purchased cooking pots, utensils and a kerosene stove. It was years since she cooked for herself but some skills are never forgotten.

Today, as Bordertown celebrated the general's wedding, she was not going to spend the evening in front of her shack cooking or washing. She was not even going to the wedding itself. She had more pressing plans to attend to.

197

After her bath, she rubbed a cocoa butter lotion onto callouses that now formed on her hands. She also applied the lotion to her chaffed and dry skin, paying especial attention to her neck and arms. As she worked the cool lotion into her skin, she realised that the act had become an unconscious routine. It calmed her and the motion of her fingers over most of her body loosened muscles she could not recall ever using.

She slid a black blouse over her head and used a wrapper to cover the ends of the blouse, wrapping it around her hips. She recalled the wrapper as one of her simple ones, only using it at home when she knew no guest had plans to visit. *Were those the good old days?*

Over her head and shoulders, she placed a black lacy head tie. This she primarily used to block out the now heavy sun. She also used it to obscure her features from curious onlookers and mischievous children.

A small mirror was placed on the table in her room and when she stared at it, her reflection shocked her. Her face was gaunt and her eyes solemn, reflecting the sadness of her eternal restless sleep.

She ignored the reflection and stepped out of her shack. Her destination was the residential shacks located across from the main Madagali road that cut through Bordertown.

Her steps were slow and deliberate and her thoughts on the deed at hand. On several occasions she had made the trip but had yet to see it to the end. Today she had decided to follow through. She would not turn back.

I have a job, for me.

As she approached the zinc shack, a feeling of tribulation like a swarm of sand flies hung heavy over her head. Panic made her think of turning back but she controlled herself.

I have a job, for me.

The young girl was sitting at the same spot she last saw her. Young innocent eyes stared into the distance with no care or notice of the world around her. She was perched on a wooden crate long enough for her to rest her leg with her missing foot, the crutches she used to move around rested within reach. To ease her comfort, pillows were placed between her back and the shack's wall.

Kadiatu paused at the door. The young girl was alone and she was not sure how her mother would take it if she saw Kadiatu trying to talk to the child. A child, she was in no doubt, in a state borne of her responsibility. Of all the people she helped, this was the one most deserving but she had ruined a life instead.

Her contemplations came to an abrupt end. The young girl's mother stepped out of the door and was facing Kadiatu. Both women were shocked and stared at each other. Kadiatu noticed the woman seemed dressed for the wedding and may have been on her way there.

"Please, I have come to speak to you…" Kadiatu began.

The woman made to interrupt but Kadiatu fell to her knees, the movement dislodged the wrap covering her head and it fell to her shoulders. The act or Kadiatu's dishevelled state silenced the woman. Taking advantage of pause, Kadiatu continued.

"I have failed you and I have failed Allah." She raised her palms to the woman, opening them to show their emptiness. "Most of all I have failed your daughter. She did not deserve what has happened to her and I wish I could take her place." Tears she swore not to shed filled her eyes. "I will be punished for this and I accept my punishment, but please allow me to make your lives easier no matter how I can. Please."

The woman was visibly moved by Kadiatu's words but anger still shone in her eyes.

How could one forgive the loss of a daughter's foot?

As she made to respond, already voicing the first insult that came to mind, a voice shocked them both into silence.

"Aunty Kadiatu! What have you done to your hair? It looks terrible. Come, come let me make it for you."

Both women stared at the young girl in disbelief. Not only had she spoken, her eyes were focused.

The look of innocence on the young girl's face broke Kadiatu and she cried. Tears streamed down her cheeks and her shoulders shook violently.

"It is okay don't cry. Come let me look at your hair. Come"

Kadiatu looked at the girl's mother who nodded. *Go.* She mouthed. Still on her knees she crawled to the base of the crate and sat down with her back to crate. The young girl shuffled forward to place Kadiatu's head between her legs. She pulled out a comb with forked ends from behind her back and leaned forward to start working on Kadiatu's hair. The girl's mother stared at the scene, tears that threatened to soil her make-up choked her. She shook her head. "I'm leaving for the wedding. Aisha's food is inside on the stove. You will need to warm it when she is ready to eat."

Kadiatu made to lift her head to respond but Aisha pushed it back down to continue working. "Yes ma," Kadiatu said from under a pile of dishevelled hair.

She winced as the toothed comb unknotted her hair.

***

"What are you doing here, young man?" Ike asked Terfa as he climbed into the luxurious bus.   "You are supposed to be consummating your marital vows."

"*Consummate yourself there.*" Terfa responded to laughter. "*All that talk of wedding night na lie. My wife no even get strength to lift leg.*"

"*Na you no get strength. No blame our sister I beg,*" Hassan replied. This time the laughter went on for much longer.

With Terfa's entry there were now six people in Hassan's command post. Olu sat with a laptop in front of him and Ada sat next to him looking through a folder of papers. Hassan and Ike sat opposite while the Old Man stood to one side leaning on one of the bus's windows.

"She probably kicked him out because of his prying hands. If it was me after such a day *na sleep get me*," Ada added. "General is that why you have a hard and long frown?"

Taking the bait Terfa looked down at his pants, the act sent everyone in the room into uncontrollable laughter.

Once some of the gathered could breathe properly Terfa took a seat and turned to Olu.
"So, president of our Social Army of Redemption, like the soldier who came to say Jesus was under arrest, what grave tidings have you brought?"

"I'm so sorry Terfa," Olu began.

Still grinning from her joke, Ada interrupted. "The soldier probably hated Jesus and did not..." Olu's frown at her silenced her. "Sorry, just saying..." When he moved his folded fist to one hip in a show of reprimand, she swallowed the rest of her statement.

The rest around the table smiled. Watching Olu and his assistant was always a curious experience. Olu still assumed Ada's dedication was to the cause and the cause alone. He was the only one without eyes to see that Ada had other reasons to want to be around him.

Hassan knew that the life of their cause made people ignore certain human interactions, it was unfortunate and one of the reasons he wanted this to end. "Please continue." He said to Olu.

Olu placed a hand on Ada's. "Please prepare the satellite data so we can show the video." He turned to the rest of the team. "This video was released last night by one of Alihu's web links from Libya. It is worse than the rest and we believe it is the prelude to increased barbaric activities."

Ada completed the hotspot connection between the laptop and the satellite phone. While Olu wanted to bring the video in a saved drive, she had pointed out the danger of being caught with it by Nigerian security officers. She waited for the video to finish buffering, clicked play and turned the screen.

The Old Man noted the video quality was better than previous releases, it seemed the Jihadists now employed someone with the skills for proper video editing. It also looked like their propaganda was getting serious and from the background in the video he knew it was filmed in the Sambisa.

Fighters wearing army fatigues and covering their faces with a black scarf with Arabic writing, stood in the foreground. Flanking them on each side were two Humvee vehicles. This raised a flag in the Old Man's thoughts; the Jihadists had recently re-stocked.

Shit was definitely going down.

Hassan focused on the video and Alihu could be seen pacing, speaking in Hausa. In one hand he held Hukumchi. Kneeling in front of him were three men with their heads bowed. Two of the men wore tattered and bloody civilian caftans.

The kneeling man on the left could barely keep his back straight, his face was an unrecognisable mess of swollen flesh and bruised bones. The face of the one on the right was not as bad but blood dripped unto the floor from his bowed head.

Terfa gasped as the camera moved closer to the man in the middle. Unlike the men to each of his side, he was dressed in the Nigerian army uniform. The man raised his head to the camera and Terfa moved forward to pause the video.

"That was my commander at the northern border. He let Sani through and I honestly thought he worked for them!" Terfa said to the questioning faces around him.

"He still does, although looking at his current state he does not seem to agree with his current task," the Old Man replied.

"Work for them?" Ada asked.

"Yes," Hassan replied. "The man is contributing to the whole scare. An officer of the Nigerian army judged and executed in the sight of the world means the Nigerian army could not protect their own. The jihadists will be looked upon as a powerful force that controls this region." He leaned forward and played the video.

Alihu continued his rant, calling those kneeling in front of him enemies of the caliphate and judging their souls lost. After listing their crimes, which to those watching did not seem enough to kill any human, Alihu swung Hukumchi.

The body of the man on the left remained upright for a few seconds as blood spurted from the severed neck. The body then jerked and dropped to the floor raising dust. The man on the right of Terfa's ex-commander bolted from his kneeling position, trying for an escape.

He did not get far. Still in view of the camera, all Alihu had to do was take two steps. He swung his blade downwards, striking the fleeing man in the back and making him fall to the ground. He placed one boot on the man's back and swung the blade again. The man's head rolled away.

In fairness to his courage, the army officer stared at the scene with no fear in his eyes. He looked up at Alihu and said something that seemed to have been edited out. Alihu pulled out a pistol from his side and walked back to the Army officer. He placed the pistol's nuzzle on the man's forehead and pulled the trigger. A red mist behind the officer's head and dust that rose from the ground behind him showed that the bullet had cleanly passed through.

Alihu turned back to the screen but none of Hassan's team were paying any more attention to his words. They had seen enough.

In a quiet voice, Terfa broke the silence. "We must destroy that fucker."

"And everything he stands for," Ike added.

Hassan's satellite phone rang and he answered it. "My brother, how are things?" *Boni*, he mouthed to Ike. "Ah… We are as good as we can…" After a pause he answered. "Okay, hold on." He passed the phone to Ike.

"Brother from another mother, how is Manchester?" Ike replied into the phone.

The muffled sounds in the background sounded like Boni was calling from a pub or a party. "Someone just showed me a fucking video," Boni said.

Ike knew the tone. It was quiet, almost inhumanly calm. He had heard that tone a few times when he was in university with Boni. Boni was well pissed off.

"Yes, we just saw it. It is the worst they have ever released yet." Ike said.

"I have spoken to my brothers. We will be there in two weeks with flesh and metal. Be strong until then." The line went dead.

Ike glanced at the phone. The others looked at him. "He and some crew will be here in two weeks."

Before anyone could respond the sound of a helicopter interrupted their thoughts. Everyone moved to the windows to look for the craft.

The helicopter was approaching Madagali from the north. It was already hovering to land and as they watched it slowly descended.

"That, my young friends, is the beginning of our plan. Madagali must be redeemed," The Old Man said.

8

Musa and Rotimi stood across from each other in front of the main entry to the palace. Two more of Sani's companions stood next to them on steps that led down to the open area before the main gate.

Light poles had been erected around the landing zone with a big 'H' marked on the ground with white paint. Four fighters crouched facing the gate with their guns pointing ahead of them. Twelve other fighters were spread around the landing zone with weapons pointed, ready to repel any danger.

The helicopter raised dust and grass as it lowered. Even before metal legs were on the ground, two men in black suits, jumped out.

From where Musa stood, he could tell these men were well trained and well-armed. Although they held no guns, one hand was in their suit and their eyes scanned around them like predators. Satisfied with what they saw, one of them moved to the helicopter and helped a man down.

Sani, who was standing at the bottom of the steps, moved forward. He noticed the fat prince did not seem to have lost any weight. In fact, not thinking it possible, the man looked to have gained more. The second man who was helped from the helicopter he had not met before. From the way the security guards reacted, Sani realised this was *the* prince.

The man was young, probably in his late twenties. Where his uncle's skin looked pockmarked with pimples and red blotches, the young prince's pale skin looked well cared for. Unlike his uncle, he walked like someone who played sports or at least spent some time in a gym. His pace was brisk and the white caftan he wore did not hide the fit body underneath. As they approached Sani, he noticed the disgusting look the young prince gave his panting uncle next to him.

"Welcome to Madagali, the centre of our caliphate." Sani bowed and the people behind him did the same, ensuring they bowed lower than their master did. "My house is yours and everything within it is for your comfort."

The young prince looked up at the house studying the structure. The look that betrayed the disgust of his uncle's fitness was gone, in its place was one of someone taking notice. Intent eyes absorbed all that was around him. Then his eyes fell to Musa.

Musa was not sure what happened. He was looking at the young prince with curiosity, it was the first time he had seen an Arab in the flesh and he was paying attention to things new to him. The light brown skin, features that looked Indian but more similar to the Fulani. He noticed simple but expensive accessories, gold chains, cuff links and a wristwatch. When he looked up, he caught the prince's eyes and his heart skipped a beat.

Rotimi was the only one who noticed the connection, the prince's stumble was clear as day when he met Musa's gaze. For a brief moment, his eyes betrayed emotion but as quick as it came the young prince quickly collected himself and walked into the building.

***

Sani told them to retire to their rooms while he made sure their visitors were well taken care off. Musa overheard him saying once food was served, the guests were not to be disturbed as they would be jet-lagged.

Unable to concentrate on anything else, Musa paced the room. He was not sure why he paced but he did. Rotimi was perched on an arm of a chair looking at him with a grin on his face.

"Why are you looking at me like that?" Musa asked, still pacing.

"I'm waiting for the floor to open up and you fall in."

Musa stopped pacing and moved to sit on the chair opposite Rotimi. For some reason, their other companions were in the adjoining bathroom grooming themselves, expecting to entertain tonight. Musa and Rotimi did not join them; they knew it would not happen until tomorrow at the latest.

"He likes you too," Rotimi said to Musa.

"Likes me? As a *Yan Daudu* or property?" he replied, a hint of disgust in his statement.

"As a person, Musa."

They paused for a few minutes, lost in their individual thoughts.

"His eyes are nice."

"I could see that, especially when they latched on to you."

Another pause. "Do you think he likes me?"

"Seems obvious. He almost fell and broke his perfect nose."

They broke out laughing.

***

For months now, Sani had walked past her several times and still did not acknowledge her. At first, she had been weary of his wrath if he realised the girl who tried to escape with Musa was still under his roof. But after a few unplanned meetings, she realised he could not even recall who she was. To him, she was just another unappealing face in the household.

Unknown to Sani, it allowed her to continue to move around the household and act as a spy for Hassan. She was even allowed out of the house without being accompanied or questioned. And when she was in town, most fighters who knew she was of the palace household did not bother her. In some cases, they even tried to be on their best behaviour lest she reported their failings.

She stood outside Sani's quarters with her ear to the door, eyes looking around and ready to bolt. She heard Rotimi and Musa laughing and could not help but smile with them.
She tapped on the door, two quick knocks, repeat and then one knock. The laughter in the room stopped and the door opened. Musa and Rotimi stepped out and without a word, followed her to the kitchen.

Mama Amina had aged in the past year and Joy was sure it was because of all the hate the poor old woman saw about her. She had since stopped venturing into the town below or even outside the palace gates. Her emotional state was now so frail that she could no more assist in the daily chores of cleaning floors and dusting furniture. Her day was reduced to cracking open melon seeds and caring for young children. One activity calmed her and the other brought the occasional smile to her face.

When they walked into the kitchen, activities were winding down, the kitchen staff were moving to the outdoor kitchen to clean up and wash used pots and pans.

Mama Amina sat on a stool with a bowl of crushed melon seeds sitting on the floor between her legs. She looked up at them and offered one of her rare smiles. A young girl of about seven helping her with her task noticed Rotimi walking in and ran to him, crying out.

"Uncle *Yan Daudu* carry me!"

Joy made to ridicule the girl with a tap to the head but Rotimi stepped into her path and picked the little girl up. He threw her in the air then caught her again. The girl's squeal of laughter destroyed whatever tense emotion the adults in the room felt.

"What have you been up to?" Rotimi asked.

"I have helped Mama Amina open plenty seeds!"

"Oh, that is a good girl. I am proud of you. How about you go outside and clean up then we can play later?"

"Yes! We can play *10-10!*" the little girl said and practically jumped out of his hands and was soon out of the door leaving the four of them.

Joy peeked through the door behind her, satisfied with what she saw, she stepped in and shut the door. She silently walked into the storeroom to the side of the kitchen and switched on the lone electrical bulb that hung from the ceiling. She looked around for prying ears, seeing no one, she walked back out and switched the light off.

Musa and Rotimi sat opposite Mama Amina and Joy joined them, choosing a stool next to the old woman.

"We must inform them about the Saudis." Joy began. "Especially those two that came with them. One of the boys who helped them with their bags said that he saw every weapon he has seen in a war film."

"Yeah, they look like professional killers. I would not want them to catch me in a corridor alone." Rotimi said.

"Did you see the way they always have their hands close to their breast pocket?" Musa added. "I think they have Uzi in there."

"I don't care what they have." This came from Mama Amina. The others around the table turned to look at her, surprised at the rare outburst. "If they have contributed to all this, they should be dead. All of them." Her eyes seemed to be on fire. "Kill them all."

Mama Amina leaned back into the wall and fell silent while her fingers continued unconsciously working on the melon seeds.

Musa felt his heart skip at the thought of death for the young prince. He brushed the feelings aside. "We have to make sure that Fatima gets here before we do anything."

"Yes." Joy replied. "It will be easier to save her. I will find out when she may give birth; maybe she can come before?"

"No, that idiot said he wanted to be there to see his first son," Musa said. "It will have to be after."

Joy hissed and shook her head. "I have an excuse to take some things to Kadiatu. I will meet with Hassan and let him know."

She noticed the shadow that crossed Musa's face; he had not seen his brother for a year. She moved her hand across the table to his. He returned the gesture and squeezed her fingers.

"Tell the Old Man to figure a way to get Fatima here. It is important," Musa said.

Rotimi moved back from the table. To Musa he said, "We better go back, we are the entertainment for the night and have to get ready."

It was a sour joke but everyone smiled at it. They understood Rotimi. In a way, they each had a way to deal with it all.

***

On their way back to Sani's quarters, Musa realised that he had missed the changes to the corridor the first time they walked past. Although the chances of the Arabs walking this way were near impossible, the walls were freshly coated in white and brown paint a foot high from the floor. Hanging from the walls were newly made paintings from a local artist depicting a hunt. Three images were repeated with slight variations; the stalking, the waiting and then the killing. Musa felt indifference to the artist's skill, it was okay but he knew students in his class who could do better. The polished dark brown wooden frames were good though.

He turned to Rotimi. "I am surprised you are part of this."

"Don't be," Rotimi replied.

"I would not have thought you hate him."

"Hate him?" Rotimi stopped and turned to face Musa. "Do you want to know how he broke me?"

Musa remained silent. Rotimi accepted the silence as affirmation and continued. "In the morning after his breaking as you have experienced, he led me into another room. A young boy with the same look of fear as was on my face the previous night was tied to a bed." Rotimi Paused, his chest puffed as if gathering courage. "Sani went and sat next to the boy on the bed. 'Fuck him,' he said to me. I stepped backed hoping to flee but the door behind me was shut. I refused and right there he slit the boy's throat," Rotimi continued walking.

"By the second slit throat I had had enough and did as he asked. I and the boy crying, I raped him and Sani watched."

Musa placed a hand on Rotimi's shoulder. They were silent for a time before Rotimi added. "Hate is too kind a word to describe my feelings."

Musa left it at that.

***

Fatima sucked in three harsh breaths, her chest heaving with the effort and her shoulders lifting as if she wept. She expelled the air in one long deflating burst that ended with a wail. She fell backwards onto the mat. Her face a painting of pain and sorrow, complete with running tears and frowned frustration.

Mama Ajiya and another woman, a traditional midwife, sat on stools in front of her spread legs, their faces squeezed in concentration and arms bloody to the elbows.

"Almost there, my daughter," Mama Ajiya said as she dipped a bloody cotton cloth into a steaming bucket of water.

210

Fatima looked up to the canvas. Two rechargeable lanterns lit her tent, one to her right and the other on a table behind the women. She could see the faded material of the tent's ceiling and wondered what crimes she committed in a previous life to be in such squalor having her first child.

She still felt lucky; around her were people she loved. Mama Ajiya with a look of empathy on her homely face and Kurum Daya sitting next to her holding one hand. The young girl was both brave and strong and she slid a finger over the marks her fingers already left on the poor girl's hand, some already had dried blood around scratch wounds.

Outside she could hear the murmur of men's voices. Alihu insisted on waiting for the birth of his first child, gathering around him a crowd of well-wishers. One day she intended to kill the bastard, if not for all he caused but for the pain she now felt.

Once again, she could feel the contraction coming. Excruciating pain was not far off.

"The pain is a wave," Mama Ajiya said. "A way of your body telling you what to do. Ride it, follow its pace, not faster, and not slower"

This time Fatima listened, she began to suck in air again.

"That's right. Hold on to the pain, follow it, ride it… Push!"

Fatima expelled air, pushing as hard as she could. She cried out with the escape of air, willing her body to do as it only knew how. She wailed as she felt her child slide free, tearing her as it fell into Mama Ajiya's hands. She crashed back into the mat.

"Yes!" The women and Kurum Daya yelled as the baby slide out. Bloody but silent.
Mama Ajiya wrapped the child in a warm clean towel. The mid-wife tilted her head to look at the baby. Its eyes were squeezed shut but it was alive. She pinched the baby's legs but there was no response, she looked up at Mama Ajiya.

Fatima, noticing something may be amiss struggled to sit up. Kurum Daya made to push her back into the mat but Fatima brushed her hand away.

The mid-wife pinched the baby's leg again, this time much harder and the child let out a wail, hands raised in protest as he started crying.

Fatima was already up and she stretched out her hands for her child. Mama Ajiya lifted the baby up to let the mid-wife cut the cord and rub a poultice of herbs to the wound. She then passed the baby to Fatima.

Fatima collected her baby and opened her gown to free a breast. She moved her child's lips to her nipple and he started sucking.

Kurum Daya arranged pillows behind her and she leaned back into them releasing a sigh of relief, the pain of the ordeal already becoming a background noise.

Alihu rushed into the room with eyes wide. "Where is my son?" He boomed glancing to the mat on the floor.

Mama Ajiya was still between Fatima's legs, a stitching needle in one hand and looking downwards as the mid-wife cleaned Fatima.

Before any of them could react, Alihu was already standing next to the mat. "My son! The heir to the Caliphate!" He leaned forward and plucked the child from Fatima's embrace. The baby's lips smacked as it was pulled from her nipple.

Kurum Daya made to rise but Fatima pulled her down.

"I will bring him back! I want to show these men that I am a man!" he yelled to the protest of the women.

Before Mama Ajiya finished treading the needle, Alihu was already outside the tent with the bundle. She picked up a clean towel from one of the steaming buckets and wiped her hands. She stood up, placing the towel over her left shoulder and stormed out after Alihu.

Outside he was already showing his son around. The bloody towel the child had been wrapped in was at his feet and he was holding the naked crying baby above his head in front of him.

"You, stupid boy!" Mama Ajiya yelled. "The weather is too cold; do you want the baby to die? He needs his mother's milk!" She reached up and collected the baby from Alihu and wrapped him in the towel from her shoulder.

"He is a Garuba, he is strong," Alihu said looking chastised.

Mama Ajiya ignored him and stepped back into the tent. She went straight to Fatima and laid the baby next to her breast. Soon the child was back at feeding with a look of primal content on his face. Mama Ajiya cleaned her hands again and sat down. As she worked closing Fatima's wounds, she looked up at the new mother.

"What will you name him?" She asked.

Fatima winced from the needle and looked down at her son. As if knowing he was the object of the conversation, the baby opened his eyes and looked up at his mother.

Fatima was taken back to an old dream where she was lying on a wooden platform surrounded by raging waves of an ocean. She had just been saved from drowning and her head was on a boy's thigh as he cradled her.

"Who are you?" she remembered asking. Or did she?

"I will tell you my name when the storm is over," he said.

She came back to reality and looked up to Mama Ajiya. "I shall name him when all this is over."

Mama Ajiya nodded.

***

Musa and Rotimi approached the guest quarters. Two goons, as Rotimi now called them stood on each side of the door. They still wore their signature black suit with a white shirt and black tie. Legs in a wide stance and hands crossed in front of them, the guards looked beyond the boys as they stepped closer.

Musa knew, although their eyes were not on them anymore, the goons had already assessed them and deemed them non-threatening. They did not even acknowledge the presence of both boys stepping into the door between them.

This section of the palace was a recent addition by Sani. Designed as a guest wing, it contained two large lavishly furnished suites and an entertainment area. Because it was built at the front of the palace, the commotion of everyday life from the rear living areas never reached it. The wing was meant to impress guests and Sani made a good effort of it.

The floors of the entertainment area were covered with a woollen like brown carpet. Musa removed his palm sandals and stepped on the carpet. It was soft to his feet and he moved his toes into it, enjoying the feel of the material. Against the walls in a semi-circle was a row of soft leather sofa chairs with several comfort pillows scattered on them.

On a centre table was a hookah pipe with tendrils of aromatic tobacco smoke escaping from the pipe's nozzle into the air. The smoke was soon collected by two air conditioners leaving behind a tangerine-like smell.

Rotimi and Musa wrinkled their noses from the sweet smell of the smoke, they both knew there was more to the contents of the pipe than flavoured tobacco.

Sitting opposite the hookah and flanked by two of Sani's companions with one boy on each leg was the older Arab. Behind him and lying on the head of the chair was another boy massaging his neck and shoulders.

One boy served the man a drink from a gold brimmed glass and the other massaged his chest, occasionally leaning forward to pick up the hookah pipe and placing it between their guest's lips. All eyes were glazed over and Musa and Rotimi were ignored.

As they stood wondering what to do, Sani walked out of one the rooms. He looked at them from head to toe. Satisfied, he turned around and waved for them to follow.

When they entered the room, sitting by a desk with a laptop opened in front of him was the young prince. He stood up and walked to them as Sani led them in.

"Who are these?" he asked.

Sani cleared his throat as if he was about to express a speech preluding the sale of an expensive item. "These are my favourites. The best of all, before and after. The *crème de la crème.*"

He turned to Rotimi. "This one I have trained to be the leader of my harem and an expert in all things exotic and erotic." He moved to Musa. "And this one is recently broken. His eyes shine with intensity and also the uncertainty of what he now enjoys."

The prince cocked his head at that. He looked at Rotimi and then back to Musa. "Leave us," he said.

Rotimi was already turning to leave, a smile breaking on his face. Sani made to speak but the prince cut him short.

"I have never repeated myself before, Alhaji Sani. For your sake do not let this be the first."

Sani swallowed what he was about to say and followed Rotimi out. As the door closed, the young prince walked back to the table and instead of sitting behind it, he turned to face Musa and leaned on the desk with his arms crossed.

"What is your name, friend," he asked Musa.

"I am not your friend…" Remembering who he was talking to, Musa added, "I… I mean I don't know you enough to be a friend."

The prince laughed. "How rude of me." The Prince stepped forward, offering his right hand. "My name is Khalid."

Musa took a few steps forward and accepted the hand in his. "My name is Musa."

Khalid turned to the suite and Musa took the opportunity to look around. He had to admit the place was beautifully furnished. Not just the sleeping area, the connected washing and dressing room seemed well taken care off. The door was open and he could see the room was complete with a spa bathtub, shower and a toilet. In the room he now stood, a large bed took almost half it. To one corner was a walk-in robe already full of clothes and shoes.

Opposite this, was a small table with an ice bucket and some glasses. In the ice bucket were two bottles of wine, their glass bodies already showing droplets of water from condensation.

Khalid walked to the table and without asking poured two glasses of wine for Musa and himself. He walked to where Musa still stood and gave him one of the glasses. Musa accepted the glass and offered him his thanks.

"Please come sit with me." The prince walked to the bed and climbed in. He shuffled to the head of the bed and leaned his back on some pillows. "Come." He said, tapping a spot next to him. "Sit, let's talk. I would like to know more about Musa and maybe we can become better friends."

Musa hesitated only for a moment. He did not wish to upset the prince and the young man did not seem threatening. He walked to the bed and sat down.

"Tell me your story," Khalid said, taking a sip from his glass.

Musa took a sip himself. His eyes widened at the taste of the wine, he smacked his lips and took another. "Thank you for the wine. It tastes very nice."

"A popular Australian Rosé. One of my favourites. You avoid the question Musa. I ask because I actually would like to know more of you. Your eyes show a lot of sadness that intrigues me. So please, tell me about yourself."

"I am not avoiding the question, Prince…"

"Khalid." The prince interrupted with a smile.

"K…Khalid," Musa responded. "In every tale, there is a victor and also the loser. I am of the losers and I do not know if you wish to hear the story to gloat or…" He looked into Khalid's eyes. "You actually wish to know about me."

"Well said," Khalid took another sip. "Yes, my family has interests in what is happening and in fact, in some ways we may have facilitated the victories of the victorious and the fall of the fallen. But at the moment I wish to know more about such sad eyes."

Oh, you wish to know, do you? Okay, I will tell you of the devastation. Of hate, of greed.

He began his tale. At first, the nature of the tale was to shock and to let the young prince know that while he and his uncle sat on their high horses, he and his loved ones suffered. He told of the brutality of Alihu, the taking of the so-called brides of the caliphate. Of Fatima. Of Hassan and of Ike.

As the words spilled forth, Musa also began to hear his own voice. His thoughts followed the tale and soon he revisited the moments. His solace under the bed as he mourned his father, the sanctuary in the hands of his enemies and the moment of false hope when he almost escaped it all.

Words flowed unaided and so did tears, from his eyes and from Khalid's. Even as lights around the house were switched off and people went to their respective beds, Musa's tale continued.

Khalid listened, his eyes a river of tears.

***

Khalid rose from the bed trying not to wake Musa. He threw a robe over his shoulders and walked into the bathroom. He locked the door and walked to the mirror above the wash basin.

His family was part of the ruling monarchy but with so many next in line, his father had settled for influence rather than succession.

"Our alliance should be of great benefit to whomever rules," His father had said. "At all cost you *must* ensure that Shia has a foothold in Nigeria."

Khalid had come here with that goal, more so because he did not want to fail his father. However, Musa's story had hit him hard. In Alihu, he saw himself. His uncle, Saeed who at this moment was probably on a bed of *bacha bereesh* was Sani.

And in Musa, Khalid also saw himself. He remembered how hard it was to accept who he was. In hindsight, he needed not have gone through the pain, because

217

as soon as he accepted what he was, he realised they were many just like himself.

He still was not a *bacha baz* and the decision was more of a choice than anything else. Until now, there was none he wanted to own. Musa, an innocent Nigerian boy, was his first.

Is this a test? He asked his reflection. *Must I make a choice between honouring my family or myself?*

Khalid splashed water on his face. Musa was proof all was not lost, he would eventually find the right person, if it happened once it will happen again.

He would play Musa. *After all, where elephants fought, the grass always suffers.*

As Khalid sank onto the mattress, Musa closed his own eyes. Soon both men were fast asleep.

9

A few hours prior and just before the sun set at the Sambisa, Mama Ajiya stood next to Alihu as he watched his men practice. Suleiman was not far off and she tried to hide the fear she still felt for the man.

"Fatima needs proper care…" Alihu made to interrupt and she held her hand up." Let me finish. I know you wish to spend as much time as you can with your new son. What father would not? But," she emphasised. "If you have eyes that see you will notice that your son is smaller than normal and your wife is very weak. She lost a lot of blood birthing him."

Alihu remained silent and she continued. "They both need proper care. I urge you to send them to Madagali."

"And you with them I am guessing?" Suleiman added.

"No," Mama Ajiya said. "My place is to remain here and wash your buttocks for you."

At this Alihu laughed. Suleiman smiled at the joke.

"I was joking mother," he said.

"So was I," Mama Ajiya replied, she turned to Alihu. "My son take them to Madagali. The General Hospital still works and the doctors honour you. It will be a great privilege to care for your son."

Alihu seemed to think on this, his eyes focused on the training in front of him.

His soldiers were on an open clearing in front of a communal hall. They lined up in rows and held AK-47s with knives attached to the barrel. The current training was to mimic combat. Run two steps then jab with the knife under the barrel.

Alihu stepped forward and scuffed a fighter behind the head. The man crashed to the ground and all the others stopped.

"Hold the gun like a man not a fucking idiot!" He kicked the fighter on the ground. "Do not embarrass me on the battle field. Fight like you deserve to be by my side!"

Without further ado, he stepped back to Suleiman and Mama Ajiya. "I go to meet guests in Madagali, I will take them with me," he said to Mama Ajiya.

She nodded, bowed and turned around. Leaving both men to their devices.

"I do not trust that woman," Suleiman said.

"You do not trust anyone." Alihu replied. "A gift and a curse."

***

"Will my child live?" Fatima asked Mama Ajiya.

"He is strong. We are only portraying weakness so you can return to Madagali."

"I know he is underweight. He sometimes wheezes when he sleeps and worse of all at times I have to check to see if he is alive. He is a very quiet baby."

"Fatima, my daughter. You, like several women in this camp, are expected to have babies in such squalor. Your meals contain the bare minimum that an adult requires. The forest is full of mosquitoes and insects only Allah knows what type! Do you expect a healthy baby when the mother never was?"

219

Fatima paused. She was being hard on the poor woman, it was unfair. But she needed to know and now she did, her child was unhealthy.

"I am sorry," she replied.

"No, it is not your fault. I am just a little short-tempered. Between facing two monsters and the thought of you going where I cannot keep an eye on you is…"

Fatima went to her and hugged her. Mama Ajiya was a rock to her. A mother and a sister. She would miss the old woman.

"Why did you not insist on coming?" She already knew the answer.

"Because it will raise suspicion. My duty after all is to care for the camp and those in it," Mama Ajiya replied. She wiped the tears from her eyes. "I know you will be fine, you are a strong woman and you have Kurum Daya with you."

"And you mother?" Kurum Daya asked. She was holding Fatima's son on her legs bouncing the baby. "Will you be okay?"

"Yes, I will be fine. When the moment comes, I will torch this place and escape with as many innocents as I can. The kerosene is ready."

The look of sorrow was gone, in its place defiance shone.

***

It was way past the first cock crow when a series of soft knocks sounded on the door. Before Khalid responded, it slightly swung open. Khalid raised his head from the pillows, a frown beginning to register on his face but Rotimi peeped into the room and the frown was replaced by a smile.

Khalid gestured for Rotimi to enter. He moved his fingers to his lips and nodded at the sleeping form lying next to him with arms still wrapped around his own chest.

Rotimi walked to the bed and sat down next to Musa's sleeping form.

"You did not touch him," Rotimi said in a whisper.

"If you mean did I have sex with him, then no. I did not," Khalid replied also in a whisper.

Musa stirred and moved his hands up in a yawn. He opened his eyes to the stares of both Khalid and Rotimi.

"That is the best sleep I have had in a year," he said.

"You must have had a lot on your chest my friend. Being able to talk about it must have helped," Khalid replied. He stood up from the bed. "I'm going to have a bath, then I want you both to take me around the city."

The two young men looked at each other. Did they just hear right? Sani would be furious.

***

And they were right. Sani was outraged and outright refused.

"It is dangerous, my prince. There may still be some insurgents in the city. I assure you when we have cleaned up this whole area and you come back, we will walk through the streets with no problems at all!"

Rotimi and Musa standing on each side of the prince both noticed the bulging vein in Sani's neck. If it was someone else standing in front of Sani, the person would be dead. Or at least close to it when he was through with said person.

Khalid for his part seemed un-fazed, rather he looked bored. "You told us this was the capital of your caliphate. Are you telling me that you have no control over the city?"

Sani was quiet at that. "Well… We do but some of the insurgents from across the border may take the opportunity to attack!"

The last word was almost a shriek and Musa tried desperately to hide his amusement. Sani for his part tried to gain back some composure.

"I'm going with Musa so I believe no one at Bordertown would attack me. Don't you think?"

Sani was shocked into silence. He looked at Rotimi then at Musa. "How…?" Of course. Sani thought to himself. Musa spent the whole night with the prince and must have spilled a lot of beans. *What more did the stupid boy let out I*

221

wonder? I will deal with him later. After all, the prince will soon leave us.

"And don't worry I'll be going with my guards. I assure you they are quite capable of dealing with most things. We will be back shortly."

***

Musa chose his old favourite, the market, as the start of the tour. He had a lot of fond memories of the walk down the hill with Hassan and Fatima and since the death of his father, this was the first time he had returned to it.

He did not want to remember the past life that was now history, he did not want to have the feeling of hope that everything would go back to normal. Him tagging along, holding Fatima's bag and trying to stop Hassan from fighting Dambé. The laughs they had with Ike, his mother's food… *Oh, Ike's mother's food.*

And so, until this day, he had stayed away.

Other times, it was fear. All those memories were not isolated. The joys of what he had, he knew came with the knowing of what he had lost. Some feelings he locked deep in his soul, the waking or the confronting was something he was weary of. What state would he be left with? What monster was lurking beneath it all?

Somehow, after meeting Khalid he was right to face his fears. He had shared the stories and now he intended to share the memories.

Khalid and Rotimi walked at his side listening attentively. The two goons followed a few steps behind and seemed not to care for his tales, rather their eyes scanned for threats.

Musa spoke of the life of the market, the shouting and yells of haggling. The smells of leather and the sparkles of trinkets. He told of it all. Surprisingly as he spoke, the sorrow he thought would follow did not.

They walked into the market and life seemed to have left the once lively community. The hustle and bustle was gone. The sellers and a crowd of potential buyers were replaced with a meagre collection of sellers offering wares to a handful of buyers. The sellers had no choice as the jihadists now set the price of all products. For the sellers, the exchange of wares was simply a job. They owned nothing for it all belonged to the caliphate.

Ngozi's kitchen was no more. In its place was an administrative building of some sorts. The table and chairs for customers made way for office desks and on some of the chairs, women in burqas sat in front of what seemed to be officers.

"What are they doing there?" Khalid asked.

"I assume they either have a fine to pay or are being ordered to pay one," Musa replied.

"Or maybe they are just being told who to marry," Rotimi interrupted.

Khalid fell silent and continued the walk.

They came to a cleared ground with four poles marking a perimeter. A string of rope ran through the poles cordoning off the cleared ground within. Completing the scene were tree trunks arranged for an audience.

"So, this is where the Dambé fights were held?" Khalid asked.

"Yes," Musa responded.

"I would have loved to have seen such a fight," Khalid said.

"I never really liked those fights because of the violence they portrayed, but now with the violence I have seen it would be a welcomed sight."

"So why do they not fight anymore?" Khalid asked.

"It is against the teachings of the prophet," Rotimi answered.

Once again, Khalid fell silent. He continued to follow the boys, absorbing all around him. The tour took him to several other locations including the police station that was now a courthouse. A beating was about to start and he stopped to observe. Musa made to leave but the prince refused.

"I intend to see what Allah wishes me to," he said.

The girl had been caught wearing something inappropriate. When Rotimi asked some of the onlookers, he was told she wore a pair of tight jeans underneath her caftan, forty lashes was her punishment. *Was any flesh exposed?* He asked. A shrug of shoulders was the response he got.

A young officer in a blue uniform circled her as she sat on the floor pleading with him and all around her. The officer held a long whip in his hands. As he walked around her, she turned to face him pleading. Her shuffling on the ground created a rising cloud of dust.

Someone barked the young girl's name and she turned to it. The whip lashed out taking her on the back.

"*Wahyooo!*" she screamed trying to rub her back. "Mummy... *Wahyooo!*"

The whip lashed out again, this time hitting her on one of her calves. She screamed from the pain and tried to crawl away from the officer. The whip lashed out again striking her on the thighs. Flat on the floor by now, she made it to some of the gathered people around hoping the crowd's proximity would stop the beating.

Another officer who stood laughing at her ordeal stepped forward with another whip. He was much older than the previous officer and after the first lash of his whip, the onlookers realised he was also a lot more skilled. The tip of his whip connected with her left cheek, drawing blood.

"Move away from there and take your punishment," he said to her in an indifferent voice. His whip lashed out. "Move to the centre." The younger officer's whip lashed out also. "I said move."

Each officer's whip ensured more cries from the girl and the crowds reacted accordingly; some felt pity and others laughed.

Khalid turned around and walked away. "I have seen enough," he said to Musa and Rotimi.

The young woman's screams followed them beyond earshot.

***

As they walked towards the palace, Joy met them at the gate. She seemed flustered and Musa was instantly worried. She bowed to the prince, greeting him in Arabic.

"You must be Joy," Khalid said in English. "I have heard about you and I would like to thank you for all your efforts for without them, I will not be privileged to meet Musa." Khalid took her hand in his, "Thank You."

"You do not need to thank me, prince." Joy said.

"For you, Joy, please call me Khalid," He said to her.

"Thank you, Khalid. Please can I have a word with Musa and Rotimi?" She asked.

Khalid nodded and stepped to the side. His security guards flanked him. One faced the gate and the other faced the town.

"Alihu is in the house with one of his personal guards. The one that really looks like a devil." Joy said to both boys.

"Fatima?" Musa asked.

"He brought her in. The celebrations were correct. She did give birth to a boy, but he is not so healthy." She whispered. "It seems our prayers have been answered but at a great cost."

"Will the child live?" Rotimi asked

"I believe so. Fatima doesn't seem too upset."

"I have to see her." Musa said turning to the palace gate.

"No!" Joy and Rotimi both yelled.

Musa stopped. Alihu did not know he was one of Sani's companions. It was a card Sani kept to himself just in case he needed to play it against Hassan.

"Okay," he said to them. "When does Alihu leave?"

"Tomorrow morning or tonight. Who knows? They are waiting for your boyfriend." Joy said nodding at Khalid.

Musa playfully punched her on the shoulders and they all walked to the gate laughing. The prince followed them and

225

Rotimi walked to his side and whispered the new developments.

Joy pulled Musa back and whispered. "Just don't forget who your enemies are if the time comes."

Musa squeezed her shoulders and nodded.

***

Musa remained in Khalid's quarters until he returned from the meeting with Alihu. The door opened and the young prince entered. Without shame, he undressed in front of Musa and walked straight to the bathroom. A steamy bath was already waiting and Khalid slid into it, sighing as the heat penetrated his skin.

Musa dipped his legs into the bath and Khalid leaned on them. Musa started massaging his shoulders.

"Alihu has left," Khalid said.

"Good riddance," Musa replied.

"I have made my decision," Khalid said. "You must make yours; will you come with me or stay?"

"I have already made my decision." Musa kissed Khalid on the forehead and continued massaging his stiff shoulders.

10

Fatima looked down at her son. He seemed content lying in her arms and listening to her heartbeat. His old eyes looked into hers as if trying to communicate more than a baby's needs. For her part, she stared back into his with sorrow. The doctor had said he would live, connecting a cannula to his wrist. *Vital vitamins.* The doctor had said. *To replace what he has lost.*

Fatima knew better. The doctor had done all this with Alihu present and she understood the lie the moment she looked into the doctor's eyes. Her child was not going to live long and if he did, he would never be normal or healthy. She sighed.

"I have learnt to love you, to look forward to a life with you. One we shared before you were born and one you have helped me through. You must live."

226

I have already, mother. A life much longer than you know.

She turned around, but she was the only one in the room. Was she also now sick? Sick in the head at least? She looked down at her son, he stared back and then turned his gaze to the door.

There was a knock on the door and she told the person to enter. Musa rushed in and she let out a squeal of joy. They both hugged with her child in between them and her baby's eyes looked up at mother and uncle.

"I am glad you are now with us. *Na gode* Allah," Musa said, looking up where he thought the sky would be.

"We should have been here earlier but Alihu is an idiot. Look you have a nephew."

Musa wanted to pick the baby up and run around with him but noticed the plastic tube running to the IV pole next to the bed. Gingerly, he accepted the baby from Fatima.

This was a moment he both feared and wished for. Would he hate the child because of his father, or would he love him because of his mother? Worse, would he feel both? For a life that was never asked to be born, was he right to hold such feelings?

He had forced the thoughts of the dilemma to always appreciate the gift of life regardless. Push away the pain; push away the sorrow, for all are born innocent.

His eyes locked with his nephew and all he felt was love. The baby lifted a hand and Musa moved a finger to it. His nephew clutched it with a firm grip and Musa raised an eyebrow.

"Strong baby, *eh*?" he said to Fatima.

She laughed. "A strength his father believes comes from him."

"I have only met his father once and I know he is a bit of a fool," Rotimi said. "Sorry young one. But we all know where the strength comes from."

"That we do," Joy added.

"Please come forward Rotimi, my brother's redeemer," Fatima said to Rotimi.

While Alihu was around, she was only able to spend time with Joy. Now that Alihu was gone, she could spend time with Rotimi and Musa.

Rotimi stepped further into the room. It was not as exorbitantly furnished as the Arab or Sani's quarters, but it was one of the finest in the palace. The bed was the main feature of the room. An old colonial style with big bedpost and frames draped with a curtain and a mosquito net. A dresser, a chair and a set of sofas were the only other furniture in the room. The floor was covered in a lush soft carpet.

"We met once before," Rotimi said. "And you still look beautiful."

Fatima laughed. "Yes, I remember. Although I must apologize, I only had eyes for one other man."

"I understand," Rotimi said. "Sani thought he was being cruel, but he brought more joy to you and Musa than he ever thought."

"Thank you for everything you have done for our family," Fatima said.

"You do not need to thank me," Rotimi said moving next to Musa to look at the baby. "All I do is for the friendship I share with Musa and redemption for my crime." He scratched Fatima's son's nose. The baby wrinkled his nose and offered what seemed to be a smile.

"Thank you nevertheless. Goodness is lacking in this world," Fatima said.

"Goodness?" Rotimi laughed. "Wait until you hear what plans we have." He turned to Musa. "Talk to your sister. Let me carry this angel for a bit."

Musa passed his nephew over and went to sit next to Fatima. Joy moved and sat at her other side. There was another knock at the door and Fatima said to the door.

"Kurum Daya, enter."

The door slowly swung open and Kurum Daya stepped in. Where Joy was wearing shorts and a t-shirt, Kurum Daya was wearing a black long sleeved caftan with loose black pants underneath. The only reason one could tell the caftan was female, was the slits that ran almost to hips on each side.

Joy had told Musa and Rotimi Fatima's stories of the young girl and she could see that the knowledge of who Kurum Daya really was and what she was capable of now registered on their faces.

"Welcome. Come and join us, this you must also hear," Musa said to the dark mien standing in front of them.

Silently, Kurum Daya walked to the bed and sat on the floor in front of the three of them. Rotimi continued to play with Fatima's son. He and the child's giggle was a contrast to the mood of the room.

Musa carefully explained their plans to Fatima and Kurum Daya.

***

The sun had passed its zenith and was on its way to the horizon. Its rays shone over the preparations going on in the Sambisa. Everywhere one looked, people were getting ready. Checking weapons, loading trucks and painting their skins in black.

Some knew where the attack was going to be, others did not. The order was they had two hours to prepare and anyone not ready would be shot. Knowing their leaders, none wanted to take the chance.

Amidst all the hustle and bustle around her, Mama Ajiya also checked her plans. When she told Fatima she was going to burn the camp to the ground, it had not been an empty threat.

In the past few months, she had stockpiled twenty-litre jerry cans of kerosene. These she had kept in the cooking store tent until few a days ago when she moved them to several parts of the camp. The Old man's instructions on where to place them had been particular. Setting fire to one of them would set a chain of events, when one burnt it would reach the other and eventually strategic parts of the camp

229

would go up in smoke. By the time anyone returned to the camp, it would be destroyed.

***

Kilometres away, a more sombre air of preparations hung above Bordertown. Here they prepared for a battle that some knew they would not return from. New visitors had joined them with more arms and resources but they still feared the superiority of their enemies.

Hassan watched the preparations with a sad look on his face. He too knew that some of his fighters would not return. He was not even sure if he himself would return, but this was an inevitable battle. Bordertown and Madagali had become brothers bound to clash; it was never a case of if, but when.

Ike stood next to him still holding the letter Joy had given him. It was written in Musa's hand and he shared it with Ike because it was addressed to both of them. The content of the letter was another reason for his demeanour.

Today was to be a day of despondency, a day of sadness and a day of loss. Despite it all, a day, he hoped of redemption.

***

It was to be an early night for Fatima. She was already in bed before the sun set. She had watched the last trickle of the IV flow down the tube into her son and disconnected it from the needle in his wrist. She fed him, sang a lullaby and then laid him in a crib.

Her son, like her, was already asleep when heads kissed respective pillows.

***

From the chair she sat in while watching Fatima snooze, all Kurum Daya saw was Fatima rising from her bed and covering herself in a wrapper. Fatima then walked to the crib, picked up her child, who unlike the mother seemed wide-awake and walked out of the room.

Kurum Daya frantically rose from the chair and followed Fatima through the corridors of the palace. She

230

moved closer to ask Fatima where she was going but the look on the young mother's face told her that Fatima was either sleep walking or in a trance. She made the choice to simply follow.

The sleep-walk took them to the kitchen already empty and closed for the day. Fatima opened the fridge and drank from a bottle of purified water. Then she grabbed a knife hanging on the wall above the carving table and left the kitchen.

On her heels, Kurum Daya followed. Once Fatima was back in bed, she silently shut the bedroom door and went looking for Joy.

***

From Fatima's Perspective, she was dreaming.

Mother wake up.

This time he was almost Hassan's age. She had woken to his form squatting over her on the same bed she had fallen asleep in. Apart from his age, he looked normal. Gone were the wings and talons. A normal boy as she would have dreamt of his features leaned over her.

He stretched his hands forward to take her hand in his and guided her from the bed and through the door. As he walked, he spoke to her in the voice she now knew was one from her moments of madness.

Unlike others, my life is mine to choose how I live it, he said. *I choose this for the contrary is not to my fancy.*

She stopped walking and turned to him. "Do I have a choice in the matter?"

Only if you can see the future… my future at least, or yours.

When she did not reply, he continued walking.

Follow mother and do as I bid. Do not miss me, for we have spent a lifetime together, one I shall forever cherish.

11

Hours later, the jihadists were awaiting an insider's go ahead at the outskirts of Chibok. Alihu's Satellite phone rang. He answered it and after a few seconds, a frown marked his face.

231

Surrounded by his generals he listened to the voice on the other line. It was Rotimi, Fatima had just killed his uncle and tried to escape but he had locked her in Sani's rooms. She had nowhere to go but Alihu needed to send someone back as soon as possible.

Alihu turned to Abu, his 2IC. "This is your moment brother! You must lead this fight and I assure you, before you reach the centre of the town I shall return. I need to take care of a woman who does not know she has now passed her use-by-date."

As he turned to leave, Suleiman followed him already heading to a pickup truck. The drive to Madagali would not take long.

***

Rotimi walked into the bathroom and slid into the bathtub in front of Sani. The water was warm and scented and he cherished the calm moment. He took in the scent of cinnamon spicy aroma and filled his lungs.

Musa was seated on the edge of the bathtub with his legs in the warm water while he massaged Sani's neck and shoulders, this was an act Rotimi knew was one of Musa's many skills.

Rotimi took one of Sani's foot in his hands and started massaging it, kneading the stiff muscles in his fingers. He was rewarded with a sigh from Sani who relaxed backwards into Musa's spread legs.

For several minutes, all of them were caught up in their individual engagements. Sani then cocked his head as a sound approached. He raised a hand to silence the boys.

As the sound got closer, Musa reached with one hand for the floor behind him while he slid the other down Sani's chest.

"Is that a helicopter I hear?" Sani asked and made to rise from the bathtub.

Rotimi leaned forward as if oblivious of what Sani was on about. He grabbed both of Sani's wrists in his hands and started massaging. This was an act he often did to ease the beginning throes of arthritis that Sani was beginning to feel.

Musa used an arm to pull Sani backwards into the bathtub. It was not a threatening motion but it was firm enough for Sani to fall back into the water, assuming enthusiasm from his companions.

"Wait," Sani said, as the sounds of the helicopter got closer to the palace. "Be patient boys."

By this time, Musa's fingers were already wrapping around Sani's hard manhood. The expert motion of his fingers already discouraging further protest from the man. For a few seconds, Sani revelled in the experience and tried to forget about the sound.

It was short lived as the gravity of the sound sipped back into Sani's consciousness. He tried to move his wrist from Rotimi's hands to stop Musa. *Why would a helicopter be coming here now?*

Lost in his thoughts, he did not notice that Musa's other hand was already going into the water and before realisation kicked in, the knife in one hand sliced the penis held in the other. Blood already pumping to the member spurted into the water, like jets from a bursting pipe.

In shock, Sani tried once again to remove his wrists from Rotimi's firm grip. His brain still not registering what just happened. As the water started turning pink from blood, He tried to rise from the bathtub with his elbows. But Rotimi released one of his wrists and took the knife from Musa's hand. He slid the blade from one ear, over the welcoming neck Musa held backwards and up to the other ear.

Realising that his wrists were now free, Sani moved one of his hands to his bleeding neck and the other to his groin. He tried to say something but was only able to make gurgling sounds.

Both boys rose from the bathtub and Sani stretched a bloody hand to them. For aid? Accusations? The boys did not care, they simply watched with indifference as Sani struggled to comprehend the life draining into the water around him.

With cold eyes and dripping wet from the pinkish water, Musa and Rotimi stood in front of the dying man, silently watching. When the light left Sani's eyes and his last breath was expelled, Rotimi turned to Musa.

"Let's go get the prince," he said.

Still holding the severed penis in his hands, Musa nodded and walked to the lifeless body in the bath. He stuffed what was in his hands into the gaping mouth and tapped the bald head.

"What is going on here?"

It was one of Khalid's goons.

The guard stepped towards Musa, his hands going into his suit and not noticing Rotimi standing behind the open door. Rotimi jumped onto the guard's back and tried to stab into the man's neck but the guard was wise to it and used one arm to hold the knife away.

Musa ran straight for the guard, but the guard saw the charging boy and balanced his feet to take on the coming weight. Trying to topple him was not Musa's intention. Once his body hit the guard's chest, Musa grabbed at the hand keeping the knife at bay.

Rotimi stabbed once, twice, at the third stab, the man's legs buckled, and he fell to the floor. Both boys struggled to their feet, breathing hard.

They rushed out of the room and quietly closed the door. The rest of the guest wing was silent.

"To Khalid, before the goon is missed," Musa said.

Rotimi nodded but ran back into Sani's room. Seconds later, he returned with a gun, which he slipped into his pocket.

As they approached the end of a corridor, they stopped and leaned on a wall. Musa hugged Rotimi and both boys started crying. They placed their foreheads together and looked into each other's eyes.

"Almost there," Musa whispered.

"Let's go," Rotimi replied.

Musa ran out of the corridor calling Khalid's name. A door opened and the second guard stepped out with a gun in his hand. Musa could see Khalid behind the guard's back.

"The helicopter is on its way, we must go now!" Musa said.

Khalid stepped in front of the guard, "What happened to you!"

Rotimi replied in a whisper, "Be quiet! Some people from Bordertown are in the palace. They attacked Sani but we got away. We must escape through the back."

Khalid nodded and called into the room, his uncle stepped out. Saeed's face was red and he was breathing hard.

"Lead the way," Khalid said.

Musa started running for the kitchen, the guard was next and behind him, Khalid was followed by Rotimi. Saeed stumbled after them.

When they got to the kitchen, Musa ran for the back door then turned sharply to the right. The guard following stopped at the door, an old woman, Mama Amina, was standing with a bucket in her hand. She threw the contents at him and he raised his hands to protect his face. He screamed as scalding water drenched him, he raised his pistol and fired blindly.

"NO!"

Musa barrelled into the guard and they both fell to the ground in a heap. Behind their struggle, Khalid turned to run back into the house but Rotimi, who was close behind, hit him on the base of his neck. Khalid crumbled to the kitchen floor unconscious.

Rotimi turned the gun to Saeed. The man stared at the gun wide-eyed. He began muttering between harsh breaths.

"I don't intend to…" Rotimi began but Saeed's complexion had turned ashen.

Saeed's brain registered the events in front of him, but he had bigger problems. He was trying to suck in air but nothing seemed to be happening. Like a fish out of water, he tried again, *I can't breathe,* he thought in panic. Then he felt as if someone had reached into his chest, grabbed his heart, and squeezed, hard. He tried to clutch the invisible hand but only managed to hit his own chest. Suddenly, he felt the cold kitchen floor on his back, *when did I fall?* Eternal darkness followed.

Musa moved away from the guard on the floor. The man was blind from the water and his face and chest were covered in blisters, he was screaming in Arabic.

Musa turned to the woman lying on the ground, Mama Amina was already dead. Musa fell to the ground next to her, crying. He turned to the screaming guard with hatred in his eyes but noticed dark forms silently surrounding the still screaming guard. The women held things in their hands, sticks, brooms, and firewood. They started hitting the man on the floor, years of beating grain guiding their motions.

"Come quickly!" Rotimi held Musa by the shoulder, "we have to take Khalid to Bordertown"

Musa looked to the women and then at Mama Amina. Despite the multiple gun wounds in her chest, she had died with a serene look.

"Come, Joy will be waiting to show us the way."

Musa nodded and stood up.

***

"This night smells of bad omens," the man at Madagali's southern gate said. "It is pitch black and not even the crickets are singing."

"Rubbish, you are only complaining because you are not with the others pillaging Chibok." Another man behind him replied.

"Well, let's be fair we have manned this gate for three months it is about time we have some fun, no?"

His colleague laughed and climbed the back of the barricade they squatted in. The barricade was created by a circle of sand bags and wooden planks. A hole existed about halfway down to allow the 7.62 PKM barrel to pass through, facing any attack coming at the gate.

The first man who spoke was not looking through the hole but above the barricade at the lights of Bordertown.

"Even they seem to be quieter than us. Only a few lights are on and there are no sounds of their infidel ways," he replied to the man behind him.

The second man who was sitting on the barricade and leaning on his rifle, started laughing at his friend's words. A sound like a thunder clap rang out, interrupting him and a .338 Lapua Magnum bullet tore through the head of his colleague looking over the barricade and into his own kneecap.

Seconds after he yelled out in pain, another bullet passed through his skull and a red mist behind his head registered the bullet's exit.

***

General Terfa and a platoon of his men spent an hour crawling from Bordertown to Madagali's gate. With them was Ike's friend Boni and some of his *confra* brothers.

Attached to their backs were grasses to camouflage themselves as they made the slow and painful crawl. They stopped just before the floodlights coming from the gate.

The town was quiet which gave Terfa hope that Musa's daring plan to kidnap the Saudi princes had worked. He raised his hat to the young men.

Without Sani's knowledge, a couple of hours ago, Rotimi had made a call to Abuja. *Send the helicopter with the remaining Saudi guards to pick the princes up.* Rotimi had instructed.

Rotimi did not expect any hesitations as Sani's staff were used to him delivery messages from their boss. He and Musa would take care of Sani then capture the prince. The boys had also been confident that once a gun was pointed at Khalid's head, the Saudi guards would corporate.

By then using one of the Old Man's secret paths into Madagali, the Old Man, Ike and two other platoons of soldiers were supposed to be in enemy territory. The idea was to use stealth to disarm enemies patrolling the trees and bushes.

All of Bordertown's lights except the administration building suddenly went out. This was a pre-arranged signal that meant Ike was waiting for the next phase after successfully breaching the perimeter. It was now up to Terfa to execute the beginning of phase two.

General Terfa knew men amongst his were cultists but did not care. Rather, he was grateful for the extra hands and the resources that came with them. He knew Boni and despite the man's crimes, he saw a kind enough heart willing to help.

One of the gifts Boni brought with him was a sniper rifle. He pointed its 686 mm barrel at Madagali's gate. He was unable to practice with the LA115A3 beast in case the sound gave up the strategic advantage of having one. So he had prayed for his skills to be on par with using the weapon when the time came.

Lying on the ground holding the weapon appropriately so as to not dislocate his shoulders, he sighted through the night vision scope and pulled the trigger. He moved the barrel to his next target and pulled the trigger again.

His skills and the British-made weapon did not disappoint.

Leaving the weapon on its stand, he picked up the M16 rifle next to him and stood up. "FOR MADAGALI!" he yelled.

Not caring if men followed him, he ran for the gate. He was right not to care as camouflaged men rose from the dusty ground and surged forward. Their faces did not show fear; these were men ready to die.

***

The Sambisa was quiet with the exodus of fighters, leaving behind all the innocents and a few of the jihadists.

Mama Ajiya lit the wick running out of the first kerosene jerry can and hurried out of the tent. She looked around to see if she raised any suspicion and when no one stopped her, she gathered her wrapper to her knees and ran for the bushes. There, her innocents waited in silence. She walked past them whispering for them to hurry after her.

They were only a few minutes away when the first explosion shook the ground underneath their rushing feet. Subsequent explosions followed and under the hidden moon, Mama Ajiya and those she found worthy, moved through the Sambisa's bushes towards a village she knew Hassan waited.

***

Ike and his team had already breached Madagali and the gunfire from the gate told him that Terfa was on point with the plan.

The generator powering Madagali's security lights was close to the main gate and since Terfa was already at the gate, the lights would go off shortly. Jihadist fighters would instantly rush to retake the gate and with their numbers, Terfa and his men would be overwhelmed.

Ike and the Old Man were already heading straight for the hotel currently being used as a garrison. The intention was to attack from the rear with Terfa continuing the onslaught from the gate. Between them both, the Jihadists would be crushed in the middle.

The Hotel grounds came within sight and some fighters were already rushing into the trays of waiting pickup trucks. From the commands being yelled out, the gate was their destination.

Good timing, Ike thought to himself and raised a hand to signal a halt. The security lights suddenly winked out and he dropped his hand in a chopping motion. His men opened fire, their bullets blocking more use of the hotel exit. One of the men with Ike crouched with a propelled grenade launcher resting on his shoulders. There was a swooshing sound and just over a second later, the front of the hotel and a pickup truck exploded.

The Old Man and his team were already at the rear of the building and gunfire followed by several explosions told

Ike they too were now engaged. It seemed that the gods were still on their side.

***

Suleiman was already waiting outside the palace gate thinking on the sound of the helicopter that seemed to be getting closer and closer. Then he heard the first sniper fire. Confused he had started walking back to the palace gate. When the second short rang out, his walk turned into a run.

Next to the gate was a man wrapped in chains and a hyena crouched at his feet. Two other guards stood looking towards the valley wondering what was going on down below.

Suleiman barked orders at them to block the gate and started running back to the main house, Alihu had to be warned.

***

Alihu was consumed by rage and the scene from his uncle's bathroom was still so vivid he literally still saw red. Panting like a wild beast, he stormed Fatima's bed chambers looking for blood.

***

The plan was, she would stay in her chambers for a few hours then sneak out of her room with her child and hide in another room. Everyone would have seen her go to her room and if anyone asked, the bedroom would be all they knew.

She had fallen asleep, then overslept. Only when Alihu kicked open the door and she was frightened awake did she realise her mistake.

He came straight for the bed and grabbed one of her ankles. He dragged her forward, brushed aside her kicks first, then her flaying fists. When she continued to struggle, he back-handed her.

Dazed, she was pulled to the floor and then kicked in the stomach. Before she could recover, Alihu grabbed her hair and punched her full in the face. She felt her nose give way and she crumbled to the carpeted floor.

Come to me mother.

240

She turned around and started crawling to her son's crib.

Hollering obscenities, Alihu continued to kick her, each hit a surge of pain but also sending her closer to her destination.

When she got to the crib, Alihu pulled her to himself and held her by the neck. He began to squeeze, choking the life out of her.

She stretched one hand forward to her son and her fingers wrapped around a wooden handle.

***

Suleiman ran towards the room he knew Fatima was staying in. He could not hear what was happening outside but he needed to inform Alihu of what he heard.

A few metres before the door to Fatima's room, a girl in shorts and a t-shirt he did not know stood in the corridor. In one hand the girl held a knife about twenty centimetres long and this made him stop in his tracks. He started laughing.

***

When Alihu had arrived, Joy and Kurum Daya just returned from helping Musa and Rotimi with Khalid. Although Musa had told her what happened, she had been shocked to see women of the household crying and holding each other over the dead body of a guard. She had glanced at Saeed's overweight body, although unexpected, she had hoped the man had died in pain.

Her thoughts were interrupted by Alihu's bellow and she had delighted in the sound. Then she had followed, to confirm that all had gone according to plan.

From the sounds coming from Fatima's room, her heart had dropped, she realised Fatima had not left the room as planned. Before the man laughing at her had arrived, she had been contemplating stepping into the room to help Fatima.

"What are you going to do with that blade young girl?" The devil in front of her asked with an outstretched hand. "Give it here so I can cut off your tiny breasts."

***

Suleiman raised an eyebrow, surprised that the girl seemed to oblige stepping forward with the tip of the blade pointing downwards.

His instincts screamed at him from behind and he began to turn but was too late. A sharp pain similar to a razor cut but much bigger, lit his back. He turned around to see another young girl wearing black. This one he knew, *Kurum Daya*.

He made to step forward and punch her face in but another pain of similar proportions exploded on his back again, this one inflicted by the girl in shorts.

Trying to move to a more advantageous position, he missed Kurum Daya's quick movement as she tried to snatch the pistol from his hip holster. He lashed out hitting the gun away and it skittled to the floor. Away from Kurum Daya but closer to the girl in shorts.

He stopped himself from rushing for the gun. They were just little girls, surely it would not be too hard a fight.

A simple enough mistake to make and a fatal one at that, for the little girls he faced could hear the sounds coming from the room beyond and their fury was hell's own fires.

He rushed at the girl in shorts, noticing her eyes were at the gun on the floor. But after the first few steps, he crashed to the floor, a stinging pain in his Achilles tendon a tale of his incapacitated predicament.

The girl he knew as Kurum Daya was very quick.

***

Ike was watching the police station go up in flames when one of the Old Man's local spies rushed to them.

"Alihu is already at the palace, he came with Suleiman a few moments ago!"

Ike was shocked; that was quicker than they expected. The plan was to meet Alihu at the northern border and take him into custody. This development changed everything, for him and Hassan. None wanted harm to come to Fatima, but the success of the mission was critical.

"I have to go there," he said to the Old Man.

"Go with a few men," the Old Man replied.

"No! Head to the northern border and secure it! If I fail, you will have Alihu boxed in." He checked his weapon. "This I will do alone."

The Old man nodded and placed a hand on his shoulder. "Go well my son." With that, he rushed away heading to the border with the rest of the men.

Ike ran up the hill, his heart was already pounding as he thought of the dread that awaited him. When he got to Garuba's palace gates, a man was standing there. Something about the man raised a memory.

Without any warning, the man barked a command and a hyena leapt forward, heading straight for Ike. Ike remembered the beast and fired his rifle. He missed and his shots hit the ground just in front of the enraged creature. It jumped to a side, raising dust to confuse but not breaking stride as it continued its mad rush.

Ike crouched, aimed carefully, drew in a breath and released it as he fired. The hyena yelped and fell to the floor only metres away from him.

Ike pointed the rifle at the minder who was already running for the gate. He fired, his bullets took the man in the back and as the gate opened, the man's body was flung inwards.

Continuing to fire and running forwards to the opening gate, Ike's barrage of bullets killed two other fighters rushing out.

He continued to the main building at a low run, scanning with his eyes for any threat. He looked up and saw the blinking red light of a helicopter in the sky. *At least something was going to plan.* He got to the main door unopposed and rushed in.

The house was uncomfortably quiet and with extreme caution, he ran for the direction of the room Joy had described. When he got to the door, he kicked it open and crouched ready to take out any threat. It was then it hit him, he was in the wrong room.

One boy was standing by the door, his eyes wide and tear stricken. From what he was wearing or lack thereof, Ike knew he was in Sani's quarters.

Ike looked beyond the boy into a bathroom. Two other boys were kneeling over a bath crying. Seeing the dead man lying in the bath was a gruesome sight, penis and all, Ike realised this was a sight he would forever cherish.

He barked a question he hoped he already knew the answer to.

"Where is Musa and Rotimi?" His weapon still pointed at the boy's head.

"They left with the Arab prince!" The boy stammered. "They killed our…"

He did not want to scare the youngster but he was not going to take any chances. Musa's letter was specific. If the uprising failed, he and Rotimi's lives would be in danger and none of Sani's companions could be trusted. So they had shared nothing.

"Fatima!" he shouted at the boy who almost jumped out of his skin.

"The… the door at the other end of the corridor."

***

Suleiman was not going to go down to two girls without a fight. He was already enraged and he cursed his legs for giving up on him.

He struggled for a jack knife in his breast pocket and flipped it free. Just as Kurum Daya was on him with her own knife raised.

She slashed downwards but he moved to the side and stabbed with his knife. His blade sank into her shoulders and her slash missed him, scraping the concrete floor.

Remembering the girl behind him once more, he turned to her. She already held the gun in both hands and worse, the barrel was pointing at him.

He tried to throw his knife, but his wrist was slashed by Kurum Daya. Her cut was deep to the wrist bone and his knife fell weakly to the floor.

His head suddenly jolted backwards and it was only when he felt the warm trickle of blood running from his brow down his nose that he realised her aim was true.

***

Ike ran into the room just as the gunshot went off. Joy was already moving to a girl with a knife in her shoulder and she looked up at Ike and pointed to a door.

With no questions asked, he kicked open the door.

***

Alihu turned to the sound of the gunshot.

The distraction was all Fatima needed and she whirled round with the kitchen knife, which was now as an extension of her arm.

Alihu noticed the movement and tried to step back but was not quick enough. The serrated edge of the knife connected with his chest and a bloody trail followed the arc of the blade. It was a superficial wound, but he was staggering backwards in shock.

Fatima let out a near inhuman scream of frustration and rage and leapt at him. She landed on his chest, their momentum sending him backwards. She was already squatting over him when they landed on the bed.

Still screaming like a woman possessed, if not of spirits then of countless months of violence. She stabbed downwards. Lifted the knife, ignoring the blood, the gore and stabbed. Alihu tried to raise a hand for protection but she slashed at it, taking multiple fingers with her swing.

Still screaming she stabbed, stabbed and stabbed again.

The power of her rage was ebbing but yet, covered in blood and still stabbing she wept. She did not hear the door bang open behind her. Her tears mixed with Alihu's blood and hers fell from her nose into her gaping mouth. She did

245

not care. She was lost in her rage and continued to pull the knife out and then stab again.

Someone tried to hold her and she turned, her knife already going for the person's neck.

Ike was not even sure whose blood Fatima was covered in when he barged into the room. All he had eyes for was the emaciated form of the woman squatting over Alihu's unmoving body. The chain on one of her ankles told him who she was. The love of his life.

He rushed to her, calling out to her. When he got close and held her by the shoulder. She twisted round with a strength he did not believe she held.

Seeing the knife coming straight for his neck, he did what he could only do and grabbed the blade. The blade sliced into his hand but he ignored the pain. He twisted his wrist and the knife released from Fatima's grip.

She collapsed into his embrace.

∗∗

Across the room and lying in the baby crib, *the devil* and Fatima's *angel* sighed his last breath.

Epilogue

General Terfa inspected the barriers placed on the road leading into Bordertown. His men looked agitated and he did not blame them, the feeling was mutual. It had been two days since the liberation of Madagali and he was expecting an attack from the Saudis or jihadists. So far, none had turned up.

Either way, Terfa wanted to be prepared. He spoke to a few of the men, boosting morale and checking weapons. He encouraged and berated as any good general would. Hoping that somehow his confidence would steel their nerves.

Done with his inspection, he turned back to Bordertown and could not help but feel regret. The place he had called home for more than a year was slowly emptying. People were already moving back to Madagali. Some would stay to help with the clean-up and he was sure others would stay permanently. However, it would never be the same.

He sighed. He too would be going back home with his wife. It was time to leave the soldering and be a family man.

***

Khalid stared unwavering at Musa, he was not surprised that his gaze was returned with steady eyes. He opened his mouth after the boy moved a spoonful of food to it. *Not boy, young man.*

"I underestimated you, Musa." Khalid swallowed. "Why did you do it?" he asked. When he saw a question in Musa's brow, he added, "why did you not believe I would take you away if you helped me?" Khalid added pain to his voice. "The vigilante leaders were to be baited by the sound of the helicopter. No one would have been killed. You betrayed me."

Musa leaned back into his own chair. Behind him was Rotimi and two vigilantes with guns pointed at the prince. Musa did not think the guns were necessary considering the prince had his hands tied behind his back, but everyone felt safer that way.

"Everything I said about my experience to you was true, the pain and suffering I lay bare, was honest. What you don't understand my prince, is that you had no right." Musa put a spoon through the food. "This is my home and these are my family. You had no right," he repeated.

The prince nodded. If he had not been blinded by self-confidence maybe, he would have seen it coming. *Would he not have done the same thing?*

When he had regained consciousness, an old man, among others were standing in front of him. They had asked him to make a video confessing his allegiance with Alihu. The deal was simple, he would be released if his family paid a compensation, but if they failed or tried to attack, the video would be released.

Khalid could not even call it blackmail. It was a fair price for his neck, one he was sure his father would willingly pay. His failure though, was something he knew his father would not *so willingly* forget.

Well played.

Khalid nodded and opened his mouth for more food

***

For the first time, Joy saw a smile on Kurum Daya's face. She followed the girl's attention and smiled too. Since the liberation of Madagali, Fatima and Ike had not left each other's sides.

Ike had a bandage wrapped around one hand and Fatima was scarred in several places, bandages also covering wounds. There was also a sadness in Fatima's eyes, the loss of her child still strong. Joy knew that like the rest of them, deeper wounds lurked under comforted faces.

She looked backed at Kurum Daya, the girl's smile lit her usually sombre face. *At least we are healing,* she said to herself. *Nagode Allah.*

***

Hassan stood at the northern border. The army were there now but he had refused entry into his town. Thanks to Olu

248

and Ada, the world was also watching and many would see any forced action by the army.

Once Mama Ajiya was safe, He and his men had entered the burning jihadist camp and killed every grown man they could find. They had continued on to Chibok but unfortunately, they were too late. Buildings were burning and family members were crying over the killed or abducted.

Once one of his men had returned with news that the jihadists had fled to Cameroon, he had ordered a return to secure Madagali.

With Madagali secure, the reunion with his family had been short. Hassan remembered looking on as Musa provided their terms to the confused Saudi bodyguards standing next to the just landed helicopter.

Musa's back was straighter, his eyes darker and as his younger brother read the terms without fear, Hassan realised, the fight for Madagali, for family, for love, had forever changed them all.

This was his town and for as long as blood ran through his veins, he would protect it. A knowledge he hoped any now leading the jihadists would heed.

***

Mama Ajiya leaned into the Old Man's shoulders. They were sitting in front of her house watching her grandchildren play *ten-ten*. She moved closer into the Old Man's embrace.

"Thank you," she said.

"What for?" the Old Man asked.

"For saving my life. I would not be here now, if not for you."

"Ah, but you see, Ajiya. You also have given me life."

The Old Man watched the children, their laughter was innocent but the world around them was not. For now though, he was happy. Happy that at least they now had a chance to live.

THE END

ACKNOWLEDGMENTS

Like most new and aspiring writers, the journey of this work was filled with ups, downs and numerous life lessons. I was driven by stories and first-hand experiences of untold hardship in Nigeria and have allowed the knowledge of my motherland help me along the way.

Huge thanks to Laurel Cohn for her services and wealth of knowledge, my partner in life and crime, Lucia Wang, who has contributed as much blood and sweat to me as I have in telling Fatima's story. Thanks to Kate Bach for reading the first draft, my sister Jackie for reminding me of Nigeria after the second draft and to my Australian family Ian and Judith Chapman for my sanity.

For those thinking about it, what is there to lose?

Dan Agbeje, Karratha, 2017.